I0668089

The Growing Universe

Worlds Beyond Book 1

Peter Apps

AUP UK
Terrestrial And Universal Publications

Copyright © 2017 Peter Apps

ISBN: 978-0-9955713-2-7

This book is a work of fiction. Names, characters, places, situations and incidents are the product of the authors' imaginations or are used fictitiously. Any resemblance to actual events, locales, or persons, living or dead, is purely coincidental. All rights reserved, including the right of reproduction in whole or in part in any form.

Published in the United Kingdom

TAUP UK
Sheerness
Kent

enquiries@taup.uk

Preface

I've aimed this book for all ages, and probably even pre-teens could enjoy the adventure. However, I have not made the language easier or used a modern style for a simple reason; I have tried to create a Victorian flavour and modern language does not suit.

I have not set out to confuse anyone so, if a strange word seems to mean something then it probably does. Everyone knows what a brake is, you find them on bicycles, cars and all sorts of things. However, even some adults may be unaware that *brougham, landau* and *brake* are different types of carriage though I have tried to make the two meanings clear. There are words such as trivirem and quadvirem that some characters don't understand so naturally they discuss them and have them explained so in all, I hope that the story remains easy to read.

Chapter 1

School sucked but there again at thirteen, school usually did suck. Still, it was a novel way of describing his dislike at being stuck in a classroom on a warm spring day though it was not entirely the school's fault for his dislike. He was found unconscious, a bad gash to his head and blood on a nearby stone. He came round in a nearby hospital, confused and unable to clearly identify himself. He claimed to be David Pevensey, the 19th Duke of Barabourne living at his ancestral home in Kent, insisting that everyone called him 'Your Grace'. Since there was no Dukedom of Barabourne and never had been, the doctors responded by subjecting him to a barrage of tests but the test results left them as confused as David himself was.

Obviously well-educated, he spoke classical Latin and Greek, as well as being fluent in French and German, and used a very precise if slightly old-fashioned English. Anything electrical fascinated him yet he had to be shown how to turn on a light. He would also stand and stare at the traffic in undisguised amazement. It concerned the doctors that he did not so much forget his delusions as accept his new persona as plain David Pevensey, but they could hardly keep him in hospital in case he relapsed so he was placed with a foster family used to handling disturbed and damaged children.

"He's a polite and well-behaved young man." The carer from the fostering service explained, "We are concerned that his delusions may cause problems and we don't know what they may be blocking out."

However, his delusions did not cause many problems. He worried that he could not dress for dinner, he claimed to have been out riding and his boots, jodhpurs and roll-neck jumper fitted in with that. Hamburger with chips smothered in ketchup was a novel meal though he was decidedly uncomfortable eating with his fingers. He tried to make the best of the situation and fit in but it was obvious he was used to better things. His foster family's children tolerated him, the consensus being that he was weird but it was definitely a nicer weird than many of the other foster children.

Sometimes his delusion surfaced; on one occasion he remarked, "Many of my old circle would just dismiss you all as part of the criminal classes. They don't know anything."

Luckily his new family recognised a compliment but he

remained definitely weird. They got their own back, laughing as he struggled to ride a bike, then stared in horror as he rode triumphantly off, oblivious to the traffic.

His head injury healed and the doctors deemed that he was fit for school. Luckily one of his foster brothers was in the same class and after the bicycle incident kept an eye on him. Although he managed a restraining hand when David tried to stand for the teacher, he could not do anything when David was asked to tell the class about himself but David was learning.

"No-one knows who I really am." he said, "I do have memories of another life but if those memories are true then I've come from a long way away."

"You mean Australia," a girl called out, "You sure talk funny."

David bowed politely and replied, "I'm pleased to have entertained you, Miss, er… I'm sorry but we haven't been introduced."

The girl blushed as the class laughed.

"We were warned that you have amnesia." Mrs Smith, the teacher said, "But this is a creative writing class. Would you be prepared to discuss your memories as a tale of imagination?"

"Ma'am, it would be a pleasure to talk about them on that basis." David replied, "They are so real but I can't discuss them with anyone. May I introduce myself according to my memories. I am David Pevensey, the 19th Duke of Barabourne. I was due to start at Harrow soon but instead I find myself here."

"Harrow." Mrs Smith exclaimed, "This must be quite a comedown for you."

"Before staying with Danny and his family I would have agreed, Ma'am." David replied, "However you look at it, I'm seeing two worlds and there's a lot to be said for this one though I'd still prefer servants to make the bed and do the washing up."

"It's possibly a bit soon, but do you have any thoughts on the two educational systems?"

"Back home, or rather in my imaginary world I would have been set a series of tests to assess my educational standard. Speaking like this is extra-ordinarily difficult, I'm not giving orders to a group of farmhands but I had to learn to speak confidently and I suppose that I'm drawing on those experiences."

"So you think that you're so much better than us," a boy called out.

"This world says that I'm an orphan in foster care. I don't know where I am or what's happened to my friends and family. Just how superior does that make me?"

The class was silent.

"Yeah but you're still a loony nutter who should be locked away." Craig Williams called out.

Before Mrs Smith could intervene, Todd Phillips turned and yelled, "Shut it, Williams. At least his bang on the head didn't turn him into a wanker like you."

Mrs Smith should have dealt with Todd's language but she sympathised with the roar of approving laughter. During break David sought Todd out.

"Thanks for what you said." David said, "In my memories it would have got you a severe beating from the teacher."

Todd grinned, "I like science fiction and stuff. Yours is a good story but do you reckon that you really come from another world?"

"I don't know. I remember Chasebourne as a village on Lord Dalton's estate. Here it must spread onto my lands as well."

"Everyone else reckons that you're just imagining things, don't they." Todd said, "Supposing they're real. Shouldn't you try to get home?"

"You're right but everyone else tells me that I should forget them." David said, "This world is becoming more real but I can't remember anything about it before my accident. It's confusing but how can I get home if I don't know how I got here?"

"Look, I don't know if I believe you but I'd love to be in a real-life science-fiction story." Todd said.

David laughed, "It can't be fiction and real-life but I do wish to know which one of my memories are real. I'd be eternally grateful for your help."

"Have you got a tablet or a phone?" Todd asked, "We need to google maps of the area."

"I think that you're saying that we should use one of those computing machines to find maps to get our bearings. Are there not libraries that could assist?"

"Yeah, they've got computers." Todd exclaimed, "Good thinking. We'll go to the town library. Williams won't find us there."

In David's memories, he had started cadet training. He was also used to studying documents, including maps about his lands so he was adept at map-reading and was thinking in terms of detailed Ordnance Survey maps. Although Todd knew Chasebourne fairly well, he had rarely ventured out into the countryside while David scarcely knew the town. However, he spotted a name on a map on the computer.

3

"Millrace Road," he murmured, "And that's Old Mill Lane. In my world it leads past the old watermill. I wonder what's there now."

Todd grinned, working the keyboard and suddenly a picture of the entrance to Old Mill Lane appeared.

"It goes up hill as it should but I don't know those houses and it's a lot wider." Dave started as Todd clicked the mouse and they jumped a little way up the lane.

He recovered and commanded, "Go to the top of the hill. Is there a path to the left?"

David was shocked to see so much land turned into housing estates to the right of the lane but to the left, the land dropped too sharply to build on. They found the track but it was blocked by a substantial metal gate.

"That's a right of way on my world," he said, "Not even my family succeeded in closing it. It shouldn't be blocked like that."

"It's an odd way of putting it but you're quite right," the librarian said, "There's a big court case going on because developers want to build on Mill field."

"They'll never do it." David said, "There's a spring by the North hedge. The land's always waterlogged. We manage a few sheep down there but not much more."

"Your family used to own it?" The librarian asked, "It's been owned by Western Farms Ltd for twenty years."

"My apologies, sir." David replied, "I'm suffering from amnesia and my memories are confused. However, I most strongly suggest that Mill Field is unusable for the reason that I have stated."

"He speaks Greek, Latin and all sorts of languages." Todd added, "He confused our history teacher by quoting Homer. All the rest thought he meant Homer Simpson."

"Thank you," the librarian said, "I'll pass it on to our committee. Tell me, when did your family own the field?"

"That's what we're trying to find out." Todd replied, "We're trying to tie his weird memories into what's real to jog his real memory."

"I think I understand," the librarian smiled, "Let me know if I can help in any way."

"There is something, sir." David replied, "Is there any way of looking up the name Barabourne or Braborn, possibly dating back to the 1640s? The doctors and alms, I mean social workers tried but I think that they only looked on the computing machines. If the name was lost centuries ago, it might not be on them."

"Good point. You carry on with your maps and I'll see what I can find."

Todd and David found another couple of landmarks and while David was relieved that his memories could be confirmed, Todd looked at him more and more strangely.

"I've no idea how you ever heard of the Earl of Braborn." the librarian said, "He was beheaded by Oliver Cromwell for refusing to accept the Commonwealth. The name just disappeared after that."

"My memories say that Cromwell was killed when the Scots overran the New Model Army while it was being trained and there was a bloody massacre. The Earl was given the Dukedom for his efforts in preventing the Scots from marauding across England and driving them back to Scotland."

The librarian looked at David curiously, "Who are you in your memories?"

"The 19th Duke." David replied, "I know, I sound quite mad."

"If your information about the spring pans out, I'd say that it would demonstrate intimate knowledge of the area." The librarian said, "It would need some explaining but why would you think that you're the Duke of Barabourne? I've never heard of amnesia having that sort of effect."

It was not a question that anyone could answer but for now, David was content. He was sure that he had convinced Todd and although he knew nothing of conservation groups, he could see that the librarian had a reason for wanting to believe him.

He was sure that Todd also had a reason for wanting to believe him, suspecting that Todd was lonely because he did not seem to mix with the other students though David was not sure why. He was becoming more convinced that he was not mad and that his previous memories were real. Finding someone who believed him was enough for one day so he was ready to go home.

School sucked even though he excelled in modern languages, cheerfully adding Spanish to his repertoire. His English teacher came to enjoy reading essays written with great grammatical accuracy in a beautiful copperplate while David relished the emphasis on creative writing. Maths confused him. The class giggled while he was taught to use a calculator. His first instinct was to attempt every problem with pencil and paper. History was worse.

Following a remark by the teacher, he put up his hand to ask, "Who is Queen Elizabeth II?"

The class did not laugh because the question was so silly that they expected a punchline. Mr. Watson thought so too because there was real anger as he asked, "Are you telling me that you don't you know who the queen of England is?"

"Yes of course I know. It's Queen Anne, wife of Charles VII. I just don't know who Elizabeth II is. I know Elizabeth I of course. The Stuart dynasty succeeded her."

The class was still largely quiet, confining itself to a few giggles. Mr. Watson was not known for his patience and they were anticipating fireworks.

"Very well! Name the Stuart kings.

All fifteen of them, sir"

Mr. Watson knew of David's delusions but he could not be sure that he was part of some big wind-up.

"Just the seventeenth century will do." He replied, hoping to control the situation.

"James I, Charles I, Charles II, and by one year, his son, James II."

"Very well. Who did Charles II marry?"

The class was still quiet, recognising a developing battle of wits.

"Lady Barbara Villiers."

"Very well. It's an interesting take on history and your research is excellent even if you omitted his brother, James." Mr. Watson said, "In fact I'm curious. I accept that you have amnesia and it'll take time for you to catch up so it might help if you wrote a comparison of the history in your memories and the one that we're taught.

"Why? He's just a nutter at it again." Craig Williams called out but was shocked by the lack of response.

"If students insist on disrupting my class, then I prefer David's intriguing imagination to your rudeness." Mr. Watson said, and finally the class had something to laugh at - at Craig's expense. It did not stop David being close to tears for feeling so out of step.

Most other subject were as bad, even sport. It was nearly summer yet no-one was thinking about the cricket season, it was as if they would continue playing football, not even rugger, rugby he had to explain because no-one seemed to know the nickname for the game but even, the tactics and rules for football were different.

He obviously liked the novel idea of a mixed school but he treated the girls with an innate politeness that they could not admit to enjoying while everyone laughed at his nerdiness. He found modern music noisy, and had no understanding of Facebook or social trending. In short, he was a figure of fun and isolated. Danny the true son of his foster parents was not hostile but he had his own life and kept his distance so his only friend was Todd who was also an outsider.

David understood fashion and how people would be judged by what they wore but he did not understand the nuances of designer labels and other modern, or rather, this world's concepts of fashion. Being outsiders gave them enough in common to make them friends.

Todd's mother had disappeared long ago and he lived with his father who was enough of a drunk that love of a drink competed with his love of his son and won more and more often. Social Services were concerned but his was a borderline case and there were far more urgent cases.

He turned up in school in clothes from the charity shop, never the latest fashion and always shabby, not even owning a phone. As David learned about charity shops, the importance of owning a phone so he realised in his old world/memories he would have reacted like the rest of his class towards Todd, seeing him as a definite inferior, not worth talking to.

They developed a friendship with Mr. Barton, the librarian who valued David's understanding of the area though Mr. Barton was concerned. He was single and lived quietly, so a sudden friendship with two young teens was out of character and he was aware of the gossip being generated. However, the information about the spring proved accurate and the mystery surrounding David intrigued him. He had the chance to learn more about the local area so had an incentive to at least, give David the benefit of the doubt. He did not accept the idea of alternate worlds but he did accept that David's memories were real, and a mystery which he was willing to help solve.

It seemed obvious that the first step was to find out where David had appeared and it should have been easy but it was not. The Emergency Services were reluctant to give any information because of Data Protection and the hiker who had found him had moved on without leaving his details.

They could have explored the general area but the bloodied stone would have been removed. Instead, they tried adding David's memories of places to a modern map of the area. It could have been easy, country lanes and field boundaries do not change much over the centuries and although some hedges had been ripped out, the countryside remained similar. What slowed them was comparing the differences. Mr. Barton was passionate about footpaths and bridleways that David's ancestors had succeeded in closing while David became intrigued with the surveys of his lands and the uses that areas had been put to.

"You don't seem anxious to get home." Mr. Barton said one time, "How come?"

"I am anxious but I was away at prep school before and I can compare my time here to that." David replied, "The information here is astounding. If I can get back, then I must take it with me. My allowance is not enough to purchase a tablet and anyway it won't last without charging so I must draw maps and write it all down. It takes time."

"There, I might be able to help." Mr. Barton said, "I showed your plan of the mill to the local historical society and they confirm early references to it. I'll suggest that they hire you as a consultant while they plan a dig. There's a young scientist group that meets here once a month. I'll ask them to convert a clockwork radio into a basic charger. Would that help?"

"It's very kind of you. I thank you sir." David replied, "The 15th Duke insisted that the railway be moved further away from the house but here, it appears that they pulled it down. If I do stay, it would be nice to see it again, would your society be interested in studying it."

"Yes indeed." Mr. Barton replied excitedly, "Our records suggested that the railway went straight over the site but to find Dalton Hall…"

"Dalton!" David exclaimed angrily, "That family's little better than tradesmen. How dare they…"

He trailed off, attempting to compose himself, "My apologies, that must have sounded so very crass. Barabourne Hall has been so called for centuries."

"Your memories are so detailed." Mr. Barton said, "It's difficult to believe that they're not real. If you're the duke then your father is dead?"

"Yes, he succumbed to cancer of the lung about two years ago." David replied, "I couldn't go into his smoking room and I could smell the smoke just walking past the door. He believed that the smoke kept dangerous germs at bay but I understand the detrimental effects that tobacco has now"

It is not easy gathering all the information of an entire world and any boy on any world could be fascinated by accounts of trips to the moon or trips by submarine to the ocean floor. David was no exception, so although it was not easy he tried to content himself with information that he could apply to his estates and learn why his world had missed out on developing electricity where it remained a scientific curiosity and show-ground novelty.

"If I do get back then maybe the link is permanent although that would raise many questions." He said, "However I want enough to keep me busy at home whether I return again or not. If I can return, then I could bring gold to purchase equipment."

David liked his foster family and tolerated school but hated being such an outsider. The one thing he really enjoyed were his evenings with Mr. Barton. The library closing times proved inconvenient so, despite Mr. Barton's misgivings, transferred to his home and Todd was always with them. One evening he called David into his living room. Sitting on the table was a laptop and printer plugged into a strange looking gadget.

"I shouldn't be buying boys your age such expensive presents. I hope that you'll accept it though, David." He said a little nervously, "I've come to believe your story and apart from the solar power charger, you need a laptop anyway."

By answer David hugged Mr. Barton.

"Thank you," he whispered, "It's superb. I'll miss you when I go home."

He looked at both Mr. Barton and Todd, "I'll miss both of you, but I've got to start looking. There's one more thing that I want to do now that I've discovered on-line printing. You could order some of these if you try to visit."

He called up a website on Mr. Barton's computer showing a business card which read,

---

David, 19th Duke of Barabourne

*His Grace wishes the bearer to
be shown every courtesy and
offered every assistance.*

Barabourne

"Keep them safe, they're only for you or Todd." David

commanded, "If you ever try to visit after I'm gone then bring some with you. I want to make sure that you're looked after."

This time it was Todd who hugged David.

"Could I really visit?" He asked.

"Of course, the entire household from my mother down to the boot-boy will acknowledge the kindness that you have shown me." David smiled, "That was a bit dukey, wasn't it."

"I liked it though." Todd replied, "Thanks."

"I need to get back as soon as possible." David said, "There's one or two things that won't wait much longer and I hope that I'm not too late for one of them but I didn't know that I could do anything until yesterday."

"You were talking to a doctor weren't you?" Todd asked and David nodded.

"No questions." Mr. Barton said, "You've pinpointed the exact location you vanished in your world and it's in the general area that you were found in this. I'll drive you out there tomorrow."

They packed David's bag, he gave Mr. Barton a letter to post to his foster parents if needed and then went home.

The following morning he sat down for breakfast, looking around the kitchen, possibly for the last time.

"I suppose you'll be off with that Mr. Barton again," his foster mother sniffed, "He shouldn't encourage you with all that history nonsense. You need to accept that those memories are just some sort of waking dream and forget them. Why not go out with Danny and his friends."

"Thank you." David replied, "Danny is very kind to me but he needs his own time. Most brothers are different ages and have different friends, that's how it should be for us."

Danny flashed David a smile of gratitude, and suddenly David sensed a warmth that had been absent for most of his stay.

"You could come with us if you wanted to." Danny said, "I wouldn't mind."

"Thank you." David replied, "I know that I don't fit in and it embarrasses you even though you try to hide it. We'll be better friends if we both accept it."

Danny nodded and continued eating. His mother had heard the exchange and was wondering whether there was too much pressure on Danny. There was definitely something odd about David, but he was amazingly mature so he could be right.

Chapter 2

As he left the house, heading towards Mr. Barton's, David wondered whether he would ever see it again. He heard footsteps pounding after him and turned to see Danny trying to catch him up.

"I'm sorry if I've been a prat." Danny said, "You're right about my friends laughing at you, so can I hang out with you and see what you're up to."

David thought for a moment. If today went wrong, then Danny would have ammunition to make him even more miserable at school with his stories but it would be nice to leave as friends.

"Very well." David said, "Todd, Mr. Barton and I talk more and more about whether I come from a different world. Today we're going to look for evidence at the last place I remember being in my memories. I'd spotted something in the hedge and got off Jasper to look, and then the ground seemed to shake and I fell against a rock."

"Who's Jasper." Danny asked.

"My horse." David replied, "Today, we're ready to look for it and see what's what."

"Could we come through to your world, too?" Danny asked to David's surprise. He had been expecting Danny to yell out to everyone that David was completely mad.

"I need to go home." David said, "I've got to risk it, but even if it's still open, whatever it is, it could close while you're on the wrong side. I came here by accident, it'll be different risking it deliberately. Besides, you might have been right and I'm completely mad."

"And I'll be the first to know." Danny yelled triumphantly, "Everyone says that your memories are too good; there has to be something. David, this is what you said, backwards. Do you want your pesky brother hanging out with you?"

"I do happen to like you." David said, "You're nothing like my imaginary friends."

"Let's go and see if they are imaginary." Danny said.

Mr. Barton had once said that teenagers would be more likely to accept alternate worlds because their awareness of the world was expanding and other worlds was just part of that increasing awareness. Adults were far more inclined to find a *rational* explanation; one that would fit in with their existing ideas. David guessed that it was probably true which was why Danny was so accepting.

Mr. Barton's car would have been just as unbelievable on his other world he decided as he was whisked along at incredible speeds. They stopped in the lane looking at the five foot high metal gate.

"The gate at home was a lot lower and I was wondering whether Jasper could jump it." David said, "I decided against it and dismounted to open it. Then I saw something shining in the hedge."

He knelt down.

"Good grief." He exclaimed, "There's something here as well. Now what do I do?"

"Careful." Mr. Barton called out but he was too late. David felt the same tremor that he had felt before but nothing seemed to have happened. He was still looking at the hedge. When he looked around, he realised that he was in the field and not in the lane and when he called out, no-one replied.

He touched the object again and the ground shook again.

"Fucking Hell. How did you do that?" Danny exclaimed, "You just vanished."

"I went home." David replied, "At least I was on the other side of the hedge and you didn't hear when I called out. I forgot to look at the gate."

"That's too easy." Mr. Barton said, "Something like that should have been discovered years ago."

"I don't think so." David replied, "The tip of whatever it is, is in the side of the ditch. It looks to me as though the bank's been allowed to erode away and expose it. Can you all be here at this time tomorrow, please?" I'm going to take my bag and go back then cover my end. Tomorrow, we'll decide how to proceed. Todd, you've said that you wanted to come with me. You must decide and be ready tomorrow."

"Why cover your end?" Danny asked.

"So that no-one else stumbles through. This is between us."

The others nodded.

"I hope it all goes to plan." David added, "I really do want to see you all again."

He grabbed his bag then knelt down and grabbed the object again. It occurred to David that they had not even examined it but the ground shook though it seemed to take longer before anything happened.

The battery's going flat, he thought, *I hope it charges up again,* but he covered the object as best he could then headed across the fields towards his home. There were some workers in the next field. They looked up, looked puzzled then hurried across to him.

"Your Grace," the oldest one said, "Where have you been? Everyone has been so worried. We spent days looking for you. Are you all right, sir?"

"I'm fine, thank you Jennings. How's my uncle? Is his leg any better?"

"I don't think so, Your Grace. I've only seen him a couple of times and he's limping badly. There are rumours that it may have to be cut off."

David turned to Jennings' young assistant, "Tom, will you run on ahead and tell Wilson that I'm on my way. He is to tell no-one else except that I wish to see my uncle in his bedroom as soon as I arrive and that his man, Wilson and you, should wait with him. Warn Wilson that I intend to arrive by the servants' entrance and that I'm to get to my Uncle's bedroom with the minimum of fuss. Can you do all that?"

"Yes Your Grace. I'll see to it." Tom replied, turning as the other lad whispered something to him, before heading off at a run.

"He's got a good mind, hasn't he?" David said.

"Yes Your Grace." Jennings replied, "He's a good lad but he's too bright. It makes him cheeky and mischievous."

"Then I might need him for a few days. Can you spare him?"

"Anything you say, Your Grace."

"I really did mean 'can you spare him?'" David said, "I assume that you called Godfrey out to look at the pump so you're already behind. You won't have to work until midnight because you're single handed, will you?"

"No Your Grace. I'll ask Mr. Thompson for another hand. The culvert's blocked again and we have to wait for the water to be pumped out."

"I'd better go. Catch you later." David said before grinning, "That's the new way of saying 'That's all for now, Jennings'."

"Yes Your Grace."

David headed towards the house. He had forgotten the strict formality of his home and some things were definitely going to change. His heart pounded with excitement as he reached the house, now he really did feel as if he was home even if he was entering by a side door. He found Tom waiting for him by the entrance.

"I told cook that His Lordship was receiving a special visitor and she is keeping the staff out of this corridor, now if you'd follow me."

13

"Good thinking, Tom." David said, "How come you know the way?"

Tom looked embarrassed.

"Visiting one of the maids?" David asked.

"Oh no, Your Grace. Nothing like that."

"We're sneaking around this house like burglars and you're calling me Your Grace. Call me David." David chuckled, "I'd like to know that you're not planning a robbery or something but I'll not demand an answer."

"Yes David, thank you. If it doesn't get anyone else into trouble, I'll tell you."

"No, it won't."

Tom took a deep breath, "Godfrey gave me directions. He's mates with one of the boot boys, and visits him and the other boys."

"Thank you for trusting me." David said, "Right, now let's greet my uncle."

For once David was too excited to behave correctly and ran across the bedroom to hug his Uncle Jethro who hesitated then wrapped his own arms around the boy.

"It's good to see you, my boy," he said, trying to retain some dignity.

"It's brilliant to see you Uncle." David exclaimed, "In fact, it's O.P."

"I beg your pardon." Jethro responded.

"The language was different in the other place." David explained, "Over powered or over powering."

He pulled back looked at Wilson then leapt across and hugged him too. Wilson looked nervously at Jethro who shrugged, before returning the hug.

"That will do, David." Jethro said, "You've been away before and that is not how you treat servants."

"His Grace has not arrived yet." David announced, "I'm just someone who has sneaked in on some household business. Can we continue on that basis, please? I will tell you what I can, you Wilson can try to explain it to the staff while Uncle Jethro explains it to the family. Make it clear that I don't wish to be continually discussing it and all questions are to go through you two."

"Very well, young sir." Wilson replied while Jethro nodded.

"Good. Uncle, how's your leg? Dr. Hastings was quite worried when I left."

"It's not good." Jethro replied, "The infection has not subsided

14

and the doctor thinks that it should be amputated before gangrene or blood poisoning sets in. To be honest I've only delayed things because I've been so worried about you.

"I shall just call where I've been 'the other place' for now. It was an amazing place and one of the surprises was a medicine called antibiotics. Now they might not work, but if anything can save your leg, they can. Shall we try them?"

"Dr. Hastings is coming on Monday." Jethro replied, "I fear it is too late but it was good of you to remember me."

"Today's Saturday." David replied, "Shall we see what happens between now and Monday or would you rather just lose your leg."

"What is this medicine? Who sold it to you, and how can you be sure that it's safe?"

"Uncle, I'm not stupid and I've not been fooled by some itinerant salesman. I've still got the scar where I gashed my head and I had to take them in hospital. If Doctor Hastings is coming on Monday, have you got anything to lose?"

Jethro smiled, "Let's go down fighting. What do you want me to do?"

"Just remove your trousers and lay down on the bed. I have a friend who is a librarian. He knows a number of clubs and organisations that taught me all manner of things."

David put on surgical gloves before removing the dressings from his uncle's legs, trying not to heave and gag at the smell and sight of the wound. He managed to clean it. He dropped the old dressing into a resealable plastic bag before washing his hands and putting on a new pair of gloves.

David turned to Jethro's valet.

"Jarvis, my uncle's trousers need to be taken away and washed in disinfectant before they are brought back in here. The same applies to the bed linen and covers. Anything that touches this wound needs to be sterile. If you notice, I'm trying to avoid all cross contamination between the old and new dressings."

"I know that you're trying to help, but not even Dr. Hastings went to these extremes." Jethro said.

"Bear with me, Uncle." David said, "It is important."

He finished dressing the wound before taking a bottle of pills out of his bag.

"You should be in a hospital where they can administer far larger doses but these are the biggest doses that I could get. Dr. Hastings seems to have stopped the infection from spreading too far, so these may well work. Jarvis, to work, these tablets must be taken regularly, one every six hours. They can cause more harm than good if not taken regularly. At the appointed time you will nag, bully and generally annoy my uncle until he takes one. No matter what happens, you will have my protection providing he takes it."

David smiled, "You had better sit down, Jarvis. You're looking quite ill. Uncle, you'll have to take those pills if only to prevent Jarvis from having a heart attack."

"You've made your point." Jethro said, "Timing is important and I will comply but please stop embarrassing the servants."

"Very well. Next point of business. I will not be going away to school. We will be hiring home tutors to teach subjects yet to be decided."

As he spoke he pulled a flash-light from his bag and as he switched it on, everyone gasped in amazement. Before anyone else could speak, he continued, "I'm only thirteen but I have information that could lead to new and very profitable ventures. If I sit on it all while I'm away at school then I shall forget a lot and I won't be able to speak with the scientists and engineers who will make it all work."

"I understand the argument." Jethro said, "I'm not sure that I approve though. You're forgetting your position and that will not do."

"I know, Uncle." David said, "When I go down to greet Mother, I shall be the duke again and I know my duty. I also have a duty to make our estates prosper. I shall have to work hard to do that so I shall need some latitude when I relax. Time when I'm not the duke, time when even Wilson can call me David."

"You should not embarrass servants, like that." Jethro said, "Wilson knows his position."

"I mean it, if he doesn't I might start calling him by his Christian name. It's the same as mine, isn't it? It might be better if I called him Davie."

"David." Jethro began but Wilson turned to him.

"If any other boy tried to call me that I'd put him across my knee spank him in front of all the other boys."

"You'd have my permission." Jethro said, "If he wants time when he is not the duke then he cannot claim its protection."

"That is my understanding, My Lord." Wilson said, "Boys do need to release their energy and David appears to have returned with an excess."

"Bloody hell, you managed to call me David," he exclaimed, "I bet myself that it would never happen."

Jethro should have rebuked David for his behaviour but he was just as surprised. He glanced at his leg. It had to be his imagination but it already seemed to be hurting less.

"I think it's time that I greeted my Mother." David said, "I bet that she complains about my clothes before she asks about my health. Any takers?"

"You could change." Jethro suggested.

"I could." David said, "But I have other things to do and I'm not going to keep changing. Wilson, will you take Tom and my bag to the library, please?"

It was David who left first leaving the other to consider events. There was a sense of bewilderment at David's behaviour and a feeling that they were all equally bemused. It was enough for Jethro to ask, "Well Tom, what do you think of our Lord and Master."

"He's grown up and taken charge even though his ways are strange, My Lord." Tom said, "If he heals your injury and what with that light of his, he does know a thing or two. You wouldn't have worried about what I thought before today so has he tired you gentlemen out?"

"You've summed it up, well." Jethro said, "You'd better go. At least you're nearer his age and may be able to keep up."

David loved his mother. She could be kind and loving but never in public and if anyone was going to challenge his new persona then it would be her. Wilson should have preceded him and announced him but David thought that if he was ever going to change her, he had to start now so he just opened the morning room doors and marched in.

"Hello mother, I'm back," he said, "I'm sorry that I worried you but I'm so pleased to see you."

His mother nearly dropped the coffee cup that she was holding but managed to keep some control.

"Couldn't you have changed?" She asked, "Please come and kiss me, but I really cannot introduce you when you're dressed like that."

"Mother, I've been missing for all this time and you're worried about how I'm dressed."

"I can see that you're well. Please dress so that I can introduce you."

David turned to his mother's guests.

"I am David Pevensey, 19th Duke of Barabourne. I'm pleased to welcome you and I have an amazing tale to tell but I need time to adapt. Please excuse me."

He made his way to the library to find Tom and his uncle.

"How did it go with your Mother?" Jethro asked.

"Her Grace, the dowager duchess was pleased to see His Grace, the duke looking so well." David said irritably, "Unfortunately she could not receive him because *he* was improperly dressed. Tom, please sit down."

"So I have lost my bet to Wilson." Jethro chuckled, "I bet that she wouldn't even speak to you though I'm glad that she was so excited to see you."

"I thought that she was going to drop her cup, so I suppose it was a result." David said, a little happier.

"You know I'm sure that I feel a little better." Jethro said, "But we must prepare for my time in hospital. You've said you do not wish to go away to school, as your guardian, I should insist. Please justify your decision."

"Firstly uncle, I hope that your leg heals for your own sake but I also hope that I can develop these medicines here. They could be produced by others under licence and save many lives. Secondly, the electric lamp I showed you, is highly advanced but a much more basic version could be made here to replace gas lighting. Thirdly our engines are highly inefficient. Traction engines, haulage vehicles and even our steamers could be improved. If we hold the patent on all of these innovations, then Barabourne could do very nicely."

"And you're suddenly the greatest expert in all these fields so you don't need an education." Jethro said.

"No, I want to assemble the greatest experts in these fields to run these projects. I can do little more than offer insights into what might work. They could double as tutors to teach me and the brighter estate boys."

"You intend studying with village boys. School would also teach you about your position."

"That's the trouble. My position is to make Barabourne prosper and I need time to sort out the knowledge I've acquired. I can't do that at school because I'll be expected to worry about little more than the next cricket match or something.

"Very well, suppose I said that you had a month to convince me?" Jethro said, "Now I am concerned about your very liberal attitudes towards the servants. Wilson and I are concerned that discipline will suffer."

"It didn't stop you sharing a little wager." David retorted, "But you stayed on your side of the fence, I suppose."

"We retained our positions but I supposed that we were influenced by your behaviour. Would you care to explain it?"

"Not completely. Wilson will have to maintain the house in the way that he understands. I won't change that, but if I decide that I want to play football then the only boys my age are estate boys. I won't develop my skills much if they just say, 'Excuse me, Your Grace and stand aside."

"But that is why you should go to school." Jethro said, "The rough and tumble of school life will make a man of you."

"You've given me a month." David said, "If my way of doing things causes too many problems, then we'll put them down to my strange disappearance and do things your way."

"And you still don't want to talk about where you've been."

"No Uncle." David replied, "It's mainly because, I'm not too sure where I have been. I really need to get my head around it."

"You seem to have acquired a strange style of speaking." Jethro said, "In some ways it is quite charming, colourful but still descriptive, please be careful."

"OK, I'll watch it." David chuckled, "Now I told Tom, to wait for me in your room. On the face of it, he disobeyed me to come to collect me. In reality, he understood what I wanted and improved upon my instructions which is why I want him as my P.A. That means personal assistant, something like a secretary but not exactly the same."

"Secretary, Your Grace!" Tom exclaimed, "I can scarcely read or write. I'm sorry, Your Grace, for interrupting."

"You didn't. You saw a potential problem and pointed it out. That's one of your new duties but you'll practice your English though. How about a month's trial and we'll see how we both work out?"

Tom grinned, "Thank you, Your Grace. May I ask, why me?"

"According to Jennings, you're bright which makes you cheeky and mischievous." David explained, "You're also the first person I met today who might stand up to me."

"So it was luck then, Your Grace."

"Partly and we'll see whether it was good luck or bad. Tell me, why are you calling me 'Your Grace' again."

"I'm not sure. When we were creeping around the servant's stairs and you were acting more as a medical orderly than a duke then it seemed right to call you David. Now you're discussing estate business, 'Your Grace' seems right. His Lordship might prefer it, too."

"I understand what you see in him." Jethro said, "You'd best inform Wilson of his new position and where it ranks. It's as good a way as any of announcing it, he'll sit accordingly in the pews tomorrow."

"SHIT!" David yelled angrily, "I forgot church. I have to make contact with the other place tomorrow morning."

"That is far less charming language." Jethro reproached him, "You'll have to postpone your meeting."

"I can't. I have to visit the other place and the, er, path will only be open at ten. I can't miss it."

"Is it only you?" Tom asked, "If I'm your assistant, shouldn't I be able to run messages for you?"

"I don't know what the path is, or how reliable it is." David said.

"All the more reason to send me then." Tom replied, "If you survived there then I should but you're needed here. Besides, we can't have the rector thanking God for your safe return while you're disappearing again."

Jethro pulled the servants bell, summoning Wilson.

"Ah Wilson." Jethro said, "Tom is joining the household. He will be a confidante to my nephew so he won't be family or guest but he'll be more than just servant. What do you suggest?"

"That we install him in the smaller housekeeper's apartment My Lord, he should address me as Wilson but he can eat in the servant's hall when he is not required."

"Did you mean that I should call you Mr. Wilson?" Tom asked.

"No, just Wilson. You answer directly to His Grace, you're not a servant answerable through me. It occurs to me Your Grace, that if you wish to be plain David then there are some rooms next to the servant's hall and kitchens. They're used for storage but I doubt if there is anything of value. You could come and go, unnoticed while working on your projects and without confusing the staff."

"Thank you, Wilson." David replied, "I don't mean to confuse you and I appreciate how well you run the house. Please let me know if I cause too much disruption."

"I will be happier after church, tomorrow, Your Grace. For once everything will be in its proper place. I'm sure that you will have luncheon with the family. On other days I understand that you will require a more flexible approach. May I take the liberty of inviting you to eat in the servant's hall. Cook will provide sandwiches, maybe even stews to suit and dressing will not be necessary."

"That is very kind of you." David said, "I'll try not to be a nuisance."

"Why does Wilson invite you into the servant's hall?" Tom asked, "Surely you can just go there."

"You'd think so." David replied, "The servants have their way of doing things and don't need someone looking over their shoulder so it is bad form to visit without warning. Wilson is trusting me not to break the status quo."

"I've got a lot to learn if I'm to stay here."

"Be guided by Wilson. You'll be all right."

"Yes Your Grace, if I'm to make that journey for you, may I stay with my family tonight?"

"Yes of course." David replied, "And thank you, all of you."

While Jethro looked on mystified, David showed Tom his mobile phone, how to find Todd's number and what to expect when it worked.

"And when I hear your friend, he could be miles away." Tom said.

"That's right. Now let me show you where the path begins."

He led the way to the gate where he carefully cleared the leaves away showing Tom the device. Now that he could look at it without being tempted to touch it he could see that it was simply a metal rod with a domed end. David was sure that it was even shinier than before. Before he could say anything, Tom leaned forward, touched it, shimmered and disappeared. It was nearly fifteen minutes before Tom returned.

"I'm sorry, Your Grace. I was just curious and didn't think. Your friend Todd wishes to visit. He says that his father rang and was already out of it. I believe that he was a little upset. What did he mean by out of it?"

"His father's a drunkard. Are you willing to go back?"

"Yes of course and I think it's David now." Tom replied, "If Todd needs looking after then I'll send him through and stay overnight. Your Mr. Barton says that as it drains so it gets duller and they were allowing it to recharge before covering it in case it relied on solar energy. Does it make any sense to you?"

"I think so. Are you sure? If the whole thing vanishes, then you'll never get back so try to follow Todd if you can. I'll wait an hour before covering it back up."

"I've talked to my parents about leaving to join the navy or the army." Tom said, "They understand that I want adventure before I settle down. If it does go wrong will you explain that I've found the adventure that I want.?"

David nodded and watched as Tom disappeared. It seemed just like moments before Todd appeared.

"Hang on," he said and sure enough after a brief pause, Danny arrived.

"Wow!" He exclaimed, "It's all true."

"What are you doing here?" David asked, "What about your parents?"

"I told them that I was having a sleepover at Craig's. You can cover up, now."

They trudged over fields only stopping as the house came into sight.

"Is that yours." Todd gasped, "It's enormous."

"It's mine." David confirmed, "It's also yours for as long as you stay."

He led the way to the main entrance where he was greeted by Wilson.

"The dowager duchess is in the morning room still and His Lordship is still in the library."

"Library then." David said, "Please stay while I introduce my guests."

"Todd accepted me more than anyone else in the other place." David said during the introductions, "More than anyone, he helped me keep my sanity. Danny was my foster brother."

"Then you're both welcome." Jethro said, "I understand enough to believe you'll find our ways very strange but we'll try to make you comfortable."

"This is Wilson." David continued, "If you need anything, please ask him."

"May I ask about the young gentlemen's luggage, Your Grace."

"I don't have any, Mr. Wilson." Danny replied, "I didn't know that I was coming."

"Staff call me Mr. Wilson, young sir. Guests call me Wilson."

"Wow!" Danny exclaimed, "I've never been called 'young sir' before."

"If I may speak candidly, young Sir." Wilson said, "If you looked after His Grace then you have earned the title."

"Thank you Wilson." Jethro said, "I agree with that sentiment. David's mother will not agree so we will keep your arrival a secret from her if possible. What are your plans for the rest of the day?"

"Since there's no meet tomorrow, the younger boys will have this afternoon off. If they go swimming then I'm hoping that a gift of cider, bread and cheese will be enough of a welcome."

"Adding some ham and pickle would be helpful. I'll speak to cook." Wilson said.

"I'm not sure if you should be encouraging him, Wilson." Jethro said.

"I believe that we agreed that His Grace could tire the adults out. I'm hoping that other boys will tire him out."

"That I do approve of." Jethro laughed, "Go ahead."

"One last thing, Wilson." David said, "I should like to send gifts to the people who cared for me. Would you select a piece of our finest porcelain with my crest on it and a couple of our best racing pigeons. See that they're ready for transport tomorrow. I should make the selections myself but I'll leave it to the experts."

They left the house but headed for some buildings instead of the river.

"We'll visit the stables before swimming." David announced, "Danny will like it."

"I'm not interested in horses." Danny complained, "Why should I want to visit the stable."

"Well, we don't use the word *garage*." David explained, "We stable locomotives."

Danny might have replied, but Mr. Allen, the stable manager hurried over.

"Good afternoon, Your Grace. How may I be of service," he said, "It's so good to see you safely returned."

"Thank you Brian." David replied, "I'm just showing my friends around. Are the steamers ready for tomorrow?"

They had been walking as they talked but neither Todd nor Danny were listening any more. They were staring at the collection of odd looking vehicles stored in the stable.

Todd recovered first.

"You call them steamers. Are they all steam driven? Don't you have any diesel or petrol cars?"

"We've used internal combustion engines as standing engines but they're too noisy and heavy for road use. I think that you'd call them diesels. You need electricity for petrol engines, don't you?"

"And they all work?" Danny asked.

"Brian, if the weather's suitable I shall use the open landau. The rest of the family can use the steam broughams and the staff can take the steam coach as usual."

"Yes Your Grace. I'll see to it."

To Danny and Todd's eyes, both vehicles dated to the end of the nineteenth century. Instead of a bonnet there was a cylindrical boiler.

"On Monday will you service the brake, my two friends may wish to learn how to drive it." He turned to Danny and Todd, "There's no driving licence or age limit here. The brake's just a small steam carriage. We send a boy with a message or something as it can go further than a horse without tiring."

"We can learn to drive?" Danny queried, "Really! When can we start?"

"Next weekend if the bridge is still open. Today I need to speak to the estate boys and tomorrow is Sunday. That's a big deal here."

Danny nodded reluctantly and they headed back to the house collecting a massive hamper and some towels.

"I'll watch." Todd said, "I didn't bring my swim things."

"The stable boys won't have either."

"Oh!" Todd said and blushed.

David led the way down towards the river through some woodland, they could hear laughing and shouting in the distance but couldn't see anything. Seeing a narrow overgrown path he turned onto it as the shouting got louder.

The woods suddenly opened out into a clearing with what could best be described as a lagoon. More than a dozen boys, some teen-aged and others in their twenties, were there, all naked and obviously enjoying the water. David had set the hamper down and pulled off his t-shirt before anyone noticed them.

"Your Grace." Godfrey asked nervously, "Is anything wrong?"

"I'll throw the next one to call me 'Your Grace' in the water." David said.

"I beg your pardon, Your Grace." Godfrey said uncertainly.

The boy was seventeen and should easily get the better of David, but David just charged pushing the other boy. He staggered backwards and David kept on pushing giving the older boy no time to recover until he stepped back onto nothing and fell into the lagoon.

"I said that I would push the next person to call me 'Your Grace' into the water." David said.

He finished stripping off his clothes and jumped in, swimming out into the river and back before climbing out.

"I'm David." He announced, "I work in the house and I can bring more cider than Billy can filch."

He paused and laughed, "Don't look so worried Billy, I've seen you sneaking out. Next time when you're looking around, look upstairs as well. Cook complains about us making too much and haven't you wondered why it's stored in the cupboard in the passageway."

"So Billy's not in trouble?" Godfrey asked.

"No, he had permission even if he didn't realise it. Let's see what else Cook's sent us."

"You're welcome to join us and you've said what you don't want. What do you want?" Godfrey asked.

David paused until he was sure that he had everyone's attention.

"If Barabourne prospers, we all prosper. If it fails, we all fail," he began, pausing as the boys nodded in agreement.

"That puts us all on the same side. If your superior beats you for being lazy, I can't intervene because it's a chain-of-command thing. If you have a problem and tell me about it then I'll try to help."

"Yeah right. You won't do anything about Mr. Allen though. You think he's too good at his job."

"Can you show me what's wrong? I said show because, if you just told me, it would be your word against his. Can you see that Godfrey?"

Godfrey nodded, "Yes I can, Your Grace. If you want to be our friend, see what you can do about this. Come over here, Fred."

The only estate boy still dressed reluctantly approached.

"Show him." Godfrey commanded but in a gentle voice, "Maybe he will help."

"He said he'd kill me. I didn't want it, I didn't." Fred sobbed becoming hysterical."

"Fred no-one will kill you. Please, I need to know what I'm dealing with." David said.

Reluctantly Fred lowered his trousers to reveal blood soaked underwear.

David turned to Godfrey and mouthed "Rape?" Godfrey nodded.

"Two of you get dressed, help Fred up to the house. Tell Wilson we need a room where he can be examined. Another, get dressed and run for Dr. Hastings. Godfrey, you get dressed as well and come with me. The rest stay here."

Danny helped Fred while Todd stayed with the other boys. David dressed then marched, almost running, to the stables. Once again, Mr. Allen hurried out to greet him.

"I've sent for Dr. Hastings to examine Fred Hollins." David said quietly, "Depending on his findings I shall instruct him to examine the other stable lads. If he confirms what I suspect, then I shall summon the constable. It will take time so if anyone has reason to fear the constable then he should leave now."

"I don't know what these boys have told you but you can't trust…"

"Dr. Hastings and the constable will tell me. The boys will say nothing." David interrupted.

"Come, come, Your Grace, surely you understand when a maid or is it a boy succumbs to your charms."

David, almost purple with rage leapt forward only to be held by Godfrey. As David relaxed so Godfrey stepped forward and punched Mr. Allen in the solar plexus before driving his other fist into the man's cheek.

They could see the older stable hands looking on in amazement then one of them began to clap and the rest joined in.

"He reckoned that the higher ups wouldn't care about a few stable hands and if we said anything we'd just lose our jobs." Godfrey explained, "It seems he was wrong."

"God, I can't believe it." David sobbed, "I was so glad to be home. I'm sorry but I didn't know."

"You do now and you've dealt with it." Godfrey said, "If you still want to be my friend let's go back and see what we've got in that hamper. What should I call you?"

How about David? I don't feel much like a duke at the moment."

"You certainly looked like one. You deserve at least one Your Grace."

David laughed feeling a little happier but still certain that the other boys would resent him and he was still trembling and sobbing when his uncle arrived. So far Jethro had been more worried about his leg. However, David was the duke and he was dealing with underlings. Instinctively he began to remind David not to show such weakness in front of the servants but stopped, taking in the scene. David had apparently not been weak, neither had his assistants and confidantes.

"It seems that we will be walking to church, tomorrow," he said instead, "It's in a good cause though."

"Begging your pardon, My Lord." Godfrey replied, "The

carriages will be ready exactly as His Grace ordered. Zack is the senior hand and knows what to do and I will see that the hands behave."

"And His Grace's wishes concerning that wretch?"

"He can leave or face the constable, My Lord." Godfrey answered, "Again with respect My Lord, may I take David, er, His Grace, back to the river. A good swim would do him the power of good."

Jethro should have replied with a firm 'No' but David had dealt with something that disgusted even him and he did not how to help David.

"It's what he had already prescribed for himself." Jethro smiled, "See that His Grace's instructions are carried out."

Godfrey smiled in understanding.

"Come on then David. The others won't dare touch that hamper without you there and we've got something to celebrate."

"You don't know Todd." David exclaimed, "He'll eat the basket as well if we don't get back."

As the stable-yard settled down after the flurry of activity, Jethro realised that he had forgotten his walking stick. He was still in considerable pain and had a limp but his leg definitely seemed stronger. He wondered whether he should intervene but hesitated. Then realised that there was something he could do and called Zack over.

"I understand that you can have the coaches ready for church tomorrow but can you handle the men?" He said.

"I know what's needed, My Lord," Zack replied, "but as you say, I'm not one to give orders."

"Godfrey appears to have His Grace's confidence. If he were your assistant, you could pass orders through him. I noticed his knuckles, and I don't think that His Grace is big enough to have knocked that man out so I assume that Godfrey stands no nonsense."

"Yes My Lord, that's a good idea." Zack replied, "His Grace wanted to tackle him. He's got spunk..., I'm sorry My Lord."

"David has got spunk." Jethro agreed, "He's got his way of doing things and I don't think that you, Wilson or I will be able to keep up with him. He's been back for six hours and I swear that he's cured my leg as well as digging out that rat. What's going to happen when he's settled back in?"

"Whatever happens, you can rely on the stable hands, My Lord." Zack said, "Mr. Allan knew his job well enough. I feel bad about not reporting him but he convinced us that he'd see us thrown out if we said anything. He's a big man and free with his fists."

"The truth is, before His Grace's absence, you probably would have been let go. Quoting his friend, 'It's the way pedo's work and we shouldn't beat ourselves up about it'. He does seem knowledgeable on these matters and I think I understand what he meant."

"Thank you, My Lord." Zack said, "I think I understand, too. At least it won't happen again here at Barabourne."

"Oh dear." Jethro exclaimed, "I hadn't thought of that. I hope that he doesn't go rampaging across the country."

"I know hands from other estates, My Lord." Zack said, "Word about what's happened will get around so we'll probably hear things. I'll see that you're informed if I learn of anything."

"Thank you very much, Zack." Jethro replied, "That should satisfy him. For once, we oldies will be ahead of the game. Another of young Danny's delightful descriptions."

"An oldie and I'm only thirty-five, My Lord." Zack said.

"I'm thirty-one so he insulted me more." Jethro laughed, "I've just thought. Six hours. I must report to my manservant to take my medication. It's a funny old day."

If Jethro was surprised at the relaxed way in which he chatted to a mere stable-hand, both Godfrey and David were enjoying some obvious hero worship.

"He's going." Godfrey announced back at the clearing, "At least he will when he comes round. Now we both need some of that cider. Come on pass some over. Jack, you're to fire up the boilers an hour earlier, tomorrow. David's done his bit, that's yours so don't let me come chasing after you."

"I thought we were getting all pally." Jack moaned, "Now you're making us work harder."

"You're a fucking idiot." Godfrey snapped angrily. "And a lazy sod to boot. When we go to church tomorrow and it's all done properly we'll be telling the world that's everything's fine. It is going to be harder without that Allan fucker so we'll allow more time. Does anyone else object?"

"You're right, Godfrey." one of the others said, "Do we really call him David?"

"Here yes but try it tomorrow and I'll black your eyes. I'll tan his hide too if he encourages you."

There were some shocked gasps while David and Todd just laughed.

"I'll behave tomorrow, I promise, Master Godfrey." David said in a pretend scared voice.

The other boys joined in the laughter that time then Godfrey described events up to when David leapt at Mr. Allan.

"I had to pull Tiger off," he said, "Then my fists sort of slipped. I dunno, we called him the weasel but he just seemed so slimy then. You just sort of wanted to stamp on him."

If any two things could impress a group of boys then it was hearing about a fight and full stomachs. Cook had just not been able to make do with some bread and cheese. There was ham, beef, pickles and chutneys in the hamper. Although not the best, the stable boys were impressed that there were plates, cutlery and glasses. It all made it seem like a posh picnic and they only had to look across to Godfrey and David to be reassured that all was right with the world.

If anyone was not reassured, then it was David's mother. There seemed to be a constant fuss in the hall, servants were slow to respond and she could not imagine what her afternoon guests would be thinking. Finally, she could not contain herself any longer, excused herself and hurried to the library as quickly as was proper for one of her station.

Dr. Hastings was kneeling on the floor examining Jethro's leg while a plethora of village boy's loafed around showing little respect for where they were.

"I'm sorry, Jethro." she said, "Has your leg deteriorated? Were these boys assisting you?"

"On the contrary." Jethro replied, "My leg is so much better that Dr. Hastings can't believe it."

"If it was anyone but His Grace who had administered the treatment, I would suspect some sort of trickery, My Lord." Dr. Hastings said, "I could believe that relief at his happy return has caused some sort of temporary remission, but little more."

"David has been treating you?" The dowager duchess queried, "How could you let him play silly games like that?"

"I seemed to have little to lose, and it is quite minor compared to his other game but it may not be for your ears."

"I may demand standards but I'm no shrinking violet. Tell me, and be blunt, I have guests and no time for you to try to be delicate."

"The stable manger was an invert of the most disgusting kind. David discovered one of his victims and saw the nature of his injuries. He has dealt with the matter impressively and is now swimming with the stable boys."

"He's cavorting with village boys and you let him? Boys who tolerate a deviant who would use them?"

"David needed to gain their trust before they would confide in him. I am informed that inverts like this, use their position to bully and terrify their victims into silence. It's to David's credit that he succeeded in dealing with it so quickly."

"But he's still cavorting with those so far below his station."

"He's thirteen and dealt with a problem that left me sickened. I share your misgivings but I believe that he now needs the company of boys of his own age and who understand."

"And these boys?"

"None that I would have cared to receive before today though I am learning to appreciate their company."

"Tomorrow, we shall luncheon on the verandah. I will be pleased to meet any boy who looks after my son."

With that she swept out of the room.

"Whoa!" Danny exclaimed, "What was that?"

"That was David's mother trying to acknowledge you." Jethro smiled, "I think that David has impressed her."

"Whoa!" Danny exclaimed again, "You're not like that are you?"

"David was like it before he met you." Jethro said, "I was selfish. I either gave him the benefit of the doubt and allowed him to treat my leg or reject the changes in him and lose my leg."

"No contest, I'd say." Danny said, "You won't change back when your leg's better, will you?"

"No. I could see something in Godfrey's eyes. Rather than undermining discipline as I expected, David's reinforced it. I don't think even David understands it yet but he's building a team who will learn and develop with him, and Barabourne will be a better place because of it."

"Should Todd and I go to church with you tomorrow. It's a big thing isn't it." Danny asked.

"As I said to David's mother, I'm learning to appreciate your company. However, I shall remember that I'm guardian to a duke and expect everything to be in its place and I would expect you to dress and behave properly. Considering that you did not expect to be visiting and are not prepared, it is acceptable if you do not attend any formal event."

"I'd like to be there for David though." Danny said, "Back home I laughed when he said that he was a duke and he's been great to me so I'd like to make up for it."

"Very well. Let's see if we can make a gentleman of you for a couple of hours." Jethro smiled, as he pulled the bell summoning a servant.

"Would you find Wilson please. I should like to see him but only when other duties permit. Inform him that I understand that His Grace has caused considerable disruption and that I can wait."

"I may have insulted him." Jethro chuckled, "I've suggested that he cannot cope no matter what."

Chapter 3

Whatever the events of the Saturday, Sunday morning went well. Wilson had fitted Danny and Todd with morning suits, altered cast-offs from David's wardrobe, the horse landau stood at the front of a line consisting two steam broughams and the steam coach. David wore morning suit, tails and top hat and led the way down the steps from the colonnaded front entrance. He was followed by Jethro and his mother and then Danny and Todd. The servants stood in a line down the steps.

David took his time, pausing to speak to a servant who would bow or curtsey, pleased to have been singled out. David paused at the bottom of the stairs, waiting for his mother and Jethro, and once they were settled, climbed into the landau. Meanwhile, Todd and Danny had boarded the second brougham. Each vehicle had a footman, in the family's case, an adult but Godfrey attended the boys, frowning slightly when Todd tried to greet him. Although Jethro had removed his top hat before getting into the car, the boys could step in and sit as if it was a railway carriage without removing theirs. In the meantime the servants had hurried, far less ceremoniously into the coach.

Todd and Danny were startled by a steam whistle and listened as the lead car chuffed away. They laughed excitedly as their own vehicle glided smoothly off, enjoying the novel trip. They passed a group of small children cheering and waving flags, chaperoned by stern looking matrons. They drove along at a steady trot keeping pace with David's horse drawn landau and even Danny could appreciate that it was quite fast enough for the narrow lane.

The landau drew up and David alighted, raising his hat to the delighted onlookers. He greeted the rector and entered the church, and the landau moved off allowing the first car to draw up so that Jethro and the dowager duchess could alight. The car moved off and then it was the boys' turn. Todd nearly made the mistake of opening the door himself and scrambling out but Godfrey was quick and grabbed the handle and waited briefly until the boys were calmer, then opened the door for them.

Once again, the servants hurried anxious not to keep their betters waiting but it was an amazing experience as they walked through the churchyard.

"I understand that you looked after His Grace while he was lost in the wilderness," the rector gushed, "God bless you."

"It's like one of those Hollywood things." Todd whispered, "They'll never believe it back home."

David's father believed in long services and long sermons. The rector, ever mindful of who his master on Earth was, accepted that a thirteen year old boy could not sit still for long and had reluctantly but pragmatically, shortened the services. Even with the prayers of thanks for David's safe return and more thanks to Danny and Todd for looking after him, the service only lasted three quarters of an hour. David was the first to leave the family pew, standing beside the rector to greet the congregation as they left. His mother and Jethro strolled amongst the emerging congregation. Todd and Craig shook hands while they were thanked yet again for helping David.

"Do you notice how much rougher the villagers' clothes are?" Todd whispered, "Some of the kids are barefoot. It's like a Charles Dickens scene."

Danny nodded, "They seem well though."

Finally, David was ready to go and made his way towards the landau. Immediately the others followed, heading for their own vehicles. As they neared the house, Danny leaned out of a window.

"Godfrey, I want to ask David something before we go inside," he asked. "How do I do it?"

"What do you want to ask His Grace, sir?" Godfrey asked, "I'll run over as soon we stop."

"I want to get my phone and take some pictures before everything's put away." Danny said, "He'll understand."

"Very well, sir."

Events can be changed by the most unexpected incident and vanity can sometimes be an advantage. David's mother looked on uncertainly as Danny took his first picture, of David standing before the grand entrance. She became a little animated as Danny showed her the resulting picture and explained how it could be printed out. She allowed her own picture to be taken and again admired the result. In fact, she was so taken by the pictures that she looked on benignly as David's friends gathered round then watched as more were taken.

A moving picture proved even more of a sensation though it simply depicted David, solemnly holding the car door open as Godfrey alighted and said, 'thank you my good man'.

That David's friends had access to such technology, that Danny was a good photographer and had created such impressive, serious images as well as fun ones, improved their standing in the dowager duchess' eyes. A less charitable version would be that, if she wanted to show off those wonderful new pictures to her friends then she had to be nicer to them. Despite mellowing towards her son's friends, she could not help but say somewhat waspishly, "I'm surprised that you didn't invite that Godfrey boy to lunch."

"I'm surprised that you even know his name," David retorted. "You would not let him forget that he was not dressed properly and then we'd all feel uncomfortable."

"That was a bit harsh." Jethro commented when they found a few moments together.

"I am the duke and my mother won't undermine me," David said. "The funny thing is, Godfrey threatened to tan my hide if I forgot my station today. He may have carried out his threat if I'd invited a mere stable boy to lunch."

Jethro laughed out loud.

"I'll tell him that he has my permission. He's a good lad and you need steady guidance to stop you being carried away." Jethro paused, "I hope that he doesn't forget his station though."

David smiled, "Are you coming to see my friends off?"

"Thank you, no, " Jethro replied, "My leg is vastly improved, unbelievably so but I should still rest it."

"I'm not going to do it all, am I?" David said, "I don't like Dr. Hastings any more but I can't find another doctor as well as everything else, can I?"

"He annoyed you with his remarks, didn't he? Remember it's you who's changed, not him. A few weeks ago, you'd have taken them at face value." Jethro paused, "Let's see, you don't think that Fred is any tougher than you, you think that he would appreciate some mollycoddling and he should have surgery on those tears. I'm not in remission because of relief at your safe return and you were not defrauded by a quack doctor. Have I covered everything?"

"Just about." David smiled.

"Very well." Jethro said, "I don't think that Fred needs to be constantly reminded of his ordeal. It might be different in the other place that you talk about but we don't have this counselling that Danny mentioned. He may talk to other boys who have suffered but apart from turning a blind eye to little gatherings, there is nothing that you can do. You could ask for a second opinion on his physical injuries but I'd trust Dr. Hastings' medical judgement.

"I am tending to believe that this wonder medicine of yours is working, but I really don't know how you found it. Forgive me if I accept the good doctor's caution until we know for certain.

"When he returns tomorrow, I'll make it clear that he is to practice according to medical need and not according to station. He does need to be paid for his efforts so do you have some ideas on that?"

"I have but how do I do it all, Uncle?"

"Today is the Lord's day and a day of rest. Allow Wilson to prepare your offices and then we will consider a manager who can coordinate your various projects."

Jethro paused thoughtfully before continuing, "One idea occurs to me which I should consider outrageous but may solve some problems. Mr. Rogers, the village school teacher is highly qualified. He is only here because he wants time to write his books. He would certainly be able to teach you if you attended say two days a week or is it too egalitarian, even for you?"

"You mean that I could keep up with English, Greek and Latin." David said, "While I was away, I started to learn about the Great War and the rise of one Adolph Hitler. Since neither happened here, my knowledge of twentieth century history is a little confused. Geography could be worse. Apparently Canada only reaches down to the 49th parallel and not the 39th. Spain and France do not occasionally go to war for control of the Americas down to the Caribbean and Spain's puppet Mexico does not also seek to expand North. Instead, there is one great nation called the United States."

"At least in your other place." Jethro laughed.

"Mr. Rogers teaches all ages. Do you think that he could cope with me?"

"We'll think about it."

Jethro might have said more but Todd sidled up, looking unusually nervous.

"It's getting time to go but can I stay, at least for a week. I bet Dad hasn't even noticed that I'm gone. I'll work my keep as a servant if you like."

"We'll speak to Mr. Barton." David said, "You can stay providing it doesn't cause trouble in your world. We'll be going to school, some lessons will seem very strange but you can help me. You know more about electricity and things than I do."

"I suppose I'll get laughed at in history, the way you were." Todd said with a smile, "At least I know that there are two histories."

"I prefer it when you refer to it as the other place." Jethro said, "However, I assume that it has laws and might not the father accuse us of kidnapping his son? It could prove embarrassing."

"I'm more concerned for Mr. Barton." David replied, "He's the adult most closely involved there and he's the one who could be in trouble."

"Could I write to Dad a letter on some of that fancy paper of yours?" Todd asked, "I can say that I'm scared of him when he's drunk. I don't want Social Services dumping me wherever they like and I've got the chance of a good education and to live with good people. If they see that I'm OK, they'll move on to the next case."

"I've written to my foster parents explaining that I've found my way home. I've got those gifts for them but I had a case worker. My disappearance might cause more problems."

"Invite Mr. Barton for tea and we'll discuss it." Jethro said, "Surely this case worker will respect our position."

"Barabourne doesn't exist there, Uncle so our position means nothing but I don't want people who were kind to me getting into trouble."

"Very well." Jethro said, "We'll wait until Tom returns and Danny goes. Arrange for the path as you describe it to be open on another day and we'll monitor events. How does that sound?"

"You mean, I can stay?" Todd asked.

"Providing Mr. Barton agrees." David replied, "If he starts getting problems with the authorities then you'll have to return."

Todd nodded happily.

David's mother played safe and decided on a buffet lunch though a servant stood by to fill her plate. She managed to mingle, speaking to both Todd and Danny, managing to hide her shock at their crude manners. However, she mentioned to Jethro in passing that she could understand what David saw in them. It was high praise about someone who did not appear in Burke's Peerage and Jethro was happy to agree.

Once they had adjourned to the verandah overlooking the gardens, David's mother whispered something to the servant who hurried off. Both David and Jethro were startled and concerned when he returned with Godfrey. His hair was still dripping and his shirt was almost invisible as it clung to his still wet body. She beckoned David over.

"I'm not sure that swimming is becoming for a Sunday," she said. "What do you think?"

"It's resting for boys and enjoying God's gifts." David replied.

His mother actually managed a smile, "Have Wilson fetch him

a bath robe. He'll catch his death of a cold in those wet clothes even if it is warm enough for gentlemen to remove their coats. I have no objections."

It was not so much later that Danny and David needed to change anyway as Danny prepared to return. Todd had written a far simpler letter to Mr. Barton, asking him to forward a copy to his father in which he explained that he was spending a few days with David. David and Danny set off laden with parcels and a wicker cage containing two racing pigeons. Todd went with them helping with the parcels and they gathered around as David cleared the rod.

"You know, it's shining and I've touched it a couple of times." David said, "I'm still here so I hope it's working."

"We'll soon find out." Danny exclaimed, "Put the parcels against it and I'll touch it."

To everyone's surprise, the parcels and the pigeons vanished but Danny remained where he was. Puzzled Danny glanced at David wondering what to do when Tom appeared, his face lighting up when he saw the others.

"Danny and Todd should go through." Tom said, "Danny's parents have been trying to phone and appear to be worried so Mr. Barton needs to get him home as soon as possible. He'll be here on Wednesday at 7.00pm."

David nodded, "You can visit again Danny and will you explain that Todd is staying."

"Thanks Dave." Danny replied as he hugged him, "You've been fantastic."

They separated, Danny touched the rod and disappeared. David covered the rod and they returned to the house with Tom excitedly describing his adventure. Friends touching a rod and disappearing was almost normal that afternoon but what really startled David was to see Godfrey, sitting next to his mother, sharing some joke. She looked up as she saw Tom.

"Thank you Godfrey. You may go," she said, "You must be Tom, come and sit beside me. David, you and your visiting friend should go with Godfrey. I'll send Tom down shortly."

Although concerned for Tom, it seemed like a good idea so David and Todd complied.

"I never thought that I would dare say this but I like your mother." Godfrey said as they walked down to the river, "She understood about Brian Allan and was impressed that we coped so well without him. I got the impression that she's warning me, Tom and

Todd that we'd better look after you or it would go very badly for us."

"Be careful though." David warned, "She relaxed you long enough to get the measure of you but when you were dismissed it was back to normal. When Tom escapes her clutches, Sunday or no Sunday, the four of us will decide what needs to be done next."

They managed to swim for a time before Tom arrived.

"Electricity's amazing," he said. "Are we going to get it here? What about that Internet thing and all that knowledge, will we have it?"

"The canals and the railways were enough of a battle." David replied, "You saw how electricity was carried along those big cables. Landowners are not going to allow another invasion of their land. Except, I learnt about something. Smog."

The others stared at him, waiting while David paused theatrically.

"London relies on coal. When the weather conditions are right, or rather wrong, all that smoke creates smog as it's called over there. It's so bad here that there's a competition to find a solution. I'll ask Uncle Jethro to find out how we enter."

"Isn't that my job?" Tom asked.

"Things like that will become your job. You said yourself that your writing isn't so good so you're coming to school with me." He grinned, "Don't look so alarmed. You might be fifteen but Godfrey is seventeen and if he can cope then so shall you."

"What?" Godfrey exclaimed, looking aghast at David.

"I'm hoping that Mr. Rogers can give me some of my lessons. I want to find scientists and engineers who can develop electricity here. They'll give me lessons in more subjects and I'll find tutors to continue studying the languages I'm learning. I want you three to learn with me. Remember that apart from Godfrey we're the only people who understand what electricity can do. Maybe he can take a trip to the other world as well but we've got to sound and act well educated so that the science people don't laugh at us."

"And we can't pretend." Tom said, "We have to take it all seriously. I understand that but I still don't understand this competition and smog."

"I have been thinking about it. I want to convert Barabourne to electricity and run it down to the village. If we win the competition then we'll run electricity into London, including the poorest parts. The only people who won't get it will be the landowners and the provinces unless they help. Well at least, something like that."

"You're talking about the National Grid or something." Todd said.

"Or something." David agreed, "I know that I've got to get a lot of powerful people on side even if I'm not sure how it all works. For now, I don't want you and Billy sneaking off somewhere tonight. I want you fresh for school tomorrow."

They swam some more until it started getting dark. Tom headed for his parents cottage while Godfrey headed for the stables. Todd and David strolled back to the house.

"Are Billy and Godfrey gay?" Todd asked.

"There's some gossip." David replied.

"Oh, somehow I thought that it would be a big deal here." Todd said.

"Getting a maid pregnant would be a bigger deal." David replied, "Father used to say that ideally, all sex should be confined to the marriage bed, but he wasn't sure if he knew any ideal couples. I never understood until I visited your world where sex was so open. If we had naked maids and menservants cavorting through the house then the whole structure would break down. If a couple sneaks off but are discreet then it's one of those things even if some couples are illegal."

"That's just your attitude." Todd said, "In other places, Godfrey and Billy could go to jail."

"If they're too blatant." David smiled, "I'm supposed to read the newspapers and there's quite a few stories about who's been arrested in Molly houses. I understand what they are now. Billy and Godfrey would do well to keep clear of them."

"What about you?" Todd asked, "Do you like sex?"

David stopped frowning thoughtfully.

"I suppose I want it but I could so easily be like Brian Allen. I could take anyone I wanted and who would stop me? That scares me now."

"You're not like that. Who do you fancy?"

"I don't know. You know that it's my duty to produce the twentieth duke and I think that I like the idea but sometimes I wonder about what Godfrey and Billy get up to. I don't know."

They had been serious for too long.

"Come on. I'll race you." Todd yelled, charging headlong for the house and David, suddenly more cheerful, chased after him.

They were a conspicuous and somewhat self-conscious group as they headed for the school house the next day. Nationally, children were required to attend until they were fourteen for five mornings a week. For the rest of the time, it was assumed that were learning a trade. In reality, most were just labouring and in some places they did not even attend that much. On the Barabourne estates, children attended the minimum required but little more.

David's group were older of course and although they arrived early there were enough younger children to stare at them curiously. Mr. Rogers also stared, puzzled before recovering and inviting them in.

"Could you cope with teaching us English and the classics?" David asked, "We also need to study mathematics, including algebra and arithmetic but not so much geometry."

"I could teach those subjects but you should also learn more of the quadvirem and include music and astronomy. By English, I assume that you mean grammar so what about the other parts of the trivirem, logic and rhetoric? You look puzzled young man."

He was looking at Todd as he spoke.

"I don't get all those subjects that you were talking about," he replied, "OK English grammar but what about composition or creative writing? I do maths and you don't need computer studies here but what about history and geography?"

"Now I'm puzzled." Mr. Rogers said, "What are computer studies?"

"Word processing, googling..." Todd trailed off, seeing Mr. Rogers looking even more confused, "Maybe David could bring his laptop in... That's not helping either. Can we come back to it when we can show you?"

David thought it time to change the subject, "You used to teach Tom and Godfrey, so you have some idea of their standard. Todd will surprise you, both with what he knows and what he doesn't. We need to be able communicate with scholars without appearing to be country bumpkins and for myself, I need to be able to convince my uncle that I'm receiving an education suitable for my station. Village boys speak highly of you and I'd rather study under someone I already know rather than find a tutor. Of course your extra duties will be reflected in your salary."

"Very well. If you would all care to take your seats at the back of the classroom, I think for today, an essay from each of you about your plans for the future, it may help me understand more. I'll find some writing materials for now, Your Grace, but my budget is limited."

"I understand. I'll see that we have everything we need and increase the budget for the others." David said.

They all stared as Todd took out a folder and some pens, then blushed.

"I do my homework at Mr. Barton's now," he explained, "I just keep all my stuff in this bag."

Mr. Rogers asked to see one of the ball-point pens that Todd was handing around and tried it on a pad on his desk.

"Interesting," he said, "I have no objection to you using them but now, it's time to call the rest in."

Chapter 4

Much to Jethro's surprise, the estate boys/workers settled down without any fuss. He had expected the younger boys in particular to take advantage of David's relaxed style but if anything, the reverse was true. True, the younger hands no longer waited to be spoken to, before greeting him with a cheery smile and a 'Good morning, My Lord', but if anything they seemed to work harder. It also fascinated him how they could mix the respectful and the informal in a single sentence. For example, he might be asked, 'Is His Grace busy today or is David coming swimming?'

At first, the older men looked on horrified, and he was sure that more than one lad had got a clip round the ear or a stern telling-off once he was gone. However, as he relaxed, he learned to respond then discuss the work that was going on. It had always happened, but where the older hands spoke cautiously, not offering more than a careful answer to a question, the boys talked freely, offering a little gossip, generally bringing the conversation alive.

"How's your leg, My Lord?" One boy asked, "David hated using you as a guinea pig so he's quite relieved that you seem to be improving."

"Thank you." Jethro replied, "His experiment seems to be working and it's finally beginning to heal. I'll make sure I don't walk into another scythe, though."

"In that case, I don't suppose that you could assist, could you My Lord?" The boy asked, "We can't get a straight pull on that log and it snags. We need a second rope to guide it. I was about to run back and ask someone but it'll take time if everyone's busy. We want to paint that strange box that his Grace has had built in Lower Field today so we can start on the fences, tomorrow."

"I'm sorry, My Lord." The older hand said, "You boy, report to Mr. Davis. You'll as like be let go for that."

Once, Jethro would have agreed but he was curious.

"Just a moment," he said, "If you had gone back, you could have loafed around pretending to look for someone. By the time you got back then you would have had an easier morning tomorrow just painting the box."

"Maybe." The boy said, "If David did it that way, that man Allan would still be here."

Jethro could see that the boy was completely sincere and he had not realised just how deep an impression the incident had made on the younger estate hands. Boys, which included those in their twenties, were assigned to older hands to learn their skills, in this case repairing fences. Suddenly Jethro remembered something.

"You're Jennings and this is Tom's replacement. I take it he's as bright as Tom and just as cheeky."

"Yes My Lord." Jennings replied, "I do seem to get them."

"I'm surprised by his comments though."

"About His Grace, you mean, My Lord." Jennings said, "Begging your pardon, but he's come home with some strange ideas. The lads seem to understand them but I'm jiggered if I do."

"I know how you feel." Jethro sighed. In fact the boy was not a boy but a young man in his late twenties, big and strong from hard work. As a mere farm boy he had no status yet Jethro felt as if he was being assessed. Was he fit to be David's uncle? Jethro shook himself, trying to clear his head of such a ridiculous idea but it persisted, together with the idea that he could lose authority if he was found wanting.

"Very well." He said, "How can I help?"

Jethro returned home unusually happy. Ever since he had stumbled against the scythe in the barn, the threat of losing his leg had hung over him. It ached certainly, but he had got the use back so he felt ridiculously pleased with himself at being able to help Jennings and he was impressed with the attitude of the younger estate workers.

Although he had taken the initiative Jethro was satisfied David was taking his education seriously so it was becoming more unlikely that David would be sent away to school.

It was another incident that finally decided him. A Mr. Garfield visited, sent by his father to negotiate some work that David wanted to be done. Jethro did not like the man, thinking him pompous and arrogant, but the negotiations were going well until David asked, "I hear your launch had some problems passing through our lands, Mr. Garfield."

"Oh that. The hand was incompetent but at least he was able to fix it. I've let him go. I suppose you heard from those estate boys. I didn't mention the incident because I didn't want to complain but they were loud and rude, jeering while we struggled to get her to the bank."

"According to them, a couple swam out to help guide your boat in. A boy was ready to run up to the house to warn us, in case you could not continue and another stood by in case you needed some tools. Yet another helped your man, then showed you why the valve needed replacing."

"It took quite firm words to make them dress for the ladies who were embarrassed at their immodesty. They milled around trying to swamp the boat and were quite rude when I wanted to send for help." Mr. Garfield said, "Common folk have no manners and do not need praising nor should they be listened to, especially if they speak against a gentleman."

Only Jethro noticed David's growing anger, wondering what was wrong. There was a long pause where even Mr. Garfield became uncomfortable.

"Thank you, Mr. Garfield." David said with an icy calmness, "We'll not detain you because we won't be doing business with you."

"Because of the word of that scum." Mr. Garfield gasped.

"No, because you lied to me." David said, "You see, I was one of the boys that swam out to collect the line that you tried to throw. Your aim was appalling by the way which is why we couldn't catch it from the bank. We did dress as quickly as possible but some of us were making the boat fast. I was ready to come back to the house to greet you properly rather than embarrass you for not recognising me and Godfrey did show you why the valve was unsuitable. What I cannot forgive is that you said that you would put in a good word for the boys. When I gave you the opportunity, you insulted them. I should say that you insulted us. You said today that you can guarantee the delivery even though it's tight. Please explain how an unsolicited promise beside the river can be meaningless while a promise to deliver no matter what, should be trusted?"

Mr. Garfield turned to Jethro.

"Surely you see the difference in placating a gang of wastrels..." he trailed off, realising what he had said, "I mean if His Grace chooses to mix with the likes of them... Surely you see, My Lord."

"Yes I do see." Jethro said, "My nephew would have respected you if you had relied on your position and treated them as servants, himself included. It is that you chose to be kind and generous towards them to achieve your ends but now choose to denigrate them because you do not wish to be beholden to them. I shall write to your father directly, informing him of our decision and why."

Mr. Garfield glared angrily at David and stormed out.

"I did do right, didn't I Uncle." David asked.

"Yes you did. Our word can be trusted by anyone so we should expect the same courtesy. His father's word is also good but it won't stop him trying to get the measure of you so he'll respect you for catching his son out so effectively. On another matter, is it such a good idea to mix with the hands so much?"

"I think so, Uncle. I didn't think much about class before I went to the other place but now I see it everywhere and it can be most entertaining."

"Explain."

"On Saturdays, river traffic is mainly pleasure. With the lower classes, it tends to be skiffs being rowed. The young men see us and may make some remark, but their young ladies tell them that they should not engage with the likes of us. You see, they want to appear posh. The middle classes are embarrassed by our lack of dress though the females do try to look. The upper class ladies offer a regal wave as if they were in some procession and the men find it amusing to engage in a little banter."

"It's the reverse of what I'd expect." Jethro said, "It's an interesting observation though."

"It's the variations that become interesting." David continued, "Mr. Garfield is one, but there is another that I was going to tell you about."

"It involves a tailor, I hope that we don't owe him money, and his family. He had his children in a small steam skiff and the lads called out as he sailed past. He turned then headed for the bank. We thought he might be angry but he asked if his boys could join us for a swim. It seems that the children's grandmother is dying and the mother has gone to look after her.

"Now I've never realised just how soft and sentimental our lads could be. Once they heard the story, they made a great fuss of the boys. I'm afraid the father also relaxed and got a little tipsy on our cider. Apparently they all got home safely though, because I received a letter from him, thanking me for the boys' hospitality and hoping that he hadn't intruded."

"So very different to Garfield." Jethro said and David nodded.

"Tom will reply saying his thanks will be passed on to the boys in question. His Grace knew and approved of their hospitality and that he is also aware of Godfrey's invitation to see our steam vehicles. Apparently the boys are fascinated by anything mechanical and as I say, it was Godfrey being soft. Godfrey may fire up the steamers and generally entertain them."

"You don't mind?" Jethro asked, "You're as soft as Godfrey."

"Maybe I am and maybe we're thinking the same thing. We can't ease Fred's pain, but maybe we can ease theirs. I kept the letter formal because people get so flustered around a duke, I can't think why. His Grace will remain aloof and distant."

"I'm impressed." Jethro said, "I said that I'd give it a month before I decided, but since your education appears adequate, it's time to put our plans into practice but there's one caveat. I'm still uneasy that you forget your station so easily. In truth, I believe that Barabourne is running more smoothly than I expected but should discipline deteriorate then I shall reconsider."

David breathed a sigh of relief. He may be the duke but until he was twenty-one, his uncle was his guardian and could intervene so he needed Jethro's support.

Even in the first few days it was obvious that Wilson was also supporting him. The rooms that he had mentioned were duly cleared, and somehow he found the furniture to make them usable. One resembled a classroom, another was bare except for a couple of stout kitchen tables while the third was a staff room.

"I regret that neither the décor nor the furniture is what you would normally expect, Your Grace, but I shall obtain new as soon as possible."

"You've done wonders Wilson, thank you." David said, "Uncle Jethro can begin looking for the people we need. I need to speak to him now."

"I intend visiting the other world again." David announced, "It's up to Todd whether he comes too but I'm taking Godfrey. I want to talk to Mr. Barton and Danny about the gate. They've been researching it from their side and I want to see their work."

"Can't you send for them?" Jethro asked.

"No. Don't forget that I'm not a duke over there." David replied, "Besides, a lot of their research will be on that Internet thing. It doesn't work here."

"And your projects here?" Jethro asked.

"You've agreed to place advertisements in various journals." David replied, "It'll take time to assemble the engineers we need and I only intend to be away for a few days. Mr. Rogers is already seeing himself as a grammar school headmaster and has set us assignments so that we do not fall behind. I was worried about getting started with him and he's already worried about us falling behind."

Jethro laughed cheerfully.

"I visited him when you started," he said, "I made it clear that he should not stand any nonsense from you and that it was in your best interests to accept his discipline. I may have convinced him too well so be warned. I understand that he can be quite severe with pupils who do not give of their best."

"Thank you, Uncle. That was most thoughtful of you. Maybe I should remember my station more."

"Then you'll go to school where they're used to dealing with aristocrats."

"I'll stay with Mr. Rogers then though the other world is becoming more attractive. Teachers there are not allowed to beat pupils."

"A strange world indeed." Jethro chuckled, "God speed and I shall endeavour to carry out your wishes, including your extraordinary treatment of the staff."

Less than a week after returning, David prepared himself for a visit to the other world. Tom and Todd were there to see him off and Godfrey was nervously waiting to accompany him. David opened the box that had been built around the rod and watched as it shone brightly then leapt back as Danny, holding his bike, appeared.

"Mr. Barton's been arrested," he yelled, "The police think I'm involved as well."

"Involved in what?" David asked, "Calm down and explain from the beginning."

"OK, I'm a bit scared. Sorry. Your social worker called on Monday and Mum showed him the letter that you'd written. He wasn't happy and said that he needed to know where you were. Mum explained that Mr. Barton had seen you off and I was with him so he questioned me. I just said that we'd seen you off at the station. It might have been all right but today the school phoned Todd's dad to say that he's been absent. Mr. Barton's name came up again and it was the same social worker and he called the police. A police car turned into my street as I was leaving. I don't know if they're after me."

"Very well." David said, "I'm sorry Godfrey but you must postpone your trip. Todd, it's you and me, we've got to go to the police station. Tom, will you take Danny to my uncle. Try to explain what's happening."

"I'm not sure that I understand." Godfrey said, "You have friends that are in trouble and you're going to rescue them, is that correct? I'll go with you."

David thought about arguing but ever since Godfrey knocked

Mr. Allen out, he had seemed like a protector or something and someone worth having around if there was trouble. Moments later, all three boys were on the other side of the hedge.

"According to those maps, it's a three hour walk to Chasebourne." Godfrey said, "It'll be dark before we get there."

David checked his wallet.

"I'd say an hour." David said, "Let's see how close we can get to the Ashford road."

Godfrey was the last of the boys to cross between worlds. He'd heard the others talk about it, had experienced the strange jump across the hedge but so far everything seemed to be the same. Well, not quite everything. The lane they were walking along was no longer a dirt track but now had a smooth dark surface which felt hard beneath his feet.

They had been walking for about five minutes when Godfrey heard a strange drone behind them, steadily getting louder. He looked behind, then just stared. He could see that it was a vehicle, he could even see the driver but it was like nothing that he had ever seen before. Todd looked behind him and his eyes lit up as he held out his hand.

"How about that then," he exclaimed as it drew up beside them. "A taxi."

"I had a drop at the Royal George and now I've got a pick up in Chasebourne." the driver said, "I can take you in that direction."

"That's fine." David said, "Er, How much will that be?"

"It depends on the meter. How much have you got?"

"Forty pounds." David replied.

"You can go first class for that," the driver chuckled, "Jump in."

Godfrey's first instinct was to open the door for David but often it is the small things that are more alien than the big. He felt worldly wise in understanding that the car was a method of transport but he stared at the door uncertain how to use the handle. Grinning, David opened the door for him and allowed him to clamber in. Just as tactfully, Todd demonstrated the seatbelt while David got into the front passenger seat.

"Where to?" The driver asked.

"The police station, please." David replied.

"The police station? You're not in trouble are you?"

"No, We've been visiting my family and now we're meeting up with friends. It just seemed like the easiest place for all of us."

The driver nodded, not particularly interested. It was near the end of his shift and he was getting tired so he did not say much more. Godfrey watched the world go by, unused to the comfort especially when they hit the main road and although travelling at an incredible speed, the car just seemed to purr along. He stared in wonder at the other traffic and worked out that traffic lights and the flashing lights on vehicles were electrical. He jumped when a disembodied voice crackled into life before the driver took a small box on a wire, again obviously electrical, and spoke into it and received a reply. Shops seemed to be brightly lit and he began to understand why David wanted to introduce electricity at Barabourne.

Seventeen year olds hate to look foolish and the taxi driver was a stranger who would not understand where they came from. By the end of the journey he had a host of questions but he could not ask them. They were all about things that seemed ordinary to the rest so to mention them would make him seem like a bumpkin yet it seemed better to act like one. He settled back, enjoyed the view and waited for his master to speak to him.

Although David still enjoyed the novelty of such a journey, he was more worried about how he was going to deal with matters. As a duke in a country ruled by Charles VII, he was already able to handle people. His father and his uncle had taught him something of running Barabourne and his other estates as well as preparing him for government through his seat in the lords. He decided to be himself and act as if he was in charge. He nearly lost his nerve as they entered the police station but he was confident enough when he rang for attention.

"I am David Pevensey, this is Todd Phillips, I believe that you're holding a Mr. Barton on suspicion of kidnapping us."

"Just a moment, and I'll speak to someone," the police constable said.

They waited for ten minutes before a door opened and a man in civilian clothes hurried through.

"I'm Detective Inspector Carson," he said, "Now what's this about?"

"You're concerned about us being kidnapped." David said, "We're quite well and I'm back with my family. Todd is staying with me. Will you release Mr. Barton please because we're staying with him for a few days."

"All in good time." D.I. Carson said, "First I need your statements and then we will consider them with the other evidence."

"No. Since I am obviously here of my own freewill and consent then there was no crime. Therefore, there can be no evidence and therefore you are trying to delay freeing an innocent man. That may be something for a solicitor to look into."

D.I. Carson glared at David who calmly looked back at him.

"Social Services are involved. I have to contact them first."

"Why? Do they investigate crimes for you?"

"It's how we do things. Now names."

"Todd, here's my phone, see how quickly you can get a solicitor here. Inform him that we seek a writ of habeas corpus tonight. Tomorrow I will instruct him on actions for compensation."

David was irritated by the D.I's attitude. D.I. Carson was annoyed at apparently having wasted a lot of time but he was still suspicious. He might have suspected that David was being threatened into seeking Mr. Barton's release but given David's attitude, it seemed unlikely but he was not going to be stampeded.

"I need your full name and some form of ID." he said.

"His Grace David Pevensey, Duke of Barabourne. So far as identity is concerned, I have a distinct form of handwriting which I would say is the equivalent of a signature. Todd, have you found a solicitor yet."

"The duty solicitor is with him. He'll deal with his release." D.I. Carson interrupted.

"Ah good, he is here. I announced myself at seven minutes before seven o'clock. It is now ten past seven. Mr. Barton has been unnecessarily in custody for seventeen minutes. When will he be released?"

D.I. Carson felt as if he was being out-manoeuvred by a thirteen year old boy. He had read David's social services report but he assumed that amnesiacs were confused which did not fit in with David's confidence, but maybe he could prick the boy's delusion. He grabbed a sheet of paper and a pen, telling David to confirm his identity.

David duly wrote, *"I duly confirm that I am His Grace David Pevensey, Duke of Barabourne but I am known in the Borough of Chasebourne as just David Pevensey."*

Modern boys could not normally write so elegantly and D.I. Carson realised that he had lost more ground as David glanced pointedly at the clock.

"Where are you staying tonight?" He asked.

"With Mr. Barton." David replied.

"He's a suspect in…" D.I. Carson trailed off as he realised that Mr. Barton was no longer a suspect in anything but it all seemed wrong.

"I'll speak to Mr. Barton's lawyer," he said. "Please bear with me, David, if I may call you that."

David shrugged, "It's how I'm known here."

"As I was saying, if you'll bear with me. We have to be very careful when it comes to dealing with minors and I'm sure that Mr. Barton will understand that I must check everything."

"Fair enough, but the clock is still ticking."

D.I. Carson could have interviewed David and Todd trying to get evidence of some sort of assault by Mr. Barton but he doubted that David would weaken under pressure. Todd might but it was still unlikely. In the circumstances he had no choice but to accept that he had been wasting his time on a complete misunderstanding. If he continued with his investigation, he risked being caught up in the sort of farcical situation which the press love, especially if they could make him look like a fool. It would be safer to free Mr. Barton but keep a discreet eye on them all. He headed for the interview room.

"I'm sorry to have kept you. David and Todd have arrived. There's been a slight delay because they were not exactly cooperative but I managed to confirm their identities. They are minors and I do have loose ends to tie up so I may want to interview you again," he glanced at the solicitor, "I shouldn't ask but is he a Duke?"

"He has an impressive knowledge of the local area especially with Dalton Hall and the site of an old watermill. If we knew where the Earl was buried, I'd certainly be thinking in terms of DNA testing."

There was a mystery, but not a criminal one. He took Mr. Barton through to the boys, and watched as they greeted him, vaguely surprised that he had to be introduced to the older boy, Godfrey. The solicitor looked curiously at the scene, shook hands and left.

"I found some plans of Barabourne Hall dated from 1709." David said as they left, "I thought that they would be more useful than more modern ones."

D.I. Carson shrugged. It was an odd comment but it was not a criminal one so there was nothing that he could do. Without an obvious victim, evidence or even a formal complaint, then for all practical purposes the case was closed.

51

By way of celebration Mr. Barton took them all for a meal. It was a warm evening so they settled on buying a pizza then sitting round a table in the garden of Mr. Barton's favourite pub. For Godfrey, it was an incredible meal. He even felt a little superior as he was allowed a beer while they ate but David and Todd had to make do with soft drinks. As it got darker so the lights came on, and he took in sights and sounds that the others took for granted. A helicopter flew over. A police car tore along the street outside, horns blaring and blue lights flashing. He watched puzzled as other customers stared at small flat boxes, jabbing away with their fingers and thumbs.

He didn't doubt now that he was in a different world and one that depended completely on electricity. He was also aware that it was cleaner and there was no smell of coal smoke that he had noticed in other towns.

"Very well." Mr. Barton said as they relaxed, "David and Todd should go to school tomorrow and David should phone Danny's parents now. Godfrey can spend the day at the library with me, or take a stroll around town but either way he can get an idea of why electricity is so important here. I'll be covered because I'll be in the library and Danny will get away with a sick day. The only real problem is if your social worker gets awkward, David. How about your father, Todd?"

"I tried phoning him." Todd said bitterly, "He was pissed and muttered something about a win. I don't think he remembers that I've been away."

David put his arm around Todd.

"You've got us now. We'll look after you," he said and Godfrey nodded.

There was a pause while Todd recovered then David asked, "Do you have any idea what that device is?"

"None whatsoever." Mr. Barton replied, "There's plenty of science fiction and fantasy about the notion but we can't find anything that can explain it. There are theories about quasars and black holes being the same thing and balancing energy levels between universes but that's all. Mini black holes may exist but no-one has found one yet though they may have created one in that Large Hadron Collider thing in Berne. To be honest I've got no idea about what's happening; I've seen you boys vanish but that's it."

"We see the rods," Todd said, "but are they connected to anything?"

"You mean, they could just be consoles like a keyboard. It

makes sense, if we just touch it we go through. If we put goods there they go through but we don't. How do you say it, there's an 'app' running it?"

"So what do you suggest?" Mr. Barton asked.

"When everyone is on their side of the er, what do we call it?"

"How about 'portal'." Mr. Barton suggested, "Go on."

"We look for the controls. When one side is covered, the other side looks as if it's camouflaged, it's obviously working so I wonder if that's when it can be adjusted."

"And you're thinking that if you alter the controls then you won't be able to reset them and the portal here will be closed for good."

David nodded, he might have said more but his phone rang just then. Puzzled he picked it up, surprised to see that it was Danny's father, Terry Lambert.

"Danny keeps claiming to be sleeping over with Craig but according to Craig's mother, they haven't seen him." He said, "What's going on?"

"We're dining at the Blacksmiths Arms, well eating a pizza in the garden. You're welcome to join us."

While they waited, they did not feel like continuing with the main topic of conversation so they showed Godfrey how the phone worked and answered his many questions. Mr. Lambert was angry as they met up but they settled down around the table.

"I can understand that David's memories are grounded in fact." Mr. Lambert said, "What I cannot understand are your appearances and disappearances. Where does Danny disappear to?"

"It's difficult to answer." Mr. Barton said, "David's memories are more real than anyone can understand. I could say that we can disappear into them and perhaps you could accept that as a poetical description rather than an exact answer."

"You mean, a form of hypnosis or something." Mr. Lambert said.

"Or something. I wouldn't allow boys of this age to tamper with each other's minds."

"I can understand that." Mr. Lambert said, "Is Danny in any danger?"

"I'm planning an expedition." David said, "The biggest risk is that I won't be able to come here any more but I'll be alive and well."

"Right. Why don't you tell me what's really going on." Mr. Lambert snapped angrily.

53

"You have a right to know because Danny is involved." Mr. Barton said, "David's problem is that he needs to defend his home and the authorities here could prove a threat. The first thing that you need to understand and fully accept, is that David's memories are not delusional but real. You are sitting with the Duke of Barabourne."

"Mr. Barton, I'm not worried about that; I want to know if my son is in danger."

"Is he in danger if he rides his bike into town? I'm not dodging the question, I'm trying to say that there are risks but any adventurous boy is at risk.

"Fair enough. There's this big secret about where David comes from but Danny is more excited than worried. He's coming up to fourteen and he's seen a lot through the kids we foster. I have to trust him but it's all so unusual."

"That's fair enough." Mr. Barton said, "David?"

David nodded in agreement.

"I think that the easiest thing is for you to visit," he said. "I'm going home tomorrow night. Why don't you come along? You too, Mr. Barton, Uncle Jethro would very much like to meet you."

"No thanks." Mr. Barton replied, "I retire in a few years and then I'm just going to potter around with the Historical Society and my garden. I'll help but I'll leave the adventures to you."

"Thank you, David. I must admit that I'm curious but if the police are satisfied then I'll let Danny have his adventure without his old man checking up on him."

David nodded then said, "We'll be staying with Mr. Barton until tomorrow night. Danny thinks the police are after him so he's staying at my place but he'll be home tomorrow or do you want us to fetch him now?"

"No." Mr Lambert replied, "Let him have his adventure."

It was Todd who changed the subject, "Why do we still call you Mr. Barton? What's your first name?"

"It's Richard. You're probably too young to understand why I dislike being called Dick Barton so I prefer Mr. Barton."

"I probably come from the wrong planet to understand." David chuckled.

Danny's father looked on puzzled as the others seemed to agree so he contented himself with, "It's getting late and don't you have school tomorrow"

"We've got assignments to do so we're going to show Godfrey the wonders of television and Harry Potter." David said, "Then we'll settle down."

Chapter 5

Even Mr. Barton needed time to relax but they slept well and were up early the next day. Both Todd and David had work set by Mr. Rogers so they decided to complete that. Godfrey was left to explore the town on his own.

He rode a bus to some destination, he could not remember where, then caught a train to the next station and back. For lunch, he bought a hamburger and a cup of coffee. It should have been easy, fast food it was called, but everything is done for the first time. The queue behind him became increasingly impatient as he struggled with the menu board and the list of options thrown at him by staff who had asked the same questions all morning and had received almost automatic responses back.

Godfrey's idea was to learn about electricity, not so much technical data but about what it could do. Watching television was fun but from automatic barriers to lighting to traffic lights, it was the things that everyone else took for granted that really fascinated him. In all he enjoyed a quiet uneventful day missing the only drama that occurred. Around midday there was a knock on the door and when David answered it, he found his social worker, John Hemmings standing there.

"You've been causing a lot of trouble," he said, without preamble, "I need you to come with me while I decide what to do with you."

In any trade or profession, there are those that excel, giving everything they can to their work. At the other end of the scale there are people like John Hemmings. He was lazy, had little interest in his clients and got by through making sure all the boxes on the forms were ticked. He used being overworked and understaffed as an excuse for delaying and doing the minimum necessary to avoid trouble with his superiors. At forty five he was already counting the days until he could retire. Although David did not understand the nuances of John's life, he did recognise his apathy and complete lack of interest.

"I'm back with my real family so I'm all right, thank you." David replied, "I'm only visiting and I'm going home later today."

"Your foster mother says that you ran away." John said, "We'll need to find you a place for tonight."

"I told you." David said, "I've found my way back to my real family. I don't need anything."

"That's not good enough." John said, "I need to speak to your parents. They didn't report you missing so there's a question of neglect."

"No, there's a question of communication and transport." David said, "Really, there's no problem."

Normally, John would have accepted it, mentioned something about going to the school then disappearing into the nearest café for a leisurely cup of tea. However, the police had become involved and his superiors were picking up on a possible high profile child abuse case so he needed to be far more careful filling in his reports.

"For a start, you're staying here. Mr. Barton has been arrested for kidnapping you and possible assault. Even if he's on bail, you'll be at risk if he's released."

Typically, John had merely skimmed through the report, not caring about the detail.

"He has been released without charge." David exclaimed, "It was all a big misunderstanding and it's sorted out now."

"So you say but I need to be sure."

John was not interested in explanations, trying to understand the situation would take time and effort; putting David into a home would confirm that he had acted positively and would look good.

"Don't make me come back with a policeman and a court order," he said.

David shrugged, "Please yourself but if you do so, make sure that the paperwork has no errors. If it does, I'll have a solicitor suing you and your department for negligence."

David spoke confidently, the situation was not as straightforward as John had thought which meant more work if he pushed it. A thought flashed into his mind. If the police we're satisfied, then a calm response, keeping the department out of an embarrassing mix up would look good. His next case was a two year old whose parents were drug takers so he could claim that it was more urgent but first a pub. He could phone the police station then 'carefully weigh up the information', in other words, have an extended lunch.

"I expect you back at school tomorrow and I'll be keeping a close eye on you."

He turned on his heels and strolled back to his car. David watched him drive off. He was uneasy, knowing that he needed to tie up loose ends but he felt that he had got the measure of Mr. Hemmings. He also had the feeling that Todd was slipping through the net. For some reason, Mr. Hemmings had forgotten about Todd, even though he was also mentioned in the police report. The pub beckoned and when he looked later Todd's file was mysteriously up-to-date.

There were still loose ends but on the whole, as they set off for the portal, they were satisfied that everything would settle down and the remaining questions would be forgotten.

Mr. Barton had steadily saved during his life, not out of meanness but because he was not interested in having the latest gadgets or going on exotic holidays or other material possessions. His passion was local history and David had offered him a chance to learn more about his locality than any other incident in his life. He saw the need for communications so had no problem buying half a dozen mobile phones, albeit the most basic models. He saw that David had needed a way of storing information hence the laptop. He was happy to do so because they were necessary tools and not fashion accessories. Each boy had a phone now and so David phoned Godfrey. While David had used them often enough to be quite blasé, Godfrey was startled when a strange tune emanated from his pocket. It took an effort to remember to take the phone out and he was definitely nervous when he pressed the talk button and put the phone to his cheek.

"Hello there," he said still not convinced that he was not talking to himself.

"Ah good." David said, "Carry on with your day, Godfrey but instead of returning to the house, would you make your way to the railway station. Wait outside and we'll collect you."

"OK." Godfrey replied, "That's what they say here, isn't it?"

"Very good. I believe that I should finish with, 'have a nice day'. Oh and don't forget to press the red button."

"No Your Grace." Godfrey replied but David was sure that he was more sarcastic than respectful.

Mr. Barton had also ensured that his visitors had plenty of spending money. He could go out for a day and not spend anything but teenagers liked treats and to do things that did cost money such as Godfrey's exploration of public transport. Despite his generosity, the maps and plans that David had given were worth ten times what he had spent so he was happy as they arrived at the portal where Danny was waiting for them.

"Tom's on the other side and he says that all's well," he said.

"Of course." David replied, "Tomorrow's Friday. We'll open the portal at the same time."

Danny leapt forwards to hug David, "It's fucking fantastic. I'm sorry I laughed when you tried to tell us."

"I'd have laughed too." David exclaimed, "Great metal tubes flying through the sky, pictures coming through the ether. Who on Earth would believe such nonsense? We'd better hurry."

Later when David was alone, he sent for Wilson.

"Can you cope with my friends?" David asked, "I'm including Tom and Godfrey as my friends as well. I liked your comment about you maintaining order while I wreck it but it does make life difficult for you."

"I've served your family all my life in one way or another." Wilson replied, "I see a lot of your father in you but since your return I see more. You command respect, not obedience or fear and your friends do not take advantage of you. May I suggest that you all behave more appropriately in the West wing or the main entrance and I shall endeavour to see just a group of friends in the rest of the house."

"I let you and mother do it your way in half the house and you do it my way in the other half." David said.

"I think that visitors would appreciate a little more aristocratic behaviour from you but in general, yes."

"You could be right. There are times when a little formality and order would be useful." David said, "Will you remind me if His Grace is needed, I'm not going to do it all on my own."

"I will, Your Grace." Wilson said, "I do understand that you have undergone a highly unusual experience and that you're undertaking very important new ventures. I will see that the staff offers you every support, no matter how unusual."

"Thank you Wilson. I just needed to be sure."

"I didn't like to suggest it before but in line with this conversation, I'm thinking that despite what I said, you should also only enter the kitchen with cook's permission. She would not appreciate her soufflé collapsing because you wanted a glass of water and the staff were curtseying to their lord and master.

"Health and Safety." David smiled, "Kitchens tend to have pots of boiling water and the like. The other place tends to make a fuss about avoiding accidents."

"A good idea. Feel free to knock at the door and wait for an answer but if you really want to forget your station then beware Mrs Mason if her latest culinary efforts are not perfect."

David laughed, "Thanks for the warning. Any other tips?"

"None for the moment." Wilson replied.

"Then that will be all, Wilson but there is something that you might do for me."

"Yes Your Grace."

"Would you keep a decanter of our best whisky in your pantry. I'm not that fond of the stuff but I do have adult guests so would you sample it regularly to ensure it is suitable to be served."

"It would be my pleasure, Your Grace. Good night."

It would never do to invite a servant to drink his master's best supplies but David had wanted to thank Wilson. Turning an invitation into an order maintained the niceties of servant/master relations and David had made his gratitude more tangible.

The following day, David and his friends chose to go swimming. Most of the estate boys were working so they were alone and in between dips in the water they were discussing their situation. It was Billy who burst in on them then hesitated as he grappled with the message he had been given.

"Mr. Wilson says that David should put these clothes on then return to the house via the stables. His Grace's presence is required to greet Lord Carlton. The rest should stay here."

David looked at the clothes and nodded. Everyone was looking at him with varying degree of puzzlement and worry so he explained as he dressed.

"Lord Carlton is trouble so Wilson wants me to be seen as a young duke who has been out for a very respectable ride and not cavorting with commoners. I'm sorry but I think he may be right."

"Of course he is." Godfrey exclaimed, "You have your duties like any other estate boy. Now be off with you, and make sure you carry them out properly. Billy can stay here. We don't want too many idlers sneaking around."

David nodded his thanks and hurried off, drying his hair with a towel.

"I'm not an idler." Billy said huffily.

"It's looks that count and it's just in case His Lordship's nosing around." Godfrey said, "You look out of place. Relax and behave like one of David's guests. "

It was exciting for David to hide behind the hedgerows as he made his way round the house to the stables then strolled nonchalantly to the main entrance to find Lord Carlton standing on the steps.

"Good morning, Your Grace." Lord Carlton greeted him, "I think that your mother fusses a little too much. You're attired as a gentleman and a morning's ride is good for you but I should like to speak to you in private. May we take a stroll."

David nodded and they headed for the rose garden.

"I wish to ask for your mother's hand in marriage," he said, "Courtesy demands that I ask the head of the house and it would mean you agreeing to me becoming your father."

"Step-father." David corrected, "It'll be less confusing when I refer to my late father. His will stated that Lord Westerham should be my guardian and I wish to respect his wishes. If you wish to marry my mother out of love, then you have my blessing. However, would you agree to a marriage contract where you agree that my uncle continues as my guardian and you have no say in my affairs."

"Your mother is concerned that you forget your station and have become too wild." Lord Carlton replied, "Especially now that he is injured, I don't think that your uncle can handle you and you need firmer guidance."

"These are my family's estates." David replied, "Uncle Jethro understands the plans I have and is helping me."

"I would review the plans you have." Lord Carlton said, "I would certainly support the sensible ones."

"And my application to the board of commissioners." David asked, "Would you support my plans to use electricity to end the London smogs?"

"I can understand a young man's imagination believing such a thing possible." Lord Carlton replied, "Your uncle should not be encouraging you."

"He's at the hospital today." David said, "Dr. Hastings asked that his leg be examined by a specialist. He cannot believe how quickly it is healing."

"Healing?" Lord Carlton exclaimed, "I'd heard that he was about to lose it."

"It's another of my plans that he's encouraging." David said, "A new kind of medicine."

"Are you playing games with me, young man?" Lord Carlton asked angrily.

"Not at all. Can you stay until he returns. We'll all hear what he has to say."

"Very well. If you'll excuse me, I'll speak with your mother. I assume that you wish to change for luncheon."

"If you were my guest then I would. Since you are mother's guest and you may wish to be alone then I shan't bother."

"That's what I mean about taking you in hand." Lord Carlton said, "You're letting your personal standards slip."

"No, I simply relax more when I'm alone."

"You can't afford to relax. If the hands think that you're soft, then they'll take advantage of you."

"I think that we should stop this conversation." David said, "I know my duties and it's for me and Uncle Jethro to decide how I discharge them."

David made his way round to his offices.

Sitting in the staffroom, he was not surprised when Wilson arrived.

"Sit down please, Wilson." David said, "That was good thinking on your part. In case you're wondering, I did appreciate a plan already thought out and clear instructions for my part in it."

"Thank you, Your Grace." Wilson replied, "With respect, I suggest we maintain our roles until Lord Carlton has left. May I assume that young Billy is still at the swimming pond?"

"You may. I didn't want too many slipping back to the house in case Lord Carlton was on the prowl."

"Very wise. I suggest that you rejoin them. I'll send for you when it is time to dress for dinner."

It was just David, his mother and Jethro who sat for dinner; Lord Carlton had left. Wilson aided by an adult footman served, and it went smoothly if a little boring for David, envious of his friends far more relaxed meal in the staff room.

"I thought that Lord Carlton was going to propose today." David's mother said, "I'm so glad that he didn't. It's always so embarrassing refusing."

"He did speak to me." David said, "I approved providing father's will was honoured and Uncle Jethro remained my guardian."

"Yes. I always thought that control of Barabourne would have been part of the dowry," she replied, "I'd much prefer a gigolo who would sweep me off my feet and not discuss the business advantages of a union. Would you object to me having a lover who would spend my money without wanting the responsibilities?"

"David may be a little young for such a conversation." Jethro said.

"It's all right. Mother, by all means find yourself a toy-boy."

"A toy-boy?"

"A young man who is a companion and offers sex. Whatever people may expect of widowhood, you are too young to be alone and a toy-boy would not be a replacement for Father."

"And you learnt this worldly wisdom from your new friends." David's mother asked.

"The place where they came from. Billy may spend time in Godfrey's quarters and I'm wondering about my duty to produce an heir and what those parts of my body do. I'm sorry, this is not appropriate dinner conversation but I'm not going to stop anyone finding companionship and happiness. That includes you, Uncle."

"I'm happy as I am." Jethro said, though David thought that he spoke a little too vehemently.

"You haven't married." David said, "Whoever your true love is, would be welcome here."

"Let's change the subject." Jethro said, "It has been dealt with thoroughly enough."

David was content though. Whether his mother would ever find someone, was one question, but her obvious reluctance to re-marry would make his life far simpler.

"So, Uncle." David asked, "What news of your leg. With Lord Carlton visiting, we've not had a proper chance to talk."

"The doctors are agreed that the infection is all but gone." Jethro said, "They were a bit miffed when I insisted on your sterile procedures but Dr. Hastings agreed. He did not want to disturb a treatment that was working either. You look surprised David."

"I didn't think he believed in it." David responded.

"He doesn't. As he said, something is happening to me and he's not going to interfere with it but you should accept that his mind is more open than you believe."

David nodded.

"That's good because he persuaded a Doctor Miller to speak to you with a view to researching antibiotics. Congratulations, you've got another project under way."

"I want to look into the portal, which is what we're calling the pathway to the other place now." David said, "That'll be my main project. Godfrey and Tom understand just how important electricity could be so they're going through the school books that I've also brought back and Todd can help them. We'll all discuss things as we go along but it would help if we could concentrate on specific projects."

"And there is nothing that a mere woman could do?" his mother asked surprising everyone.

"I rather assumed that you would be keeping an eye on the

house, ensuring that it remained a ducal seat and did not turn into a factory." David said.

"There is talk that medical services are less than they might be, even for the aristocracy." Her Grace replied, "Would you allow me to join the committees that are investigating?"

"By all means. We have some knowledge of germs and viruses but few ways of tackling them. If we can produce antibiotics here, then maybe you could lead other changes that are needed."

David thought for a moment, "Maybe you should hire a handsome young medical student to act as secretary."

"Really David," his mother smiled, "Such ideas. You wouldn't mind though?"

"Not at all. I have my offices and the library where I can work. We should set aside rooms so that you can work as well and we'll ensure that there are public rooms for our guests. Wilson and I have already begun a version but we should agree on what's needed."

"Wilson should agree as well?" Her Grace queried, frowning.

"Wilson's role is to see that standards are maintained." David said, "We succeeded with Lord Carlton and it was because of his quick thinking. I know a very little about a lot of things. Once a plan has been decided, I'm happy to think of myself as just an estate boy with duties in the house, learning from my betters and Wilson is far better at running the house than me."

"And your present duty is to dine with your family rather than eat with your friends." Her Grace said.

"It's a pleasurable duty, but yes." David replied, "Everything I do seems to have another, important reason, even when it's just fun."

"I understand," his mother replied, "I think that perhaps, once a week, your friends should join us for dinner or would you wish Wilson to join us?"

"I think that I see him shaking his head." David chuckled, "It would be fun, seeing you cope with Billy but some of them are servants and I'm not sure that it would be fair on the other servants."

"Your group of friends do far more than can be expected of mere servants, do they not?"

David nodded.

"I could dispense with a dinner once a week so a soirée with a buffet may be in order. We could dismiss the regular servants and look after ourselves."

"I'm surprised at you Mother. Such egalitarian nonsense."

"I know that you're engaged in a number of ventures and that you would not succeed without your friends. If Jethro believes that they're important then I'll accept it and I'll support Wilson's efforts to maintain standards. It's time to change the subject. Do you have any plans for tomorrow?"

"Yes mother, I want to explore the gateway, the place where our two worlds meet."

Chapter 6

Standing close to the portal David was amused when Billy said: "What are you all looking at? I can't see nuffing."

"I can't see anything." David corrected absent-mindedly, "He's right though, it's excellent camouflage. I know it's there and I can see it and not see it. Does that make sense?"

"It's like seeing something in the corner of your eye but when you look, it's gone." Godfrey said.

David leant forward to touch what he thought was the rod. It shone bright silver again and a screen appeared above it. Tom and Godfrey knew little about computers, the portal revealed something new each time they visited, so they just assumed that it was normal. It was all completely new to Billy who glanced nervously at Tom and Godfrey then tried to act nonchalantly. It was Todd and Danny who gasped in surprise at seeing a holographic image.

"Whoa, I want one of those." Danny exclaimed.

"Now what do I do?" David muttered.

By answer the screen changed to a mass of incomprehensible hieroglyphs.

"In English, please." David said and the screen obliged to reveal three columns of numbers, one with a green background, the middle yellow and the third red. In the green column, one number was deep blue and another pale blue.

"Is one of those numbers for here?" David asked and the dark blue number started flashing.

"Display Danny's home number." David commanded and the pale blue number duly flashed.

"This is going well. Can you save my home number so that it's stored and I can always call it up?"

The numbers changed to 'Home – saved'.

"How about Danny's?"

Again the numbers turned to 'Danny – saved'.

"Is there any way of seeing what's on the other side?" David asked.

The screen dissolved into a view of the lane.

"But we can't go through at the moment."

Psychic link incomplete so instructions limited, the writing which appeared said, *Oral instructions understood. If both sides are uncovered, transfer is automatic.*

"Understood. Where's the control centre for this device?" Todd asked.

Here.

"No I meant the base, where the owners are."

Here.

"I think Todd means the people who built you. Where are they?" David said.

Nowhere.

"Which world were you built on?"

The columns of numbers reappeared and the red column scrolled rapidly, stopped and a number began flashing.

"Can you show it on the screen?"

No.

"Does the red column mean danger or destroyed."

Both. It is unwise to link with any of them.

"Why not just delete them?" Todd asked.

To cross reference new discoveries.

"I think that I understand that." David said, "What I don't understand is why you said that the base was here."

Question vague. Extrapolation attempted. You match the curiosity, leadership and benevolence of the creators.

"You're saying that you like us and want to live here?"

Question vague. Extrapolation attempted. Algorithm complex. Your knowledge limited. Excluding temporal displacement you could be creator. Your world will decline, Danny's world could destroy itself, other worlds need help. Reactivation requirements met.

"We need to learn." David said, "Connect to another world that we can safely visit."

Define safely.

"I suppose where people will accept us for who we are and will not try to stop us."

Description vague. Extrapolation attempted. Link set. Assume all travelling.

There was a pause and David nodded uncertainly.

Acknowledgement detected.

The ground shook and they stumbled but as they straightened up they found themselves in a large hall much like a temple. A monk who was sweeping the floor looked up staring in amazement, and dropping his broom hurried over.

"Welcome Honoured Travellers," he said bowing deeply. "My

apologies at such an inadequate greeting but it has been so long."

"That's quite all right." David replied, "How long has it been?"

"Seventy five years, Honoured Traveller. Surely you know."

"A lot's happened and we'll try to explain later, but first we want to know what you know."

"My apologies for my rudeness but it is so exciting to witness the end of the Long Absence."

"You weren't rude, maybe it's me who's a bit blunt so let's worry less about perfect manners and more about learning from each other. My name is David. The others can introduce themselves as we go. First question, this place reminds me of a Roman temple."

"We chose a temple design out of respect to all Honoured Travellers. Since we are Roman, how else would we design it?"

"I think that we should leave." David said, "We are not Honoured Travellers. We're just a group of friends learning about the portal."

"If the sacred door, portal if you wish, allowed you through then you're Honoured Travellers. I promise on the Gods of my ancestors that you will come to no harm and that you may return home whenever you wish."

"Godfrey, you and Billy go back now. I'm uneasy about it being unguarded on our side."

"No, Tom and Todd should go." Godfrey replied, "They can guard it and they understand computer things better."

"And you think that you should protect me." David smiled, "Very well, since it's Billy's first trip, we'll do it your way. Later Danny can go back and the other two come through again. That's if it's acceptable to our hosts."

"Honoured Travellers may travel as they wish," the monk replied, "Why not control it from here?"

"I'm not sure if I can." David said looking behind him. The rod appeared to be embedded in the floor.

"I don't want to travel," he said as he bent forwards to touch it. A screen appeared.

Explain what you do want.

"I want you to camouflage yourself on my world, so no-one else will come through."

No-one else authorised.

"Explain authorisation."

Algorithms authorise you, you authorise others.

"If I allow someone through the portal then I authorise them, is that right?"

Yes.

I'd authorise anyone to return to their home world but I'd like to limit who goes where."

Define limits.

"At least three people must travel together."

Be aware. Limit can only be rescinded in presence of those who witnessed instruction.

"I mean no insult to our host but don't include him. We may not be here if we do need to rescind it." David said.

Protocols established.

David turned to the monk, "May we look around, please?"

"Certainly. This temple is part of Cantium University. I could arrange transport to Rome if you wished, a lot would depend on how long you intend staying."

"Forgive me. I haven't asked for your name." David said.

"It's Marcus."

"We're trying to understand the portal so we didn't plan a long journey." David said, "We'll alarm our families if we're not back by this evening."

"It would be plenty of time to visit Rome. The Emperor would wish to greet you but Your Honour is correct and it would be a rush. I will inform His Imperial Highness that you wish to arrange a formal visit. May I offer you and your people refreshments?"

David wondered how they could travel to Rome so quickly and he also wondered why the others had been described as his people and not his friends. As they arrived at the refectory Marcus asked, "Do you permit your servants and slaves to eat with you?"

"They're my friends." David said, "Some are employed as servants at home but they're all off duty at the moment."

"Curious. You don't respect your patricians or Emperor then, that's like the other Honoured Travellers."

"I suppose that I'm a patrician." David said, "I get shown respect when it's needed. This sort of travel is equally new to all of us so…"

He trailed off as two youths, left the refectory holding hands.

"Is something wrong?" Marcus asked.

"No, I've never seen two boys be so close before."

"As a priest, I prefer it if men just do their duty to produce children and concentrate on higher things but our young tend to be less disciplined."

"I think that Godfrey and Billy would be happy here, though." David chuckled as they blushed.

It occurred to Danny that they never denied anything and that maybe it was a mistake because it seemed to fuel gossip but just then, he was more disconcerted by Marcus' reply.

"I'm sure that there are suitable students for them to serve," he said.

"Do you see all of us as just servants." Danny asked.

"If the sacred door accepts orders from Honoured Traveller David then we must acknowledge him as noble. We accept that his ways are different and will respect them but our way would be to demand simple obedience from the rest of you."

"You'd make us slaves." Danny exclaimed.

"If you proved incapable of looking after yourselves then yes. None of you own land here so you would certainly be in the servant class."

"Including me?" David asked.

"Not for as long as the sacred door obeys you." Marcus said.

David glowered at the monk.

"I can see that I've upset you. My apologies but, should you become subjects of His Imperial Majesty you would be treated accordingly. I should not be thinking that any of you are servants since Honoured Traveller David has made his wishes clear."

Lunch was pleasant though none of the boys felt truly comfortable. The waiters who wore a uniform of simple, white knee length tunics, were obviously slaves. Diners wore a mixture of clothing from togas to business suits. Some wore clothes that were visibly more worn and frayed than the slaves' tunics. Even then, there was a difference between them and the slave/waiters.

"There was nuffing in their eyes." Billy said later, though during the meal Marcus proudly explained how students were recruited from all ranks.

"Physicians were considered little better than slaves at the beginning of the Empire but then a series of plagues struck," he explained. Suddenly medicine became highly respectable. Other sciences followed suit. Today a master can allow a slave to enrol as a student. If he succeeds he is automatically freed and has the same chances in those fields as a patrician."

A lot was left unsaid though Marcus drew gasps of surprise when he said he remembered seeing the last Honoured Travellers leave.

"That would make you at least eighty years old." Danny exclaimed.

"Eighty-four to be precise" Marcus replied, "Another thirty-six years before I retire."

Marcus introduced them to professors whose eyes initially lit up but on discovering their lack of knowledge, lost interest and hurried off muttering about waiting for adults.

"Like I said, Marcus, we're not Honoured Travellers." David chuckled.

"Priests run the temple because we revere the sacred door. I do not question its decision to allow you to take control."

For Billy, the strangest part of the day was later when they all gathered in the library to tell Jethro about their adventure. He settled into a comfortable armchair while David happily sat on the floor. Godfrey also sat on the floor leaning against Billy's chair while the others made themselves comfortable.

It was as Billy made his remark about the slaves eyes that Wilson served them all lemonade. Billy looked nervously at him.

"Don't worry Master Billy." Wilson said, "Today you are one of His Graces' travelling companions. Tomorrow you will be up early to clean the shoes as you should and if His Grace doesn't need you then you will lay out a dinner setting as I showed you. His Grace won't help you if you don't get it right, either."

"Yes Mr. Wilson." Billy replied.

"It was safe enough but I didn't feel comfortable." David said, "I told Marcus that I'd return when I could but I don't know if I will. There was that threat in the background and I don't want to spend too much time there."

"So you won't be travelling again, then?" Jethro asked.

"I'd like to but it could be dangerous, couldn't it." David replied, "The portal said something about worlds needing help and ours declining. I need to find out more but I can't ask anyone else to come with me."

"I will," said Todd. "This is my world now so I'll help you any way I can."

"My place is beside you, Your Grace." Godfrey said, "I'm the head stable boy, that's where we house transport and the portal is transport. It's my duty to assist."

"Jumping to other worlds is way beyond duty." Jethro said, "So thank you both."

"That priest bloke looked down on you because you didn't have no servant." Billy said, "I'll do it. I can be all quiet and obedient like those slaves."

Wilson seemed to have a choking fit.

"I can if I have to, Mr. Wilson." Billy exclaimed, "You know I can."

"Yes, you can when you try." Wilson said, "Discussing David's adventures then it should be just Wilson, Master Billy. When you're back to your regular duties, you'd better not forget the Mister."

"Nah, I'm just Billy and you're Mister Wilson." Billy said, "I'm not clever like the others so I'll just do as I'm told. I like sitting here though. It's real posh."

"Be my guest." David chuckled, "You did well today and you've made a couple of interesting points. One was about the slave's eyes but the other was about who should go through. I'd like Godfrey to come with me because he's older, and I feel like he's my bodyguard. Whatever the teasing, he and Billy are friends and Billy was useful so I'd like him on the team. Danny and Todd know more of the sciences so one of them would be useful. Tom I'd like you to work on our projects here and keep me up to date."

Tom breathed a sigh of relief, "That would suit me, I don't think that I like travelling after all."

David nodded, he had noticed Tom's relief when he was sent back from the Roman world, and turned to address Wilson. "Can you manage without Billy, Wilson?"

"We do need a boot boy and he did make an adequate footman when he was needed." Wilson replied, "Perhaps we should take on another, preferably one who does not wish to join in your escapades."

"I'll leave it to you." David said, "Uncle, I think that you should stay in town for a couple of weeks while we recruit staff. I also think that I should visit this new Earth and learn as much as I can from them. Would you take Tom and Todd with you. Tom is supposed to be a personal assistant so could you show him how to make the travel arrangements, place the advertisements and so on. Todd can help and at the same time, learn more about our world and see if he can get any clues about how it's in decline."

"How about I visit that new Earth with Billy and Godfrey." Todd said, "I could take a laptop and try to download data."

"No, I think that Billy might have the right idea with them." David said, "I'll go as the Honoured Traveller and Billy acts as servant. How about you Danny?"

"I've been thinking about it." Danny said, "I want to spend

time with my parents. Mum and Dad are pretty cool with the way they're trusting me so I'd rather live at home and just visit. I can do research at home and visit at weekends if that's OK."

"I think that it all makes as much sense as this situation ever will." Jethro said, "David, I really do admire the way that you're handling it all. I'll be delighted to assist."

The next few weeks were relatively quiet for them in that there were few surprises or dramas. Jethro found himself busy in London and although he should have been scandalised at the breakdown of social barriers, his travelling companions proved to be fun.

Wilson should also have been scandalised that a mere boot boy and a stable boy had become his master's close confidants and he was expected to serve them. However, Billy loved to tell him about their day's adventures. On one occasion, he described how they had been whisked to Rome in less than two hours.

"It just looked like a wing," Billy said, "It didn't have windows but it was as comfortable as the lounge. We was pressed into our seat, then we was as light as feathers and then it felt as if we being thrown against the ceiling. We was warned, acceleration, free fall and er, oh yeah, deceleration. Then we was in Rome. The Emperor didn't want to see the likes of me, only David, so Godfrey and me was stuck in the airport."

On another day, he was even less enthusiastic when he described how a slave was whipped.

"It was near a courthouse and his back was a right mess when they had finished. Someone said that his kidneys had been ruptured and he was being left to die. Marcus didn't care though. I wanted to come back but he saw this girl they brought out of the court. They chained her to a post and stripped her with hands tied above her head. Marcus said that he might make an offer before the dealers arrived. I don't like him now or that world much, Mr. Wilson. It's so much cleverer than us but it's so cruel. They think that David's a god but Godfrey and me are just slaves. They offered to have me whipped because I asked a question. David had to explain that he needed intelligent servants. They still wanted me whipped though."

"I've often wanted to see you whipped for your cheek." Wilson said, "However, wanting something and it being right are two different things."

"Good point." David said, "They think that Honoured Travellers are some sort of oracle who come to warn them of some great disaster. I hope that they're not disappointed if I can't tell them anything."

"If I might suggest Your Grace." Wilson began.

"Please just speak, Wilson." David said.

"Very well if I understand correctly, your portal is a computing machine so it does not do anything that it was not told to compute. Did it simply send you to a random safe world as you requested or are there other parts of the calculation. Does it indeed have information that it calculates that you can relay?"

"Is that what it meant by helping worlds?" Godfrey asked.

"I'll ask it tomorrow and thank you." David said, "Are you sure that you don't want to make a trip?"

"Thank you but no, Your Grace." Wilson replied but then hesitated, "On second thoughts, I think perhaps that I would like to make a trip to Young Master Danny's world but just long enough so that I understand."

"Godfrey can arrange something with Danny and Mr. Barton." David said, "Supposing that I suggested that you considered buying in some wine from over there. It really is only a suggestion but it would give a purpose to the trip."

"Yes Your Grace and I agree that it's better to have a reason for going." Wilson replied, "Thank you."

"No! Thank you." David said, "Without you, I'd have to choose between Barabourne and travelling. I wonder, do you hate serving Godfrey, Tom and Billy?"

"May I say, it is you who is harping on the question and that it bothers you more than it does me." Wilson replied, "It may be harder for Billy than anyone since he appears to be answerable to both you and me."

Very well. Billy can take charge of the offices as one of my personal staff but he receives instruction from you, Wilson. Technically that will make you a tutor so you should be entitled to the same privileges in here."

"I'll accept that distinction, Your Grace." Wilson said, "I suggest that your time would be more usefully spent discovering how to instruct a computing machine while I begin Billy's tuition."

The fourteen year old boy in David caught the adult's instruction and nodded. Wilson had used the same tone with staff and they knew that to ignore it would mean trouble. With so many projects and ideas whirling around his head and lacking experience in prioritising his tasks, David needed advice even when he was unsure what advice he needed.

"Why must you wait until tomorrow?" Wilson asked, "I would not release Billy to go swimming if he had tasks that needed completing."

David shrugged, "It all seems so big. I'd like to think about it."

"I understand but they will only seem bigger tomorrow and they will keep growing. That is the nature of big problems. It occurs to me that the machine might have some answers. Why not ask it questions about what puzzles you the most. In my world, laying a dinner for fifty people is a big event. A new footman might ask why guests place napkins on their laps. It has nothing to do with laying the table, neither is it for him to question his better's actions, but it is distracting him and it is part of the background of the event, so I would answer."

"So if I ask something, it doesn't have to be important, but I'll move on to something else that may be."

"I believe so." Wilson replied, "What bothers you the most?"

"When the portal writes something like, 'Question vague. Extrapolation attempted'. I worry that if I'm too vague then we'll run into real trouble."

"Then I suggest that you run along and ask it." Wilson said.

"But what about the message for the Roman world?" David asked.

"Learn to communicate with the portal first. You'll have a better chance of passing messages on."

David nodded thoughtfully.

"Wilson was right." David said later when he, Godfrey and Billy were at the swimming place.

"I told the portal that I was worried about asking vague questions and giving vague instructions and I wanted to know how to do it properly. Guess what it said."

"Question vague. Extrapolation attempted." Godfrey laughed.

"Gotcha. It actually said, 'English language vague so warning issued. Extrapolation always needed. Consider developing mind control."

"So it struggles with English." Godfrey smiled, "We should send it to Mr. Rogers."

"It knows more English than it lets on." David said, "*Consider developing* mind control? That sounds more advanced than it usually speaks."

"But how does that help?" Godfrey asked.

"I tried an experiment. I said, 'Designate safe world you sent us to as Roman World' and got the reply, 'Saved'. I then asked, "Does Roman World need help?' The reply was yes. To be sure I asked, 'from us?' The portal replied yes."

David paused letting his friends consider the conversation, "I tried asking the questions in as few words as possible. I didn't say please or try to be polite and it seemed to help but I wasn't sure how to phrase the next question. The obvious question was *why does Roman World need help* but I could see the portal explaining why they *deserved* help so I tried 'Define the problem'."

David paused again, this time just to add to the tension, "It seems that one of their deep space probes disturbed an asteroid which is now heading towards them. By the time they spot it, it will be too late to do anything. Our task is to tell them where to look."

"Why doesn't it just tell them?" Billy asked.

"To stop them becoming too dependent." David replied, "They know that something is watching over them, if they blow themselves up then it will be their own stupid fault but this is a genuine accident so they're told to look for something. It's up to them to find it and sort it. They can't rely on a rod, buried in the temple floor providing all the answers."

"I think I get it. I still don't get how we speak their language though." Billy said, "You're all right, you learn Latin so you get it."

"I don't speak their modern Latin." David said, "I tell you what though, it's another reason why I think the portal knows English better than it lets on. It speaks all those other languages and teaches us when we go through. Don't ask me how though and don't ask me how it printed this."

David held out a flat plastic square, resembling a clay tablet including a series of numbers inscribed on it.

"I'm to give them this but only reluctantly tell them what I've been told."

"I don't get it." Billy said, "Why all the arsing about?"

"Me, oracle's messenger. Tablet, its latest message." David quoted, "Messenger should be man of wisdom. Message given more weight."

"It's still arsing around." Billy said.

"Maybe but we'll make a show of it. We're just about done there so we'll make it the last visit and I'll dress formally. You two can dress as footmen and be the perfect servants. Oh and we'll take the brake round the lanes. I'll feel ridiculous if we just stroll across the fields dressed like that."

"I'll drive." Danny said excitedly, "It'll save any of you from getting all sooty."

"It's a good thought, but the brake's not big enough." David said, "Do you think that you can handle a brougham?"

"Who me?" Danny gasped.

"Why not?" David asked, "You like driving the brake, the only difference will be that we'll be content to drive along at a walking pace rather than trying to match the speeds on your world."

Danny grinned, "The brake's faster than my bike. It's fun. I'll give it a go. I'll fire one up."

"Godfrey, will you take Danny on a practice run today and we'll go tomorrow." David said, "

The trip proved to be an anti-climax. David formally thanked Marcus for his hospitality and then offered the tablet with the coordinates. Marcus studied it, puzzled.

"They are the coordinates of an asteroid. You have time to stop it being a threat." David explained.

"I see." Marcus said, "Such a gift should be made to the Emperor. It may restore relations but you can never be sure. I'll arrange for an Imperial courier to take it."

David nodded in understanding and bowed. It was over and David could leave. On an earlier visit, David had been offered gladiatorial games in his honour which he refused as politely but as firmly as possible. David's refusal was a personal insult to the emperor, and relations cooled to the point where the emperor nearly forgot that David was an honoured traveller.

Chapter 7

After the Roman trip the friends were busy as their research teams arrived and settled in. Even David's mother helped, she decided that anyone who had been to university could only be of noble birth or with wealthy parents and invited them to dinner. She apparently ignored the fact, that Jethro had selected by ability so that there were a number who had received sponsorship or grants. She increased her soirées to three a week and made everyone feel welcome.

David suspected that there was more than just support. She could boast to her friends how Barabourne was at the centre of a second renaissance which promised to be more exciting than the one which lasted from Charles II's long reign through to Duncan I's, a change in history which at first confused Todd. She kept an interested eye on the younger members of the team and an even more interested eye on their even younger assistants.

Now it was Todd who took the initiative. He might have wished that he taken more interest in science lessons but he understood more than anyone else about the new technologies.

David had very little to do. Everything was in the hands of engineers, scientists and managers and it was Jethro who carried the authority. David did not mind; he could relax and enjoy the tail end of summer. The portal still fascinated him but it also scared him a little so he was reluctant to experiment further. However, as memories of his fear and confusion at being so lost dimmed, so his curiosity increased especially when he became increasingly distracted by developments in his projects.

He was aware that Godfrey had taken over the brake and was tinkering around with it but he was surprised one evening when it was nearly dark that Godfrey asked him outside. David obliged and watched amazed as Billy drove the brake confidently around aided by two enormous lamps mounted on either side of the boiler.

"I've tried not to be a nuisance but I wanted to try my own experiment." Godfrey said sounding unusually nervous, "That glass blowing firm is getting good at making the bulbs and I used one of the test dynamos. I tapped the main boiler for the steam and Mr. Grant helped me make up a small engine from the spare parts we had lying around. You can see it strapped to the side of the boiler so that it drives the dynamo. You're not angry, are you?"

"I think it's brilliant. I wondered where you'd been over the last few weeks, I thought you might have had enough of my projects."

"Bloody hell, no." Godfrey exclaimed, "I'm ready for another journey when you are. I thought you might be angry that I used stuff without permission."

"Come on. Billy can drive us into the village." David exclaimed, "I want to see if we can get to Dr. Hastings' surgery and back."

"Your Grace? Is someone ill?"

"No, but you've given me an idea." Supposing we had a new brake built that was ready for immediate use. Maybe it should have a feed from the engine room boiler to keep its own boiler under full steam, a properly designed electricity generator so that it's ready for an emergency, even at night. We could also start thinking about building a viable road diesel. Come on, let's see what night driving is like."

The steam brake could go about as fast as a galloping horse but on a moonless night, it was usually too dangerous to use in the narrow, twisting lanes. That night, two beams of light shone out in front of them and Billy drove confidently. It might be slow compared to Danny's world but listening to the cheerful chuff of the steam engine, and feeling the wind in their faces, it was exciting to be tearing along through the tunnel of light. The village was quiet, though a few villagers peeked out wondering at the lights and watched as the boys drove around the green to head back in the opposite direction. On the way back one of the lights failed and the other flicked out as they reached the drive to the hall. Godfrey found a lantern and he and David leapt off the brake to guide Billy back to the stable.

"Perhaps it's not such a good idea, after all." Godfrey said sadly.

"The bulbs were a bit fragile, that's all." David replied, "We know it can be done so we'll still build that emergency steam brake. I'm glad you're learning about electricity because I'm going to need a lot of help if I'm to convince the commission."

David was right to be concerned because not long after, he was summoned to London to present his ideas for supplying the capital with electricity.

"It's a preliminary hearing." Jethro said, "You'll be convincing one or two of the commissioners that you're not wasting everybody's time. It'll be tough because their job is to weed out the crackpots."

Jethro was wrong because waiting for him was non other than

King Charles VII himself presiding over a full board of commissioners.

Among his other concerns, David's disappearance had also caused alarm. Could he have been kidnapped by a foreign power? Agents were still reporting on strange events since his return and the king had even heard of the lights that Godfrey had installed on the brakes. Barabourne was close to London and he could not allow the dukedom to descend into chaos because of David's unconventional attitudes to the lower classes.

Being openly worried could undermine confidence further but the commission provided an opportunity to assess David though he tried to appear unconcerned as the board settled.

"Welcome Barabourne," he said, "You must be the youngest ever to submit a proposal as well as the highest ranking. I must say, I'm intrigued. Let's hear your proposal and don't worry, I doubt if you can be worse than other ideas that we've heard."

David swallowed nervously. He was defending his reputation as never before and everything depended on this presentation.

"Your Majesty, my Lords Commissioners, most suggestions revolve around refining the existing system, either cleaning coal or filtering smoke. My proposal is to dramatically reduce the amount of coal used in London and to confine it to areas where weather conditions will not trap the smoke." David said, "Now if my assistants can stop shaking as much as I am, we have a model to demonstrate the principle."

The King chuckled and so, following their ruler, the commissioners also laughed.

"Please take your time. I understand from your initial report that you intend conveying power by electricity. Isn't electricity just a fairground toy?"

"At present, Your Majesty. We have considerable knowledge on the subject but certain key ideas have never been followed up and since we have abundant coal there's been little incentive in developing new forms of energy, or energy transmission."

"We're ready, Your Grace." Godfrey whispered.

"We heard," the King said, "Gentlemen shall we gather round."

The commissioners left their seats gathering round the two tables that had been set up.

"This table represents the power house." David began, "The array of lamps on this table, a home or a city in need of heating and lighting, and the gap, represents the distances involved. The power is generated by this steam engine which can be purchased from any good toy shop, but it now drives the generator that my engineers have designed. The power is carried along these wires to the display. Start the engine, Godfrey."

The little toy spun into life and the bulbs began to glow.

"You need to be careful, but you can feel the heat rising from the bulb."

The King cautiously stretched out a finger and nodded.

"And these little levers control each lamp?"

"Yes Your Majesty. It's quite safe if anyone would like to try."

"It could still be a fairground novelty," the King said, "Is this the end of the demonstration?"

"You are quite right, Your Majesty." David replied, "At this level it is little more than a children's toy but there is one more part to this demonstration."

David picked up a hammer and smashed one of the bulbs.

"As you saw, electricity does generate heat so it can cause fires," he continued, "Equipment and lines have to be maintained properly but if a gas lamp fails it leaks gas which is poisonous and explosive. Usually damage to electrical equipment just stops the supply. The other thing is, we did think of demonstrating a water turbine to replace the steam engine but it may have confused the issue."

"Why?"

"It requires a head of water and would be of more use in Scotland than London."

"This is going to put a lot of coal merchants out of work," one of the commissioners said, "I foresee considerable resistance."

"Not if they can adapt to being energy supply shops. Each house will need fittings, and bulbs like these have a limited life. As demand for coal goes down so demand for electrical supplies will increase."

"You've patented your devices and you're claiming our prize." another asked, "Forgive us for seeing a very mercenary approach. It's to your advantage to convince us to approve an incredibly expensive scheme that may not even work."

"I'm converting an old watermill to drive a larger version of the generator on my estate, a second generator will be steam driven. I intend replacing all the gas lighting at Barabourne with electrical lighting. I then intend running wires down to the village. Initially it will provide street lighting but as our capacity increases it will be fed into the cottages."

"Yes we believe that it was part of your original submission. I invited you here today to explain your ideas in person. Your answer to Aberamle's question is that when it comes to London, it is not so much the prize money as the authority to do what's needed."

"Yes Your Majesty."

"Have your man run your demonstration again please," the King said, "He seems quite competent. Tell me, is he merely a servant? What about the other one?"

"When they need to be, Your Majesty. At other times they are my friends."

"Indeed, we've heard that you have some strange ideas and that you forget your station. God gave you your position, you should not hold it so cheaply."

Godfrey made to speak though he remembered just in time but the king noticed.

"Speak if you wish," he said.

"His Grace does not forget his station, Your Majesty. He sometimes leaves it behind so that he can run, swim and do things that dukes are not expected to do but boys are."

"And dukes are not expected to have such an impressive knowledge of the sciences as he'll be expected to have this afternoon. That was well said. You have sent plans, costings and the like for us to consider. Does anyone have any questions?"

"Yes, your plans suggest that the wires have to be buried underground. Isn't that an unnecessary expense?"

The grilling continued and for David it was the hardest part of the day as it focussed on the costs and financing more than the technical side. Finally, the king intervened.

"Gentlemen, Unless His Grace spoils his demonstration by crumbling under questioning this afternoon I suggest that we consider his plan in detail, at least until we can assess His Grace's efforts at Barabourne. I cannot invite mere servants to lunch but I could invite your friends. How would they address you?"

"As David, Your Majesty."

"And we have been known to manage with a simple, sir. We would like to hear more of your plans."

David was more nervous than Billy or Godfrey. His Majesty was known to be suspicious of anything that disturbed 'God's order' and he would never tolerate two lowly servants forgetting their position. David was even more concerned when they were shown into a cosy little room with a buffet on a long table against one wall. The King dismissed the servants.

"Very well." Charles VII said as he sat down, "Please make yourselves comfortable. There's no-one here to witness bad behaviour so may we concentrate on plain speaking. You, Barabourne, disappear for several weeks then return with a considerable knowledge of science and strangely egalitarian views. It does concern us. Would you care to explain?"

"I can but it's difficult to believe." David said.

"Try us!" The King commanded.

"I spent time on a different world." David began, "Coal is more or less banned from their London. They have not had a smog for over fifty years because the air is so clean. They use electricity for all sorts of things including communications and can send messages from the Admiralty to ships in the middle of the ocean in seconds."

"And you did not think that we would find this important?" King Charles asked, "It's a fantastic story and I'm not sure that I believe it despite the reports I've received. However, assuming that you do have access to a wonderful new communication's system, why have you not mentioned it?"

"Would you believe me, sir?" David replied, "I've just said that I travel to other worlds. How many wild schemes could I mention before I became a laughingstock?"

"A good point," the King chuckled, "We agree that your explanation is fantastic but accepting it for a moment, is this other world a threat?"

"No, sir." David replied, "I keep the door closed except when my friends on the other world expect me. The door itself has some safety features. It chose me for some reason and now only I can give permission for someone to pass through."

"And in this strange world of yours, you mixed with commoners and had no contact with your own kind."

"Yes sir."

"I see. So now you trust them more."

"Not quite. Lord Trevallion was asked to resign from the bank. I think now that he should have faced court because he tried to steal nearly a £1,000,000. If Godfrey or Billy tried to steal a few pence they would face a birching or hard labour. Thieves are thieves and should be treated as such for they spoil everyone's reputation."

"Radical but we see the argument. What do you say, Godfrey?"

"That His Grace is right, Your Majesty." Godfrey replied

standing up with Billy following suit, "We all rely on trust, and there are liars and cheats in all classes."

"Please sit down." King Charles said, "We said that you should relax."

"Begging your pardon but you're asking His Grace to defend himself not to demonstrate his ideas on energy. Both Billy and I know our place, even if His Grace does not remind us all the time."

"Given Barabourne's position in the order of precedence, we have to be sure," the king said softly, "You must admit that it's an unbelievable story so allow us to defend the realm with the same vigour that you defend His Grace."

"I'm sorry, sir." Godfrey said, "I tend to think of him as one of the estate boys trying to do too much. Whatever the rank, adults don't like uppity youngsters."

"Sit down, Godfrey." King Charles said, "You make a fine champion. David is indeed an uppity youngster as you put it but he has our support now that we're more certain of his ideas. The board definitely regards him as uppity and will endeavour to discredit him. They'll question him far more intensely than an adult this afternoon so I suggest you continue to forget your position and your manners if needs be."

He paused, "These London smogs are getting worse. They disrupt everything including palace business and it could be that the major offices of state will have to abandon London altogether. Although your reasoning appears sound, your proposal is so radical we're not convinced that it will work on such a large scale, so we will not directly support you. However, we can see how such a scheme could be supremely beneficial to the country so there is something we can do."

He summoned a page who hurried off then returned carrying a sword on a velvet cushion.

"Godfrey, please kneel," the king commanded who then tapped his shoulders with the sword.

"You may stand," His Majesty commanded, "Sir Godfrey, you may consider this as my tacit instruction to look after and defend His Grace. The obvious support that we're showing you may help with the commissioners so we look forward to a more entertaining afternoon than is usually the case with enquiries such as this. I'll leave you to prepare."

Billy and Godfrey were standing, dumbfounded, staring at each other as David hurried over to congratulate him.

"That wasn't for real, was it?" Billy asked.

"Oh yes." David grinned, "You'll have Jennings and Zack knuckling their foreheads and calling you sir from now on."

"But why? I don't understand." Billy persisted.

"I suspect that His Majesty is more worried than we realise." David said, "Can you imagine the repercussions if we had to abandon the Empire's capital city. It would make us a laughingstock."

"Yes but surely all cities have the same problems." Godfrey said.

"Agreed but we owe our position to the development of industrial power. Imagine if we had to admit to being beaten by it. If we can make our scheme work then we will not just be buying a little time which is the best that other schemes have offered but keeping our world lead by introducing an entirely new industry. That's why he wants us to succeed and indirectly he's given us his backing. It costs him nothing to bestow such a title and you're still a commoner but he does not give them to idiots, so congratulations."

"But how will it affect me?" Godfrey asked.

"It won't for most of the time but on Sundays you will wear the badge and be behind the family but ahead of the servants. If we have guests who are commoners, you will take precedence over them."

David paused thoughtfully, "Be careful. Despite his friendliness today, he would not normally speak to a mere servant. If we fail, then he may seek to blame you for the breakdown in order, and view me as an immature boy who should not sit in the Lords."

"That's all right because we won't fail, will we." Billy said, "I've seen that world as well and he won't be disappointed."

"At least it's technical questions and not financial ones this afternoon. Billy, you've got the file and know how to find information, Godfrey, you're following the building of the powerhouse, feel free to answer for me. Remember, you'll be expected to earn your new title."

Later it was Godfrey who was tackled by one of the commissioners.

"You can compare it to water." Godfrey was saying, "Electrical power is a combination of quantity and pressure. The higher the electrical pressure, which we call volts the less quantity which we call amps."

"And is that how you taught your man to answer, Your Grace?" The commissioner asked.

"I don't employ parrots." David snapped, "*Sir* Godfrey is trying to explain the complication of adding transformers to the system, if you don't wish to listen, then he needn't waste his time."

The commissioner looked nervously towards the king before saying, "Please continue."

"We have one question," His Majesty said. "Those names have a French flavour to them. Is there any reason?

"It's to do with something we discussed over lunch, Your Majesty." David replied.

"We understand. Please continue."

The questioning continued until finally, David and his friends were allowed to go.

"Do you think that we've still got approval." Godfrey asked.

"I think so." David replied, "From what I understand, at least half of the applicants don't make it to lunch and we even managed the financial stuff. I bet that his agents are among the new staff so he may even have heard of our new brake."

"You mean, he's spying on us?" Billy exclaimed.

"As he says, his duty is to protect the realm and my disappearance was odd. He seemed to accept the portal very easily so I wonder."

"Billy, write a note for the town-house staff. Tell them that we're heading straight for the station. They're to close it up and come down in their own time. They can also fetch our things at the same time."

It was about 5 o'clock when they left for the station and it was nearly eight before they arrived at Barabourne.

The following morning David called a meeting. He arranged chairs around the largest table he could find in his offices so that everyone could sit comfortably. He ensured that his friends and Wilson were there as well as the senior staff running various projects.

"As you know, the summons to appear before the commission was sooner than we hoped," he began, "I need to know how we're doing. Wilson, is the hall in good running order and have we given Mother a nervous breakdown yet?"

"No, Your Grace." Wilson replied, "You must redouble your efforts to reduce the house to chaos."

"That's good news." David chuckled, "Mr. Thompson, how about the estates?"

"I'm worried about the harvest, Your Grace." Mr. Thomson replied, "My men seem to get roped in to other projects and at times we're short staffed. We're definitely falling behind."

"I know." David said, "It wasn't so bad in early summer but

we're getting busier. Mr. Grant, the actual harvest time depends on the weather but at the right time, the harvest takes priority. We could use all able-bodied help and it would be useful if some of your staff could be available."

"I can do something, Your Grace." Mr. Grant replied, "My main worry is getting the building work completed before the bad weather sets in."

"Fair enough." David said, "Bear in mind that the harvest is an important part of our income at the present."

"I wouldn't worry about that at the moment." Jethro said, "You're not exactly destitute."

"I'm delighted to hear it." David laughed, "I still want all our ventures to prosper. Anyway, how are we doing on our new projects?"

"What you call the infrastructure is well under way. The senior staff are already in permanent accommodation and even the electrical system has performed well under tests. Junior staff still find living in a tented city a novelty so there's no problem there. Number 1 generator is delivering more power than we expected though the gearing between it and the water wheel is still giving problems. However, it's enough to look at the practical problems of distribution and the rest. Number 2 generator is so much bigger and construction is slower but we're getting there."

"Thank you." David said, "Doctor Miller?"

"Those books and notes that you supplied take resources for granted that we just don't have." Doctor Miller replied, "However, we found references to naturally occurring moulds including those on bread. We know what to look for, we have the facilities to develop the right strains so we're searching for them and that means overcoming our innate snobbery and speaking with those we regard as charlatans, the village witch who acts as a doctor for the poor, that sort of thing. Some really are charlatans but some having been growing moulds for years and the results are impressive. We can hardly go against your ideas on equality so we are following it all up."

He paused, marshalling his thoughts, "There is another side to our work that we've already published papers on and that's sterility. We do preach the idea of *cleanliness being next to godliness* but we understand now that we have to take it much further than we did. I'm thinking of your comments on the harvest and income. With Todd's assistance we might be able to develop a few lines and patent some ideas which could bring in an income."

"Have a word with my mother." David said, "Introducing new

techniques might be just the project that she'd like."

Dr. Miller looked surprised but nodded.

"Godfrey." David said, "You're looking into improving road transport and you've started with night driving. I'd like you and Danny to investigate flash boilers as well as look at the basic flaws in our diesel engines. If you can get enough practical data, then we'll look into developing them."

"I've never heard of a flash boiler." Mr. Grant said, "What is it?"

"It's something I came across while I was away." David said, "That place didn't have steamers but I was curious to see if they'd done any work on them. Apparently they had and had experimented with flash boilers but they were prone to overheating. I'm thinking that we might develop them and use electrical apparatus to control them better."

"I'll do what I can, but the lights on the brake didn't last long." Godfrey said, "Tom's spoken with the glass blowing firm and they reckon that they can come up with a better design now that they understand what we're doing."

"Tom's proving to be good at dealing with our suppliers." Jethro said, "He also translates the technical jargon you all use. I'd like him to keep him as my assistant."

"That's cool." David laughed, "He can translate that later. Now the project I like the least. Uncle, do you find any problems with our schooling?"

"Technically, I'm only responsible for yours but I get good reports from Mr. Rogers about all of you and he coordinates your studies with these gentlemen. No, I have no problems as your guardian."

"It's about four months since I returned and we've made a lot of progress so I'm happy." David said, "Are there any problems that I don't know about?"

No-one spoke until Todd said, "Not about work but Danny has got something on his mind and there's something else I have to tell you."

"I thought that he was back at school." David said.

"He is and that's the problem." Todd said.

"OK." David said, "If there's no estate business then we'll head for the swimming hole."

And with that announcement the meeting broke up.

Chapter 8

Outside David and Todd talked quietly as they walked to the swimming hole.

"I went for a walk yesterday and wandered down to the portal," he began, "I was thinking of jumping across and phoning Danny and forgot about the box until I got there. Anyway I swore a bit and said something like 'I bet you won't even talk to me. Guess what, the screen appeared and a message said, *You lose*."

"Anyway I did talk to it." Todd said, "It wouldn't let me through because this is my home world now. I said something about wanting to talk to Danny and it replied, 'Mobile phone link activated'."

David stared at him as Todd continued, "It'll act as a mobile phone system on this side and an ordinary phone on that side."

"That's clever." David said.

"Apparently it monitors radio frequencies on various worlds. It's a pretty neat computer and apparently it's easy creating the link because our system is basic compared to other worlds. It gave me a message to give you. I was going to tell you but you called that meeting and I haven't had a chance."

"So what's the message?"

"It needs to talk to you urgently." Todd replied, "The only thing that it would say to me was, *crisis soon*."

"I was going to visit it myself this afternoon. That'll have to do. Now what about Danny?"

"I didn't get all of what Danny said, but you cleared Mr. Barton and now the social services people are wondering why you turned to him and not to your foster dad. You're still down as having been abducted, and they're worried that they've never spoken to your parents and that they never reported you missing. Your case worker tried speaking to your teacher and a couple of kids overheard. Now they're saying that we're all some sort of pedo ring. Danny's father is about to lose his job."

"Is it that bad?" David asked.

"I timed it so he was on a break but Danny didn't have much time. He said something else, no-one's mentioned me."

"Right, would you go and find Billy and Godfrey, please. Meet me at the portal."

When he arrived, David studied the box.

"I need to talk," he said and the portal obligingly displayed a screen, "Do you know what is happening to Danny?"

Partially, only clear information on computer appeared on the screen, *Events based on emotion, not logic.*

"So no-one is actually suspected of kidnapping me but people are jumping to conclusions. It's a pity that I can't take the brake across and drive into Chasebourne."

Why can't you?

"They've got all sorts of regulations and licences." David said, "We'd be stopped."

Godfrey licensed, vehicle licensed, Godfrey should bring brake into field.

"What?" David exclaimed, "How come?"

"*Danny's world does not believe eyes, it believes computers. Their computers basic. Monitored since inception. Number plates needed.*

The others had arrived and had stood listening to the conversation. All four boys gasped as two plastic plates appeared and it took a couple of moments to realise that they were number plates. As always, there seemed to be a lot more than the portal was actually saying but David was content.

"Has Todd told you what's going on?" He asked Godfrey and Billy.

"Todd talked into those fone fings." Billy said, "Now you're worried."

"They still think that you've been kidnapped or something and you're planning something." Godfrey said.

"Our world is steam driven." David said, "Theirs has moved on but they still like steam driven gadgets. There's something called steam-punk and it's about things not driven or controlled by electricity. With Godfrey's electricity system, the brake even looks odd to us so imagine how it would look over there."

"It'll sure attract attention." Todd said.

"There's a shop that sells all sorts of steam-punk stuff." David said, "If we could dress up and go to one of their festivals, I'm thinking that it could be fun and offer an explanation as to why we're so friendly."

"Even the duke stuff could be part of it." Todd said, "All a big set-up."

David nodded, "Most importantly we wanted to keep it secret until the festival but too many people got the wrong idea."

"It sounds like fun." Todd said, "Can I come with you?"

"Why not." David replied, "Portal what do you think of plan?"

Not programmed for humour and fun so question vague. Extrapolation attempted. If plan is to provide alternative source of pointless chatter, then it should be attempted. Correct additional response may be, 'good luck'.

"Thank you." David said, "You said that you had a problem. What is it?"

Critical point soon. Deal with current activity. Will inform when you are needed.

David nodded.

Godfrey, Billy, are you coming?"

"Of course." Godfrey replied, "I'm the driver but I'm not so sure about driving over there. Maybe Billy should stay behind because he doesn't have to go."

"I'm His Grace's travelling servant." Billy piped up, "It's my duty to go."

"Very well. Billy go and find Wilson, we need six top hats and footman's waistcoats. Godfrey, will you fetch the brake. You can bring Billy back with you."

While he and Todd were waiting, Todd had an idea.

"Portal," he asked, "Could you create a false address, say Barabourne, Barn's Lane or something? Then if people looked for it, make them think that there was something here and I know; question vague."

Extrapolation indicates letter box, phone number and suggestion of lane to distant house. Possible and may assist current plan. Modification suggested. Visit art shop first. Collect leaflets for festival. Distribute at school.

"Good idea but I don't know where it is or what it's called." David said.

Accept language, accept other information.

"Very well." David waited, "I still don't know where it is."

Godfrey will.

"I know where it is." Todd said then he paused, "About me coming, I want to but I don't want to see Dad yet. I'd like to know how he is though."

"Portal. You say that you can monitor computers." David said, "Can you find any information on Todd's father?"

Still working as cleaner. Vodka purchases steady. No discernible change in status

91

Todd nodded.

"The more I think about this steam-punk thing, the more I like it." David said, "If the portal agrees then I'm even wondering if we could build more brakes and sell them. We'd have a source of income over there. Let's think about it."

When Billy and Godfrey returned, Billy was still giggling at Wilson's outraged concern that they would be dressing so badly. It was true though, bright yellow waistcoats edged with silver, and worn with a top hat should have looked out of place on either world. On Danny's world, the brake looked decidedly eccentric and putting the two together, the effect was extraordinary.

Once across the portal, they headed off. To his surprise, Godfrey knew the way and understood the road signs. The lanes were deserted and there was no-one in sight as they drove through a village. They had no choice but to join a wider road and there were now people about. Almost as if they were playing to an audience, they raised their hats to anyone who stopped and stared while Godfrey gave a cheery blast on the whistle. In their turn the passers-by stared at the three lads sitting on a vehicle rather than inside it and in front of a vertical boiler blasting out smoke from a chimney.

David was nervous as the traffic built up but they were in town so nothing moved quickly and it was still fun. When stopped, Godfrey allowed the pressure to build up so the brake could accelerate smartly away to loud chuffs from the engine which made even more people turn and look.

They reached the shop which was on a road just off the High Street and pulled up with a final blast of the whistle. The owner and a couple of customers came out as David leapt off and raised his hat to them with an elegant bow. He did not even have to ask about the festival before he was being invited to take part and was filling in the forms. Then they were off to the school, arriving just as lessons ended for the day.

There were cars parked, waiting for students but they drove slowly into the grounds distributing the leaflets that they had picked up. By the time David had managed to phone Danny and explain where they were, they had been forced to stop by the crowd excitedly examining the brake. David could sense the hostility against Danny as he arrived but he waved for him to come forwards. A teacher also pushed his way through.

"You're blocking the traffic here," he said, "Drive it into the staff car park. I'll try to clear a space."

"I've got a better idea." David said, "Godfrey, Billy and I will walk in front while Danny drives. Hang on. Billy, give Danny his coat."

Danny did not wait for a reply as he removed his school jacket, donned the waistcoat, then clambered into the driver's seat. Progress was slow but it took on the air of a parade with three oddly dressed boys preceding the extraordinary vehicle.

The teacher should have stopped Danny from driving but he was startled and was caught off guard. By the time he recovered, the car was already edging forwards and Danny obviously knew the controls so he contented himself with walking beside it.

Students were still jostling around and a picture built up of Danny and Todd spending the summer helping to build the brake but keeping it secret until it was ready. With such tangible proof and Danny's obvious confidence in driving the brake, other rumours simply vanished

The chaos gradually subsided, the last of the leaflets for the festival were given out and students dispersed more intrigued by their activities rather than scandalised by now forgotten allegations and gossip.

When they were ready to go, Godfrey drove with Danny, Todd and Billy as passengers, with David riding Danny's bike as they headed for Danny's home. Danny's family lived in one of the older housing estates, nowhere near a slum but also far from fashionable. Many of the residents were elderly couples who had lived there all their lives. They had watched the trees along the road grow from saplings to a pleasant display of greenery and on into oversized menaces blocking out sunlight and threatening overhead telephone cables.

One thing that the brake was not designed for was parking in tight spots and like many roads, this one was lined with cars. Luckily, they arrived as workers in nearby shops and offices were preparing to leave and before residents got home. One obliging resident moved his car to create a big enough space then worriedly watched as Godfrey manoeuvred the brake. He need not have worried, for Godfrey handled it expertly though even he breathed a sigh of relief when he finally stopped.

Again a crowd gathered, many knew Danny and he spent time talking about it and what it was like to drive it. David was surprised at how many people recognised him, asking him how he was and how was his memory. Danny's mother was busy in the kitchen preparing snacks and food, she did not know about the fuss outside until her younger son, Darren looked up from his computer game then rushed down to tell her.

Mary Lambert hurried out, saw that her own children were well and happy so diverted her energy into giving David a welcoming hug much to Billy's amusement. After all, it was not the way to greet a duke, was it? Mary was a kindly woman and even the most belligerent of her foster children had a sneaking regard for her. A more practical manifestation of her kindness was that whenever anyone came home from work or school, there would be a snack to tide them over. She told Godfrey to put the fire out or whatever he was supposed to do then ushered them through to the kitchen.

For a time it was bedlam but fun as they all tried to settle down. David only remembered a remark by Darren, "I'm Darren, my brother's Daniel and Mum only takes in kids if their name begins with 'Da'."

Finally, David managed to speak quietly with Mary.

"There's new papers coming in," she said, "The course, loss of earnings and the rest is just too much. We can't afford it and it's cheaper for the company to hire new drivers who have already got them."

"So it's got nothing to do with all the allegations against me and Mr. Barton." David asked.

"No. It's just this new driving test. Well, and his blood pressure. The doctor says he should rest more."

"Can I help?" David asked, "If you were prepared to move then I could offer him a job in charge of the stables, er, and garages. It's different to here but it's far slower and Terry would find it easier. I need to find a way of transferring funds reliably but when I do and if you want to stay, I'd happily pay for his courses if that's what you'd prefer."

Mary hugged him again.

"You're a good boy. I'll talk to him then you can explain more." She replied but before she could say more, Darren charged over.

"Can I spend the weekend with David. I'll be able to drive their steam cars and everything."

"You're a bit young for that." Mary said, "And you should wait to be invited, it's very rude to just barge in. David's family might have other plans."

"He really is a duke and he's in charge so can I come, please?"

Darren asked.

"It's a bit more than a drive to my house." David said.

"I know." Darren said triumphantly, "You're not mad; you're a duke from another world. Danny says it's cool and you've got a big house so can I come, please?"

"We were worried about all that fuss about you disappearing again and we didn't want Danny to vanish as well." Mary said, "I don't understand this other world business but you seem well enough so I suppose it's all right."

"Can I go then?" Darren interjected.

"Not this weekend." David said, "I'm only visiting to sort out some problems and I've got another journey to make. I'm not so sure about that one."

"You mean it could be dangerous?" Mary asked.

"It *could* be." David agreed, "That's why I'm going alone."

"No you're not." Billy called across the room, "I'm your servant so I'm going and Godfrey's your bodyguard so he's going with you too."

"You're just a boot boy." David said, "You do as you're told."

"Stuff that." Billy exclaimed, "If that's what you wanted, I wouldn't be here, would I?"

David looked at Mary and shrugged, "You just can't get good servants nowadays, can you?"

"You're all a bit young for this." Mary said, "You need the army or something."

"Back home, I command the local militia." David said, "I don't think it would help if I brought a squad of soldiers across and led them into Chasebourne."

"Perhaps not." Mary conceded. "You shouldn't be putting yourself in danger though."

"I don't think that I am." David said, "The portal was built by very clever people. I know something went wrong but I'm only visiting places that the portal knows about and just carrying messages. Driving a car or riding a bike can be dangerous and I know someone who drowned because he ignored warning signs. I promise you, I'm not going to ignore any warning."

"No I don't think that you would." Mary said, "According to Danny you're doing all sorts of things…"

She tailed off thinking, "And Todd seems happy enough."

"He's working on my projects and he's doing well at school." David replied, "Thinking about it, you could all visit as his guest and he can show you around while I make my trip."

"Are you inviting all of us?" Mary asked.

David nodded, "Why not? You can all come Friday evening and stay for the weekend. Uncle Jethro would love to meet you."

"That's tomorrow." Mary said, "I'll talk to Terry this evening. Can we phone you?"

David nodded, "Thanks to Todd. He worked out how to do it."

Mary looked puzzled while Darren looked even more excited. At eleven, he was younger than the other boys, slightly awed by them but seeing the adventure of a lifetime. David was satisfied though. It seemed that his appearances and disappearances were not causing problems for his friends. Indeed, as he learnt about the portal's abilities it seemed that they could all live in both worlds. The portal had said that his own world was in decline and he thought he understood why. It centred around a remark that he had made to his uncle some time back. If he had tried playing football with the estate boys, then they would have held back out of deference to his rank when he tried to score a goal.

He still expected his position to be remembered when it was necessary but he was aware that if there was a problem and he was plainly dressed, then the younger hands would approach him direct. At first the older hands looked on aghast but as time went on, he was sure that the older hands suggested that the younger ones talk to him. They could not bring themselves to do it but it did not matter for David was not aloof, unaware of what was going on but involved in all aspects of his estates and they were prospering because of it.

Although David had a valet who looked after his clothes, whenever he was dressed and preparing to act in an official capacity, it was Wilson who might send him back to comb his hair again or speak as sharply as he would to Billy leaving the valet appalled. On the other hand, David accepted it and instead of the dukedom crashing into chaos, Barabourne was a lively, vibrant place that could impress any guest. Even David's mother was satisfied that they were maintaining standards when needed and ignored what happened when they weren't.

It was something that he would have to ask the portal but he was sure that it was all connected with stopping the decline that the portal had mentioned. Whatever the reason, it certainly seemed to be trying to make visits between the worlds easier. David was curious about the problem that the portal had mentioned but it seemed that the warning and the understanding that David would help was enough for now.

For now, Godfrey wanted to be home by dark so they left not long after. Curiosity got the better of Mary and she persuaded her husband Terry, to take a weekend break.

Of course, Danny often talked about parallel worlds, and David being a duke but somehow it had not really registered. Terry had the image of a big house at the end of a long, muddy lane. Danny was a town boy and any house that remote would be a foreign world. Adding in engineering workshops and steam-punk would only enhance the otherworldliness.

Mary had heard of Danny's adventures and if she did not believe them, accepted that there was something. Even so it took time to realise that they really were somewhere different. The real problem was that everything was so similar. The lane, the fields, the gate were all there and since it was mainly hidden by a hedge, not even the lane losing its metalled surface and becoming a mere dirt track really registered.

It was the household staff and the old fashioned manners that convinced them that David really was a duke but another world remained a difficult concept. Remembering that David had been treated kindly by them, Wilson and Jethro made them feel welcome. His mother also tried but they had been warned by Danny and Todd so it was not too much of a disaster. The worst part of the weekend for Mary, was remembering how she had tried to persuade David to forget the silly nonsense about him being a duke. In his turn, Terry, her husband wanted to talk to David privately.

"I have Mary and the boys to think about," he said, "Back there, I've got insurance to cover the house if anything happens to me. We might moan about it but the health service is far better than what you seem to have. I reckon the doctor's right and I should slow down a bit. I could do a bit of taxi-driving or something. There is something though. That portal thing could be temporary so I don't want to rely on it but I'm wondering if we could trade while it's open. You've got a lot of craftsmen here making all sorts of stuff and you want technology."

"That's an excellent idea." David said, "We need funds on your side and that would be a way of getting them. Normally, I'd talk to Uncle Jethro and he'd say something about our solicitors working out the details. That's not going to work for us but I think we'll get by. Mr. Barton may want to help."

"Aren't you worried about too many people knowing about the

portal?" Terry asked.

"Not greatly. You can go home whenever you like but once you're on the other side, I doubt if you'll even find it. This is designated as Todd's home so he can't just nip across to see his friends."

"I still can't believe where I am." Terry exclaimed, "It's incredible. I'm so proud of Danny handling it all. I'm glad I trusted him and you too."

Chapter 9

If David was finding it easy to deal with his cross dimensional friends, it was his relatives, in particular Lord Carlton who were proving difficult and plotting against David.

"I've had a letter from Sybil," his mother said to David, "Jeremy and Isabella are coming to stay. They'll bring a tutor so that they can they continue their lessons. You could work with them instead of going to that other place."

"The village school, you mean." David retorted, "Why do I wonder if it's her brother-in-law's idea?"

"Lord Carlton? Don't be silly, dear," his mother exclaimed, "Sybil just remarked how happy Barabourne always seemed to be so it would be good for her children. She did wonder if you were a little lonely without suitable companions but that's all."

"I could work with a suitable tutor, have friends of my own rank and they'll be happy here." David said, "When was the last time that they went anywhere to be happy?"

"I know that you don't like that part of the family but your father always tried to make Sybil welcome. For his sake, let's try to be hospitable with her children."

David's Uncle Jethro agreed with David.

"The father's as bad as Carlton," he said, "They're both schemers but there could be another far simpler reason for this visit."

"Go on, Uncle." David prompted, puzzled by the twinkle in Jethro's eyes."

"You're fourteen, becoming an extremely handsome young man, and one of the most eligible bachelors in the country."

David stared and then blushed, "Oh, I hadn't thought of that... I mean I do wonder about it all but you're talking marriage, aren't you."

"One of the benefits of your methods is that I do hear a lot more gossip, including those rumours about Godfrey and Billy. I'm trying to be delicate here, but is your embarrassment just shock at the subject coming up so soon or is there something that we have to deal with?"

"No Uncle. I don't have any trouble looking at girls, sometimes I have trouble looking away but Isabella? I don't think so."

"She'll have grown up a lot since you last saw her, you may

find yourself unable to look away again but you've answered my question so I'll not embarrass you further."

"It doesn't embarrass me, Uncle." David replied, "We don't talk about the weather at the swimming hole either, but I'm not getting married for a few years yet, OK?"

"OK!" Jethro grinned, "A funny expression but succinct. Changing the subject, what's happening about the task that the portal has for you."

"Nothing so far, Uncle." David replied, "All it says is, 'situation volatile but all is not lost'."

"Do you know what it means?"

David shook his head, "No, but I'm happy to wait to find out. I like visiting Danny's world because I'm anonymous, taking the brake there was such fun and I want to be part of that festival. It's useful to us as well, even Billy is learning about their technology and can talk to our engineers."

"Yes I know. You're all working hard, and I can see the results of your experiments. Even Godfrey is busy, working on his new engines."

"He's also involved in the design of the electric light bulbs. Apparently fitting them to the brakes shakes them up so he's after more robust designs."

"You know that you have my full support." Jethro said, "However, I think that entertaining your cousins has to be another project and it'll demand your full attention. The more you act as the perfect host then the more you'll please your mother. She still tolerates you more than supports your activities so consider it as a way of easing her fears."

David nodded thoughtfully, "You could be right."

It was a couple of days before his cousin's arrival that David called his friends into the library. Wilson and Jethro were also there as he explained the situation.

"The last time I saw them, Isabella complained because her glass was out of position on the dinner table and Jeremy nearly rode down a stable lad who had to jump out of the way." David said, "That was on good days. I will not have any of my staff abused so my instructions to Wilson and Godfrey are, if they don't show the courtesy of guests, then you needn't show the courtesy of servants. On the other hand, you both know that I don't want to embarrass my mother or give Lord Carlton grounds to say that I need firmer supervision and I know that's contradictory. I'm asking you to please use your discretion to balance it all out."

David paused, "Tom has become Uncle Jethro's assistant and Billy likes to understand what's going on in the offices so they have free use of the library. If you're questioned about it, then the safest answer is that you're acting under instructions. Todd you're a guest but you're a commoner. If you can just swallow as many insults as possible, then I'd be grateful."

The others all looked thoughtful before Wilson said, "I will inform the staff that you are concerned for their well-being. They will appreciate your thoughtfulness and I will keep an eye on things."

"I could go back to just being a boot boy." Billy said, "I wouldn't mind."

"No, but I would." David snapped, "You're my friend and I don't treat friends like that. Neither am I going to be ashamed of you. I hope that all I'm doing is asking my friends for a bit of help in dealing with my cousins. I hope that I'm not being rude or insulting."

"You're the duke, Your Grace." Godfrey said, "Your cousins need to see that, and we understand that you need help in discharging your duties. We wouldn't be your friends if we didn't offer that help."

Jethro, impressed as the others including Wilson, nodded.

"Lord Carlton would like to prove that I'm ineffective as guardian. I'm more inclined to David's notion that there's more to this visit than just a family reunion." He added, "David do you have any plans of your own?"

"A couple." David replied, "Godfrey doesn't make a big deal of his knighthood because it confuses the older employees. It was awarded to help him to protect my interests, so it could prove useful if there's trouble and I might ask Godfrey to take them into Chasebourne. You know that I visit the portal each day and I'm learning a lot from talking to it. One thing that I've learned is that it draws energy from an imbalance between universes. Don't ask me for details, I've got the idea and that's enough but it's got limitless energy except for one thing.

"The raw energy has to be converted to usable energy, again don't ask me to explain more and that is limited on a daily basis. It's partly to stop armies charging through though there are other reasons but it's shown me just how imaginative it can be in using that power."

David paused, looking around, pleased to see everyone was fascinated before he continued, "It could expand the portal so that it spread across the lane and create a hologram inside the transfer zone. We could take the brake round into the lane and you would see a bit of mist and the road on the other side. My cousins wouldn't have to know about the portal or even know that they had jumped worlds but they'll have the trip of their lives."

"Surely they'll want to know what happened." Jethro said.

"There's plenty of rumours about our magical trips." David replied, "They could easily pick up on them. Instead of us denying them, show them, let them try to convince others when they won't have any evidence. It'll be easier."

"I see some sense in that." Jethro laughed, "Let's hope everything goes quietly."

In the event, half of the problem did not exist for Isabella greeted him warmly.

"I've heard a lot of stories about you," she said by way of a greeting, "I hope that they're true because I'd like your help."

Jeremy barely managed a handshake and there was nothing warm in his greeting.

"And are there any other guests my age or am I stuck here on my own?" He asked.

"There are friends of mine who come and go." David replied, "There's a number of engineers and scientists. The house is quite busy."

"But no-one worth knowing." Jeremy sneered.

"Now, now Jeremy. You should give David's friends a chance." David's mother said, surprising him.

"I don't think so. I know my station."

David turned to Isabella, "You said that you wanted to talk to me. Why don't we go to the library. We won't be disturbed."

Billy was already there, he looked up from his book and immediately moved to put it away but Isabella smiled and said, "You look like one of the rumours that I've heard about."

"Your Ladyship?" Billy queried.

"Forgive me if I'm mistaken but you're dressed like a servant but you weren't sitting in that chair like one."

"No, you're not mistaken." David said, "Billy is a boot boy, a travelling servant and learning to run my suite of offices. He's also my friend."

"Then please do not leave on my account." Isabella said, "Let's share secrets. Mine is that I'm a published writer. I've had a collection of short stories published and a novel is due out shortly. Mother knows and is encouraging me but Father would never allow it. I'm seventeen so next year is my débutante year. I simply could not be associated with a common trade if I'm to meet a suitable suitor."

"Mother says that not coming out until eighteen is creating a country of old maids so I'm on my guard." David laughed, "How can I help?"

"Father and Uncle Reginald want to know what you're up to." Isabella said, "Mother has heard that you're much more relaxed socially so she suggested to Father that we visit to see what's really happening. Jeremy's relishing his role as spy or guardian of morals, I'm not sure which, so be warned. Since there are also rumours that you are close to the king, we thought that a little patronage from you might help me."

David nodded thoughtfully then rang for a servant. Wilson arrived soon after.

"Isabella is a guest of the East Wing." David said, "She needs an office where the West Wing lot won't disturb her."

"Since Tom chooses to live with his parents and does not need the apartment we offered, may I recommend that? I assume that Her Ladyship requires a desk and other fittings."

David glanced at Isabella who nodded.

"I shall also enquire whether Tom can extend his duties to assist, Your Grace." Wilson added.

"Thank you Wilson," David said before turning to Isabella, "Wilson maintains order in the house. He doesn't allow me into the West Wing unless I'm in full ducal mode."

"Full ducal mode?" Isabella queried.

"An expression I picked up." David explained, "I simply can't behave like the duke all the time, there's too much to do. Wilson reminds me when I need to be formal."

"I see." Isabella said, "Wilson, I should like the relevant bags moved as soon as possible. Perhaps someone could show me to this apartment."

"I'll do it." Billy said, "I'm done here anyway."

"If I may suggest, you should both return to the morning room as soon as possible. Your other guest may become bored, and that may lead to mischief."

Isabella looked curiously at Wilson but did not comment as they followed his advice.

"How about going for a ride?" David suggested after he had greeted his mother and Jethro.

"Now?" Jeremy snorted, "I don't suppose that my useless whelp of a valet has even unpacked yet. We'll never get a decent ride and be back to change for luncheon."

"David is so busy that he rarely dresses for lunch," the dowager duchess said, "It would be nice to have a chat with Isabella without menfolk listening in so please go ahead."

David rang for Wilson again.

"His Lordship's valet may need time to find his way around. Would you find someone to guide him and help him. We wish to go riding as soon as possible."

"Certainly Your Grace, I'll also advise your man." Wilson replied and withdrew.

Jeremy seemed quieter when he said, "I must say, he seems to know his business."

"I've never known a situation that Wilson can't deal with." Jethro said, "Anyway Jeremy, from what you were saying, you appear to be less lucky with staff."

The conversation continued about nothing in particular until David decided that it was time to change. David contented himself with his last pair of jeans, jumper and proper boots while Jeremy wore tweeds, collar and tie.

"You look like a servant." Jeremy said, "Surely you don't intend going out dressed like that."

"I'm going out to have fun." David replied, "Have you ever had a pub lunch before?"

Jeremy looked puzzled but did not reply.

As they reached the stables, Godfrey hurried over.

"Hello Godfrey." David said, "Not tinkering with your engines?"

"No, Your Grace." Godfrey replied, "Most of the lads are servicing the machinery after the harvest, and the rest are putting up the poles for the power cables so I'm stuck here."

"Well, I'm giving you a little break. Will you help His Lordship to find a suitable mount and saddle it. I can saddle Jasper myself and I'd like you to ride with us as far as Barns Lane."

Jeremy was not really listening for he was looking curiously at the lighting in the barn. David hurried off, but Jeremy could not risk appearing uncertain by asking a mere stable hand. However, he was less certain and so could not be quite as haughty as usual.

Jeremy had to admit that David was an excellent rider and Jasper jumped the first two gates almost without breaking his stride so he was surprised when he pulled up at the third and Godfrey dismounted to open it. Everything was as it should be as they made their way through the gate until Jeremy became aware of a curious shimmering. He blinked in astonishment, for the lane had changed. Instead of the usual farm track, it was smooth, hard and far wider than he remembered. He might have put it down to a trick of his imagination but the gate was now a tall metal affair and Godfrey, together with his mount had disappeared.

"Is anything wrong?" David asked innocently.

Jeremy's pride and his confidence was seriously dented but he still could not admit to his uncertainty though he sounded far less confident as he replied, "Er, no."

David was contented with a steady trot until, hearing a rhythmic droning behind them, he dropped back to the rear. Jeremy could only stare again, this time at the vehicle that edged past. It was sleek, quiet apart from the drone, it had no obvious means of propulsion but it smoothly accelerated away from them.

"What sort of carriage was that?" He asked as David caught up with him, "Do you know who owns it?"

"I've no idea." David replied, "You see quite a few of them around here."

"Oh!"

At eighteen, Jeremy thought himself a man of the world and something was very wrong, yet his cousin seemed unconcerned. Still unable to ask questions, he allowed his confidence to drain as he continued riding in a state of nervous bewilderment.

David had mentioned a pub and it certainly looked as if they were riding towards one but Jeremy could see it was obviously different to the usual sort of place where yokels wasted their time instead of working. Firstly there was a pen for those strange vehicles, second, he could see well tended gardens behind it and thirdly, even in the bright daylight he could see more of the lights like those that illuminated David's stables.

Neither did things seem right when David simply turned the horses into a field. Where was the ostler? It got even worse inside the pub as the landlady glanced across and simply smiled and greeted him, "Hello David. I must say, you've brought along a very dapper replacement for Godfrey."

"This is my cousin, Jeremy." David said, "You'll have to excuse him though. He's not used to things yet."

"Sit yourselves down and I'll bring the menus across though before you do, here's a couple of quid. Put some music on. I like your choices so we may as well start with it before the philistines arrive."

The conversation was gibberish so far as Jeremy was concerned, and he watched as David fiddled around with a box on the wall, again brightly lit, and jumped as a band began to play. He looked around for the orchestra but saw only tables and other guests. So where was it?

"It's called swing." David said as they made their way to a table, "The locals say that I'm old-fashioned but I like it."

With Jeremy's grasp of reality still steadily slipping away and with it, his bravado, he finally surrendered to the situation.

"What's going on?" He asked, "Why isn't she more respectful?"

David threw his head back as he roared with laughter.

"You're priceless," he spluttered between breaths, "Is that all you're worried about?"

"No, but you forget your position too easily. Are we still on your estates?"

"No."

Jeremy stared as more cars drove past.

"What's going on? Where are we?" He asked, all pride gone and with a desperate need to understand.

"It's easier if you try to work it out for yourself." David said, "I learnt a lot when I first came here and I'm using it to claim the prize for tackling the London fogs."

"Those lights. There's no smoke."

"Very good, but it's not only lighting, it's heating." David said, "We're working on it all at Barabourne."

Just then the landlady came over to take their orders.

"The trugs are still selling well," she said as they studied the menu, "Can you supply some more?"

"Yes of course." David said, "I'm glad you said that because I'd like you to settle the meal out of my account."

"That's no problem. There's far more in it than that. Are you ready to order?"

"I think that I'll have the garlic mushrooms followed by lasagne, please. Jeremy?"

"I'll have the same," he mumbled.

To Jeremy the prices on the menu seemed extortionate, if not ridiculously high, and what did £9.95 mean anyway. If not £9 19s 6d, then surely 9 guineas. He recognised some dishes but the side dishes seemed more suitable in a fashionable French restaurant. It was safer to follow David's lead.

Unable to judge from the price of the bottle, he found the house wine pleasant, surprised to find that David was not allowed alcoholic drinks and that he did not use his rank to insist.

David was drawing on Godfrey's experience and focussing on small things like the lights, the jukebox and the selection of ice-cream, available courtesy of an electric fridge.

Jeremy remained tense and quiet so they did not stay long. As they left, Jeremy noticed the display of baskets, made of thin, hand carved wooden boards.

"Your trugs," he said, glad to find something he recognised.

"Yes." David replied, "Estate workers earn extra by making them and as you heard it's helping me to build funds here. Even Uncle Jethro has eaten here but I've never persuaded Wilson."

Jeremy should have protested at the idea of taking a servant to lunch but he was still at a complete loss. He simply followed David home. On reaching the stables, he dismounted and walked as briskly as possible to the house and his room.

Godfrey watched him go and smiled, looking quizzically at David.

"I thought parallel worlds would be too much for him." David said, "Cars and electricity seemed to upset him."

"That is so cruel." Godfrey laughed, "All the sights and no explanations what must he be thinking."

"It's when he tries to tell someone or tries to make his own way there." David said, "More importantly, Terry was right. Apparently the trugs are selling well so when he's ready we can sell even more."

"Action Stations, Your Grace." Godfrey whispered, "Another cousin in sight."

David glanced round.

"Hello Isabella. This is Godfrey." David said, "Another friend."

"Hello Godfrey. I'm pleased to meet you. Now, what have you two done to Jeremy?"

"Nothing." David replied, "I took him for a ride and we stopped for lunch."

"There's more to it than that; he babbled about engine-less cars and music coming out of nowhere then retired to his room."

"Supposing I said that he's learnt that the universe is a little bigger than he thought." David said.

"Another rumour." Isabella said, "You go to magical places. May I visit sometime? Godfrey perhaps you would accompany me."

"Yes of course, Your Ladyship." Godfrey replied and David

thought that he noticed an unusual eagerness in his voice.

"Call me Isabella." she said, "It was an invitation, not a command. I would think that you would make an extremely handsome if unsuitable escort."

"More suitable than you may think." David laughed, "May I formally introduce you, Lady Isabella Darrow this is Sir Godfrey Lowe."

"Sir Godfrey?" She queried.

"The king appointed him as my champion but I'm sure that he can tell you all about it. You're not the Isabella I remember."

"The stuck up bitch, you mean?" She laughed, "I have my own story. I was romantic enough to believe that a handsome young man would sweep me off my feet and whisk me off to a life of wedded bliss. Anyway, after Father had introduced me to the umpteenth vacuous, preening dullard, I began to question what I wanted. Mother was sympathetic but pointed out that sometimes a marriage can work if the wife accepts that the husband is more in love with his horses than with her, while he accepts her discreet interests elsewhere. I knew what she meant but I considered a discreet interest that I already had and did the unthinkable. I wrote down all the strange fancies I had instead of putting them out of my silly little head."

"I can hear your father speaking." David said.

"You were meant to." Isabella said, "It was after yet another of his speeches saying that 'telling silly fantasies' was most unladylike and would bore a real gentleman. I sent the best off to a publisher. I expected a rejection saying that Father was right and they were silly but instead they were published."

"Congratulations," David said, "They must be good and not silly."

"I think that the only word that Father knows is *silly* because my stories revolve around a young lady who goes around solving mysteries with a male companion who may well be more than just a servant. The mysteries are always gruesome, sometimes murder most foul and other times, it is a dark legend that seems to have come to life."

"And they are popular?" David asked.

"Oh yes," she replied, "At least once in each story, the companion is comforting her near the bedroom door and she makes a comment about being unable to sleep, she is so upset. It's the hint of raciness that people seem to like though as I gain experience in that direction then so might she."

"I assume that you don't publish under your own name." David said.

"Oh no, I publish as John Sanders."

"A Lady is Curious." Godfrey exclaimed, "I've read it. I must say that you suggest rather more between them, but the mysteries themselves are wonderful. I've read them, then when the solution is revealed, I realise that all the clues were there all along."

Isabella curtseyed.

"Why thank you, kind sir," she said, "It's a pleasure to meet someone who appreciates my efforts. When your duties permit, perhaps we can talk."

"Ah, my duties include protecting David from his enemies so I'm doing my duty if I can divert a beautiful spy from her duties."

"How gallant," she laughed, "I must write and tell Father that I have met the charming Sir Godfrey Lowe, impoverished but apparently in the king's favour."

David felt as if he were becoming an interloper and made his way to the house to find Jethro waiting for him.

"Your mother is worried that Jeremy has a fever and is delirious," he said, "Should we be concerned?"

"No." David replied, "I just took him to lunch at the Royal George. What a name! Can you imagine Hanoverians running the country."

"Don't change the subject." Jethro said sternly as they made their way into the library, "That's all you did?"

"Yes Uncle. I'm sure that he'll recover, then try to find his way back there. He may have a relapse when he can't find the way but it'll be nothing serious."

"Fair enough." Jethro said, "That just leaves Isabella, will she be a problem, do you think?"

"I believe that she is wooing Godfrey and he may well have succumbed to her charms by now. I believe her interests lie in seeking our support."

"You have been busy." Jethro said, "You shouldn't use Godfrey like that, though."

"I did nothing." David exclaimed, "It's a matter between themselves."

"I'm not sure that her father will agree though." Jethro said.

"Somehow, I think that if she decided to marry Billy then her father would end up approving." David laughed, "She's changed but she can tell you. Have you read A Lady is Curious?"

"Yes I have. I found Godfrey reading it and his description intrigued me. Why?"

"Isabella wrote it. She needs our help and she's welcome to stay for as long as she likes."

"While Jeremy needs to go home to… What's the phrase Todd would use? Ah yes, to get his head around things."

He turned to Wilson who had entered the room, "Yes Wilson?"

"His Lordship sent for some whiskey. I was concerned that something might be amiss until he asked me why I had not visited the Royal George. I replied that it was a place for His Grace and his friends, and that I would prefer to remain in my place. I thought that you should know."

"Yes thank you, Wilson." David said, "Some slowness and incompetence in providing refills will be in order. Bad hosts would water it to save money but it might also help his liver."

"I understand, Your Grace. I'm becoming used to controlling young gentlemen."

From then on, his cousins' visit proved to be something of an anti-climax. Jeremy spent much of his time out riding, with reports indicating that he spent considerable time attempting to retrace his original ride with David. He had no success of course, even though he had taken a brochure describing local walks as tangible evidence. It might be in full colour, double sided which would have been impossibly expensive to just leave in a pub but it did not explain the rest. Wilson did not deny that a pub called the Royal George existed. His Uncle Jethro had said that David often met friends there and David's mother had said that David seemed to visit many strange places, yet no-one could give him directions.

The further away from David's immediate circle, so people that he spoke to, seemed to understand less of what he was talking about. It was unsettling as the only thing that he had learnt for certain, was that Barabourne was developing electricity and that it had capabilities beyond his understanding. However, for the life of him, he could not work out how to describe it all to his father and uncle.

On consideration, he decided that he could mention electric light. Some had been installed in the barn and it had also been fitted to the smaller steam brake. He could mention that some select servants could come and go as they pleased but they were all very closely involved in David's projects. He was also aware that David held very technical conversations with his friends and servants. If he approached, David would say, 'that will do,' or something and the servants would fade back into the background while David and his guests would try to entertain him. Even though he was three or four years older than most of them, he felt like a child being humoured. Godfrey was closest to his age and he was curious about the new brake but he could not bring himself to offer friendship to a stable boy. Jeremy lasted just three days before he prepared to leave.

On the other hand, Isabella developed a genuine fondness for Godfrey, and an interest in all the activities at Barabourne, talking as easily to Billy as to David.

"I'm considering a new book," she announced, "An evil uncle is plotting to send a young nephew mad to gain control of the family fortune. Would you mind if I modelled the characters on you?"

"Uncle, is there something that you want to tell me?" David asked.

"Oh, it's pure fiction." Isabella laughed, "It's just that your interactions are so different to those between Uncle Reginald and Jeremy. He's your Uncle too, why do you always call him Lord Carlton."

"I can't imagine him being anyone's uncle." David explained, "I always feel as if I'm dealing with a visiting dignitary."

"I know what you mean." Isabella said, "Godfrey has that amazing colour brochure stuck to the wall of his room. What is a steam-punk festival?"

"You should not have been in his room." Jethro said, "We still maintain certain proprieties."

"Yes I know, Uncle." Isabella said, "Don't worry, I'm still pure and virginal."

"Er, yes, er, I'm sure you are." Jethro said, blushing profusely, "I was thinking of gossip."

"And I should like to attend this festival. I gather that it's a fancy dress ball of some sort." Isabella said, "I know. You have this big secret and you only let Jeremy far enough in to thoroughly befuddle him. You must have noticed that I've stopped being very ladylike and I'm quite willing to use my charms on Godfrey to break him down and tell me."

"It's a couple of weeks before the festival and Godfrey needs to finish his new brake so don't distract him too much." David said, "However, if you'd like Godfrey to take you to the Royal George one day, then Billy or Todd will have to accompany you."

"I didn't think that you were that old fashioned, I don't need a chaperone." Isabella exclaimed.

"No, but there's a rule that we have to travel there in groups of at least three." David explained, "I broke it with Jeremy but Godfrey still had to come a certain distance with us."

Isabella nodded, satisfied that she was keeping her independence. She settled in and proved to be good company, content to 'let the boys play with their toys' as she put it while she settled down to her writing. David was concerned that the portal would say nothing of the task that he faced but apart from that everything else seemed to be progressing smoothly. There were hiccups. The king announced that he wished to visit to see the electric lights turned on and Lord Carlton wrote to say that he intended visiting to discuss matters of family importance.

Chapter 10

As was now his custom, David called a meeting.

"Godfrey, can you fit all the steam broughams with electric lights?" He asked.

"Yes, I've been looking at designs for a proper unit that could be mounted across the front of any vehicle providing we can tap the boiler."

"Wilson, I want to put the king off for as long as possible without seeming to." David said, "I'll suggest a two-day visit. He arrives at about lunch time, does a tour of our facilities, we have a banquet, see the house light up. We then take a trip into the village to see the lights there and finally a trip back here to a late supper. I'm thinking late November or even early December. Can we do it?"

"Her Ladyship may wish to have a say on this." Wilson replied.

"Yes of course, she is the lady of the house and we need her skills. I want you to consider how many of the commissioners we can entertain overnight and to keep the proceedings focussed on the demonstration while we stop her inviting half the county."

David turned to Jethro, "Will you take on Lord Carlton, please Uncle. I mean find out what he's up to because I've got a feeling that he's not going to leave us in peace."

"You could be right though I suspect this trip has more to do with Isabella than us." Jethro replied.

"He's coming on the Wednesday and we're all leaving Saturday morning for the festival. Billy, Godfrey and Todd will be busy but if they can stay clear of the house during the middle of day and we can pack him off on the evening train then we'll cope. If he stays any longer, then he'll just have to meet all my friends."

"Is this festival so important?" Jethro said, "Surely there'll be another time?"

"The text books we want aren't cheap and we can't expect Mr. Barton to keep giving us money. I know that you don't like me being involved in trade, but it is a way of repaying friends' kindness. By the way, it's not trade as in a regular market because we're going to have fun as well."

"Very well. Let's see what happens on Wednesday."

Two things, among many, annoyed Lord Carlton; having to acknowledge anyone he considered inferior and having to treat David, a fourteen-year-old boy as his superior. He was placated to see that David had enough respect to meet him on the steps of Barabourne but he wanted the initiative. He ignored Wilson and led the way to the library where he found a group of boys sitting around a table engaged with their studies.

He strode across, snatched a notebook, studying it closely.

"Latin?" He queried, "These louts are learning Latin? In Barabourne's library?"

"A library seems a fitting place to catch up with assignments." David replied.

"Yes, but why are they learning it at all? It's a subject for gentlemen."

"Originally I asked them to stay away from the house today but I decided that I was not going to be ashamed of my friends. Would you like to be introduced?"

"Certainly not." Lord Carlton snapped, "Why on Earth would I want to meet them?"

"They'll be dining with His Majesty when he visits in the Autumn. However, if you don't wish to meet them then I'll not embarrass you by inviting you."

"You do not play games with me, young man." Lord Carlton yelled, "Jeremy told me about your foolishness. Electricity indeed. You're demeaning the whole family with this nonsense. You people, you can leave. This room is not for the likes of you. Where's Lord Westerham?"

"This is a library and my friends are studying." David said quietly but firmly, "This is my house, not yours or Uncle Jethro's and I must ask you to lower your voice especially since you only barged in here to cause a row."

"Why you little…" Lord Carlton yelled raising his hand but he got no further because he was startled to see Godfrey scrambling over the table. Before he could lower his arm, Godfrey had grabbed it and was twisting it round behind his back.

"How dare you?" Lord Carlton spluttered, "I'll see you hanged for this insult. David, do something."

"Very well." David replied and opened the door, "His Lordship needs time to compose himself. Take him for a walk in the grounds, will you please Sir Godfrey."

"Certainly, Your Grace. This way Your Lordship." Godfrey said.

Just then, Jethro arrived, closely followed by Wilson.

114

"Do something man." Lord Carlton yelled, "Or are you allowing this oaf to treat me so."

"David?" Jethro asked calmly.

"He tried to strike me." David explained, "Sir Godfrey was defending me. I suggested that he take a walk to cool off and Sir Godfrey is escorting him."

"I apologise." Lord Carlton said with as much dignity as he could muster, "I'm afraid that his wild tales of His Majesty visiting to look at electrical toys annoyed me more than they should have done."

"Very well." Jethro said, "I received the confirmation letter today, and I was just coming to tell you, David. His Majesty will arrive on the 4th December which is a Friday and he plans on staying until the 6th."

"His Majesty is visiting?" Lord Carlton spluttered, "Why?"

"He wants to examine all of our projects and I suspect that he is concerned about your own personal one, David." Jethro explained glancing at Lord Carlton, "At least we can say that Sir Godfrey is a courageous champion."

"Why do you insist on calling this lout, Sir Godfrey?" Lord Carlton demanded angrily.

"His Majesty saw fit to make him my protector." David replied.

"As long as I'm not going too far, Your Grace." Godfrey interjected.

"Wilson might have something to say about the scuff marks on the table." Jethro said, "Just be sure that you're discharging the duty that His Majesty knighted you for and you'll be fine."

"What is this nonsense?" Lord Carlton sputtered. It should have been one of his trademark roars but even he was beginning to see that it was he who was disturbing the calm order of the library not the urchins running wild. That was the problem, they were not running wild. They were using the library as it was intended and the notion confused him. He was still ready to fight his way free so Godfrey still held him tight. It was stalemate.

"This is some ruse to humiliate me." Lord Carlton exclaimed, "You will regret it."

"David is doing work of vital importance to the crown and the country." Jethro said, "We do not have time to play games with you or Jeremy. This is David's house, we are his guests here and I suggest that we behave accordingly. Now would you care to greet David's mother and Isabella or would you like Sir Godfrey to show you the activities that are causing such a stir?"

115

"I take it that neither of you have the manners to show me. You'll foist a farmhand on me."

"If it helps then I'm still a little uneasy at David's behaviour." Jethro said, "However, I do understand his trust and confidence in Sir Godfrey."

"So you agree that he is betraying his class." Lord Carlton said calmly, "Do something about it man, or I shall. At least tell him to release me. I should not have raised my hand to David. I promise that I'll not do it again - until I have the authority."

At a nod from Jethro, Godfrey relaxed his hold and Lord Carlton pulled free but he had only promised not to attack David; he swung round to punch Godfrey in the stomach. As Godfrey doubled over so Lord Carlton brought his knee up to smash Godfrey's face but he found himself pushed sideways and, standing with his weight on one foot, he crashed to the floor. David was alert as Lord Carlton swung round and raised his fists but could not react fast enough to prevent the first blow but luckily for Godfrey, David's charge prevented Lord Carlton's knee from connecting. Although not hurt Lord Carlton was surprised by the unexpected attack and needed a few seconds to get his bearings, startled to see both Jethro and Wilson standing over him.

David was helping Godfrey up and the other boys were hovering around them, not knowing how to help, though Billy hurried off but returned with two beefy footmen. Lord Carlton brushed aside Jethro's helping hand as he stood up. Even he could see that he was outnumbered and was not going to be able to bully his way into some sort of control.

"I apologise. In my concern for Barabourne, I forgot my manners so I should leave." He said with as much dignity as he could muster, "I'll have lawyers challenging the late duke's will. You Westerham, appear to be incapable of raising a gentleman."

He turned on his heels and strode off as Jethro and Wilson turned their attention to Godfrey.

"Todd, would you arrange for someone to drive Lord Carlton to the station, please?" David asked.

As they all calmed down, Billy said, "Todd and I have been talking. If we're your friends then we shouldn't be causing you trouble and now this. We shouldn't be in here."

"I don't want to do all this studying alone." David said, "I could find friends of my own class but they are more likely to agree with Lord Carlton and Jeremy; Isabella is the exception. Do you think that I could get on with them? You are my friends and I expect you to feel as welcome as any other guest."

"As you wish, Your Grace." Billy replied, grinning cheekily as David turned to Godfrey.

"Father would pour himself a brandy after an exchange like that," he said, ringing for a servant, "Would you like one? I think I'd like a cider."

"I'm sorry, Your Grace." Godfrey was almost sobbing, "I shouldn't have done that, should I?"

"Lord Carlton has always been free with his fists," David said, "Relax, you protected him as much as me. Can you imagine the trouble he could be in for striking a duke? You're my champion you did what you had to and I must say, it was pretty impressive."

"I shouldn't have done it though. I should have been more tactful." Godfrey said, "I'll understand if you want me to go."

Wilson had arrived in answer to the servants' bell and had heard the exchange.

"With His Grace's permission," he said, "The whole household knows that you'd protect His Grace with your life. The weather is still mild, so I suggest you take the house boys and stable boys swimming, all of them. Fresh air and exercise will do you all, far more good."

"Come on, Godfrey." David yelled, "If I get there first, I'm going to push you in again, but you'll still be dressed."

Godfrey's mood switched as only a teenager's can, especially given a challenge

"You wish." Godfrey riposted, "It's tiddlers like you who get thrown back."

They rushed past Jethro who was returning from seeing Lord Carlton off.

"Fresh air and exercise?" He asked.

"Yes Your Lordship." Wilson replied, "I fear that we be may short staffed this afternoon. I suggested that all the house boys join them."

"You'll manage." Jethro said, "I may take a ride with Tom so you'll only have to worry about the West wing. I assume that the stable lads have been released as well."

"Yes Your Lordship." Wilson replied, "I'm sorry, I'll see that a couple remain behind."

"No." Jethro said, "Let David relax. We'll cope."

The afternoon went well. Everyone knew that David had taken on Lord Carlton and, defended by Godfrey, had won. Nobody liked

Lord Carlton so they approved of David resisting his attempts at gaining influence at Barabourne. Although she would have been horrified at such appalling treatment of a guest, if she had heard about it officially, David's mother enjoyed hearing about her son's determination and Godfrey's staunch defence of him. She would have preferred him to have adopted an aristocratic calm and to have taken the incident in his stride but even she found Lord Carlton to be an overbearing boor. Maybe, the estate lads would provide some balancing escape. Either way, Wilson had few problems as no-one wanted to spoil David's afternoon.

Wilson had started out as a boot boy like Billy but unlike Billy he had not attracted anyone's attention as he slowly rose through the ranks of the household staff. As he rose higher so more of the staff had to treat him respectfully until now, he reigned supreme. Had David ignored all the protocols in his rush to be friends with the estate boys then his own status would have fallen. Although it was true that his position was much more complicated, his status had actually increased because of his relationship with David.

Many of the staff were disappointed that they still had to carry out their duties and could not slack off. They ignored the fact Billy was never released until his household jobs were completed. On schooldays, he had to complete his duties before leaving, risking punishment for being late if Wilson was not satisfied. David might sympathise and Wilson had watched as Billy had told David not to interfere on one occasion.

"You don't want to be late as well so clear off." Billy had said, "Mr. Wilson's right and I've got to sort it. If I don't, you'll think that I'm a skiver and won't want me as a friend."

Wilson, suppressing a smile, said, "He's right Your Grace and the sooner you go, the sooner he can tidy the cupboard, properly."

Later, Wilson sent for Billy.

"Do you have everything you need for the weekend?" Wilson asked.

Billy frowned, "David doesn't get that I like being his servant. He wants me to be all toffed up like him but it don't feel right, Mr. Wilson."

"I've never known a boy take his responsibilities as seriously as David does. He works hard, then plays hard. Thinking about it, I do know another boy and that's you. There's a good few of the staff who wonder why you don't spend your time lounging around. They certainly wouldn't be complaining because they're not treated like a servant but I wouldn't be able to say this to them."

Wilson paused, marshalling his thoughts, "When was the last time you polished a shoe? We all think of you as a boot boy because of your age but you're not. You run those offices for him and that's your duty. Going to school with him, trying to keep up with all his projects is more friendship than duty."

"I suppose so." Billy replied thoughtfully, "He don't need to treat me like an equal to know that he's my friend."

"Never in all my years in service did I expect to say this but you should defy your master. If you want to be the servant then dress and behave accordingly. Convince him that it is what you want and how you feel the most comfortable."

"You won't even clip me round the ear, then." Billy laughed, "You've seen pictures, will you help me make a uniform so I fit in?"

"It would be my pleasure. His Grace's valet wishes to maintain the status quo and disapproves of David's behaviour so he won't help but let's see what we can do."

Others were also deciding what to wear. Clothes on David's world were approximately the clothes of the 1950s on Danny's world. David and Todd could adapt cast off morning suits to fit in. They had enlisted the help of the dowager duchess' seamstress, dyed the suits a deep maroon, added brightly coloured waistcoats, and goggles to their top hats. The result was smart, they could almost have worn them in David's London but they were definitely in keeping with a steam-punk theme.

A farm boy's normal dress was boots, corduroy trousers and an off-white collarless shirt. Godfrey had obtained a couple of 'Sunday shirts', white, with collars, with the help of Mr. Barton and he borrowed a cravat from Jethro. With Mr. Barton's help, he had also acquired some disposable protective suits.

"Coal is coal and it's dirty work feeding a boiler," he explained.

Isabella looked the most conventional, at least on David's world. A tight charcoal grey jacket, white breeches and black boots, a white shirt with a wide yellow tie. However, she still managed to raise Jethro's eyebrows.

"You look very masculine," he said, "I assume that you still ride side-saddle."

"Father considers it more ladylike and I agree if I'm riding along Rotten Row." Isabella replied, "However he's beginning to accept that it's not so practicable when riding cross-country. I do believe that goggles are de-rigour at these events, I shall acquire a pair together with a suitable hat when we arrive."

Rather than boots, Billy wore a pair of David's black shoes, standard servant's trousers though with a silver stripe down the seams, a cut down footman's shirt complete with white bow-tie. He also wore one of the silver lined waistcoats that they had worn on their previous trip.

Although Jethro could see the sense of earning money in the other world, he was concerned that as members of the aristocracy, David and Isabella would be making unseemly spectacles of themselves. However, as they gathered in the library to show off their clothes, there was definitely a party atmosphere. Jethro was also satisfied that David had planned the weekend with great care. It was an unusual trip and although Godfrey had loaded a trailer with goods to sell, it was the party atmosphere that dominated.

Both Jethro and Wilson saw David's irritation at seeing how both Godfrey and Billy were dressed.

"You get too bossy and we'll beat you up but we look after you and that's that." Billy announced.

There was a startled silence then Todd burst into laughter. Soon the rest were joining in, even Wilson was unable to resist a brief chuckle and David shrugged in defeat. Jethro should have been the most shocked but he was waiting for David to spot his one mistake but neither he nor his friends seemed to have noticed.

The following morning they still seemed to have not noticed. Jethro watched as Godfrey donned the coverall but stared as Isabella took one and slipped it on, he then looked on horror-struck as she took up the driving position on the second brake. Wilson noticed his reaction.

"I believe that Godfrey has been teaching her and that Her Ladyship is quite competent. She is also of an age when driving is permitted over there."

"A lady driver!" Jethro exclaimed, "Whatever next?"

"It may be better not to ask, My Lord." Wilson replied.

Apart from concern at allowing Isabella to drive and even more concern that she was far too close to Godfrey, Jethro found himself disappointed that David had remembered that they needed a second driver above the required age. Perhaps disappointment was the wrong word for he was proud of David but it would have been interesting to see him deal with a mistake. Instead, he sought out David's mother.

"They have set off on that expedition of theirs?" She asked, "I take it that Godfrey will use the opportunity to further court Isabella."

"You know of their relationship?" Jethro asked, surprised.

"Apart from Isabella, Sybil regrets her marriage," the dowager duchess explained, "Her one delight is that Isabella is becoming such a strong minded individual. She's aware that Godfrey is totally unsuitable socially and that her father will disown her if he were to learn of their relationship. On the other hand, Godfrey is in His Majesty's favour, is in a position to do very well out of all this new activity and, as with this carriage driving, he encourages her rather than suppresses her. Publicly Sybil will support her husband and will not receive Isabella but unofficially she's relying on my opinion of Godfrey's character."

"Good heavens." Jethro exclaimed, "This all assumes that Godfrey is not just a passing fancy."

"Of all the people involved, the only ones that do not know that they'll wed is Isabella's father and Godfrey."

"Oh!" Jethro gasped, "I'm surprised that you approve."

"Sybil's husband believes that he has a right to chastise his wife as he would a horse or a groom. It is a wife's duty to obey her husband but mine was kind and considerate. He allowed me opinions which I held dear. David is thriving because of his very unsuitable friends and Isabella is so happy here. I think I'm beginning to see our conventions as far too narrow."

"I do see a problem though." Jethro said, "There are rumours that Godfrey and Billy are unnaturally close."

"Isabella's already got to the bottom of those." David's mother laughed, "They both come from orphanages, and they share their experiences. They are also intelligent and apparently they had both read *A Lady is Curious*, enjoying discussions about it along with other books. It seems the rumours mean that they have more privacy but they were more embarrassed about having intellectual pursuits than having carnal ones. Boys can be so strange."

"I don't understand that one, either." Jethro smiled, "I'll have to see if one of David's friends from the other place can explain it."

"The alternate world where men and woman behave equally and there are all manner of strange going's on. Isabella explains it all to me. She hopes to seduce Godfrey this weekend."

"Good God Almighty." Jethro exclaimed, "We should bring her back."

"No. I promise you that her mother would not wish it. You're right and I don't fully approve but Sybil only sees Isabella's happiness."

Billy had always known that Godfrey would never love him as he loved Godfrey. It was one of the many things that they had talked about, leaving Billy a little disappointed but also content that he had a friend in whom he could confide so much. He was sure that there was at least one person at Barabourne who would be interested in getting close to him. That person would have to be very careful and be willing to risk a lot to have a relationship with Billy so Billy knew that he had to be patient. For now, it was more amusing to think that his friends were discreetly arranging a room for him and Godfrey while he was just as discreetly arranging for Isabella to slip into Godfrey's room.

Although unaware of the sub-plots in his plans, David's day was going well. The festival was in a town not far from Chasebourne that closed off the High Street at weekends, partly to promote it as a shopping centre and partly to hold events that would attract visitors.

Their arrival caused quite a stir but they were expected. Danny and Danny's father along with Mr. Barton had arranged things on this world so everything went smoothly.

They had also been lucky. Insurance company's were not known for their sense of humour but they found one that could see advertising potential in promoting the flexibility and adaptability of their policies. They were insured to drive along the High Street provided that they were preceded by someone carrying a red flag.

Danny, Darren, Todd and David all cheerfully carried out the task. As the risk assessment pointed out, the flag and regular blasts on the whistle gave pedestrians adequate warning, while a person walking in front effectively regulated the speed. Terry, David's one time foster parent and Mr. Barton assisted by Billy did a roaring trade selling trugs, corn dollies and steam driven toys purchased from David's world.

For once, it was Isabella who was overwhelmed. The brakes attracted large crowds and some were remarkably knowledgeable but she watched admiringly as Godfrey handled it all with his usual calm efficiency though there was one incident that amused her. The town mayor was being shown around and stopped to admire the brakes. Godfrey forgot where he was, pulled himself up, standing as he would in front of a visitor at home.

"They're amazing," the mayor said, "You must be very proud of them. I'd like to take a ride in one."

Godfrey bowed his head and replied, "Thank you, Your Worship, I am proud of them and I'm at your service whenever you wish to take your ride."

"And you play the part well," the mayor said, "Congratulations."

The mayor moved on while Godfrey relaxed, looking sheepishly at Isabella.

"I did that all wrong, didn't I." he said.

"No, she liked it," she replied, beckoning David and the others over.

"Other participant's clothes make us look dowdy. How about assuming ranks?" She said then seeing David's frown, added, "I know, it's not how you treat your friends but you and Billy could swap later."

"No we couldn't." Billy said, "How about it Darren? I'll be the butler and you be a footman."

Darren nodded cheerfully; still a little overwhelmed by the older boys, he was glad to have something to do.

Cook had prepared a lunch for them and since David and Isabella were involved she had not been satisfied with a few sandwiches. Packed into the trailer there were tables, chairs, full place settings and a white table cloth, not to mention linen serviettes and towels and even a parasol for Isabella. They set everything up between the two brakes.

Billy was also enjoying himself. Remembering Wilson's advice he brought white gloves, putting on a pair and offering a pair to Darren before laying out a table. Isabella was right and it became part of the event as Billy expertly laid out a place setting then told Darren to lay out a second while he prepared the food. Of course there was no plastic, just silver plated dishes complete with lids, which he laid out on another table. There was no wine but lemonade, juice freshly made from real lemons that morning. Food consisted of a cold cucumber soup, followed by a chicken salad with apple tart for desert.

Wilson would have been proud of him, or rather Wilson would be proud of him after he watched the video that Danny shot. In fact several visitors were filming it as they looked on with interest. Billy deftly tidied Darren's effort before turning to David and Isabella.

"Your Ladyship, Your Grace, luncheon is served," he announced then held the chair for David indicating that Darren should do the same for Isabella.

David felt as if he was a zoo animal at feeding time as Billy served the soup. Isabella could only think of her father's fury at such a vulgar display and thoroughly enjoyed herself. In fact, Billy was the star. He knew that Wilson would be warning him about all sorts of mistakes but his behaviour was impressive. TV shows about life in a country house were very popular and visitors were seeing a live scene. Once David and Isabella were eating, he sent Darren to fetch the others who were left to help themselves.

"Godfrey, we shall promenade in the brake after luncheon. See that it's fired up ready, will you?"

"Yes, Your Ladyship." Godfrey replied knuckling his forehead.

Danny acted as footman, assisting Isabella, then David onto the brake taking up position with the flag. The show was over and a few clapped Billy as he began clearing up. He paused long enough to bow politely.

"This really is tremendous fun." Isabella said glancing at David, "Let me guess, you're worried about Billy and Godfrey. Don't be. They're showing off their skills and we're just unimportant supporting actors."

Isabella was proved right when they returned. Billy was cheerfully passing on his butlering skills to a couple of volunteers while an interested crowd watched. In all, the day was an outstanding success and sales from the goods that Godfrey had brought, added considerably to their local bank account set up by Mr. Barton.

Neither brake had lights good enough to drive at night on this world and so, one of the organisers had offered a yard to store them in. They would then be able to take part in the evenings activities though they were mainly opportunities for adults to get a little drunk. However, they could spend the night on this world then go home, the next morning. It could have been an excuse for the younger boys to have one big sleep over but they were tired. They were content for David and Todd to stay with Danny's parents, while Billy and Godfrey were to share a room at Mr. Barton's and Isabella occupied a single room there. It was not unusual for servants to share beds, Mr. Barton did not know of the rumours concerning them so everyone assumed that it was to allow Isabella the privacy of her own room.

What they did not realise was that as soon as the house was quiet, Billy slipped along to Isabella's room and tapped on the door. As she came out of the room she kissed Billy on the forehead and whispered, "Thank you, Billy you'll always be our friend."

Unbeknown to any of them, John Hemmings had been in the crowds just enjoying the day. Like any public official, he had too big a case load to worry about cases that were considered closed but there was something odd about David and his friends and they had stuck in his mind. There were few legal records that David had ever existed,

Todd had disappeared, no-one seemed worried and there was no official investigation but something was going on.

He was not sure why it had felt so important to come, but something seemed to push him. It niggled and he rationalised it by thinking that it could give a substantial boost to his career if he found the answer. At that point, his thinking faltered; not on his day off.

In their turn Billy enjoyed the luxury of a bedroom fit for his master at Mr. Barton's, while Godfrey and Isabella enjoyed each other. David enjoyed the hospitality of his ex-foster parents and a new friendship with Darren and Danny. On his home world, David was expected to be much more adult and it was nice to be treated like a child again even if Danny did roll up his eyes at his mother's fussing.

Chapter 11

However they spent the night, they were a cheerful group as they headed for home. It was as well that nothing had gone wrong for the portal was now warning David to be ready to travel on 21st December, the Winter Solstice. Unaware of why the date was so important, he could only wait but in the meantime he could deal with his next major problem - the king's visit. It began with the arrival of the king's equerry, Sir Anthony Rowbotham about a week before.

"His Majesty insists that he should not be an inconvenience," the equerry said, "His train will arrive at 10am. Normally a support train would precede the royal train with his car but he is content to be met at the station like any other guest."

"Is he travelling alone, Sir Anthony?" Jethro asked, "No retinue?"

"None that you will see," the equerry smiled, "On this occasion he is here as chairman of the board of commissioners and should be treated accordingly. I'm here to advise so any breach of protocol will be my fault."

"I'll speak to Godfrey." David said, "I bet he takes both broughams to the station in case one breaks down. We'll hold a heads meeting this afternoon."

"I don't think that His Majesty would object." Sir Anthony chuckled, then looked puzzled, "A heads meeting?"

"With so many projects going on, not to mention the normal running of the estate and house, David holds meetings with the managers or heads of each department. They cover anything from cook complaining about too many people expecting meals at odd hours to arranging manpower for installing electrical equipment." Jethro explained.

"Do they achieve anything?" Sir Anthony asked, "Surely the people can just sort things between themselves, I would not involve myself in squabbles like that."

"Once, I would have agreed with you, but not now." Jethro replied, "Engineering apprentices and household staff helped with the harvest and now farm hands are erecting poles to carry the cables. I believe Wilson has called in some extra help for this weekend."

"Does everyone refer to His Grace as David?"

"No, it's mainly the younger staff." Jethro replied, "They see him as working in the house and see a difference when he's carrying out his duties and when he has time off. I gather that they assume that he's on duty all next weekend."

"His Majesty believes that we are given our position by god." Sir Anthony said, "It's unseemly to treat one's position so off-handedly."

"I don't believe that I do." David exclaimed, "As Duke, I have initiated a number of projects which I expect to be done properly. On Sundays, my people expect to see their master and I oblige. There are times when I have no immediate duties and then I'll play football with any of the estate lads who also happen to be free. It is not treating my position off-handedly, it is knowing that everything is going smoothly, I can trust my people and can relax."

"My apologies, Your Grace." Sir Anthony said, "It would not do for His Majesty to walk in on anarchy and we have to be sure. I am authorised to tell you that he has received a petition from Lord Carlton requesting that you, Lord Westerham be replaced as guardian. Lord Carlton alleges that His Grace is, in fact, forgetting his position and that Your Lordship is unable to control him. Lord Carlton made it clear that while he would not interfere with ventures approved by His Majesty, he would introduce a proper sense of order to Barabourne. His Majesty is bound to consider the petition but personally, I don't think that you need to worry though we are concerned that mere village boys have free rein of the house."

David tried to reply but Jethro interrupted, "Not even David's mother complains about their behaviour. David is creating a talented team to assist him and is not worried if they are more intelligent than him."

"As with his two assistants at the examination," Sir Anthony said, "I repeat that I don't think that you have anything to worry about but we have a duty to investigate. Perhaps you would go about your business as usual and allow me to deal with Lord Carlton's petition."

Many at court referred to Sir Anthony as that jumped up little artisan; he would never take offence, agreeing that it was true. His father was a labourer in a factory, and Anthony had left school at thirteen to work alongside him. He spotted a crack in a bearing which could have caused expensive damage and as a reward, he was apprenticed to an engineer. Even before his apprenticeship was completed he showed a flair for design. Most of his work was for the factory but he sold other designs. The arrangement might have

127

continued, had not the owners decided that all work done on their premises belonged to them and demanded a contract from Anthony who promptly resigned.

He set up on his own, became even wealthier and took up tennis. Sir Anthony was a skilled player so not only could he afford them, he was welcome in the top tennis clubs around London.

Todd's world was used to a constant stream of pictures of celebrities. On David's world, photography was limited by the lack of electricity. Cameras were complicated mechanical affairs, darkrooms needed expensive equipment and chemicals. Neither could pictures be transmitted anywhere. Although there were pictures of the king in nearly every home, they were formal affairs with the king wearing robes and a crown. Naturally polite and courteous, Anthony treated all his opponents with respect. He did not relate the pictures of the king to another talented player who was willing to chat with him after the game. He was later embarrassed to be told that it was the king and he had been invited to play him again, this time at Windsor.

A friendship developed that made the court nobility jealous yet King Charles found Sir Anthony' easy manner useful in dealing with situations needing considerable tact. A squabble between a young duke of England and his uncle was a good example, and if necessary, Sir Anthony would have returned to London to advise the king not to visit. Instead, Sir Anthony was impressed with what he saw. He spoke to the boys closest to David, content that they became as relaxed with him as with Jethro and David himself. His other brief was to ensure that David's projects were genuine and not some sort of hoax but he could see that those employed were enthusiastic and genuine.

He was also impressed with the calm efficiency of the staff as they prepared for the royal visit. Often the host would be close to panic, constantly interfering but only succeeding in causing chaos while Sir Anthony would be seen as an interloper; only there to find fault.

At Barabourne, he found himself part of the team, and left to complete his own tasks. One evening, he entered the library to find Godfrey sitting, quietly reading. As usual, Godfrey stood, to leave a house guest in peace but Sir Anthony waved him down.

"There's one of His Grace's projects that we haven't discussed." Sir Anthony began, "I'd like to know about the place he disappeared to. Do you think that it's a threat to us?"

Godfrey frowned and Sir Anthony quickly added, "Yes, I may be asking you to speak against His Grace but we're discussing the safety of the realm. I'd like an honest opinion."

"Shouldn't you ask David, I mean, His Grace?" Godfrey asked.

"The people here talk about his trips to magical places. You and his other friends have all mentioned other worlds. He also mentioned it to His Majesty who was then caught between pushing the commission to tackle smog and dealing with a lunatic duke."

Godfrey grinned as Sir Anthony continued, "You realise that His Majesty is half expecting you all to be living in some strange fantasy world. I have to say, half-expecting because he does receive reports on your medical work as well electrical development and it does all appear to be grounded in fact. Indeed, other worlds is a less fanciful explanation to his sudden accumulation of knowledge than other suggestions I have heard."

Godfrey grinned again, "There's a portal, it's a machine that can think but it can only think about what it was built to do. It believes that this world is in decline and that David, I mean His Grace should do something about it. There was something hidden that was threatening another place and… His Grace had to give them a message telling them where it was."

"By all means call him David." Sir Anthony said, "And do you think that we're in decline?"

Godfrey thought for a moment, "I'm just a stable lad but I'm also designing electric light bulbs and building vehicles that can be safely used at night. Lord Carlton would have a fit if he was to catch me just sitting here, I'm not even working while David says that his books are for anyone who can appreciate them. Who do you think is right, Lord Carlton or David?"

"It's not for me to say but you're suggesting that we stifle innovation because we're more worried about keeping the masses in their place while David succeeds quite well in an atmosphere that encourages it." Sir Anthony said, "We have to maintain order though."

"Yes sir." Godfrey said, "If I showed Lord Carlton the new brake that I've built, I'd be whipped for getting too uppity or for being insulting because I didn't assume he knew everything. I could even be arrested for stealing his materials."

"Lord Carlton does know everything worth knowing." Sir Anthony laughed, "At least he believes he does and I do understand. This is an establishment for developing new ideas and you use your initiative accordingly. Lord Carlton would never allow it, neither would the majority of his peers. It's getting worse which is why we're in decline."

"Yes but the portal thinks in terms of worlds not nations."

"You may be surprised to learn that His Majesty agrees with you." Sir Anthony said, "Even without the resistance to change, it's difficult to know what to do without causing chaos. However, the king cannot become involved with a house of cards which could collapse with the first draught of air." I've been tasked with finding out what it's all about so convince me that we're building on solid ground."

"Begging your pardon, sir, but it may be better to show you. Billy and I could take you."

"Providing your master agrees to share it with me." Sir Anthony said, watching Godfrey's reaction but he just smiled.

"There are rules and we travel in threes. David can bend the rules but I don't try. By the same token, I wouldn't have invited you if I thought that I was abusing my privileges."

"No I don't think that you would. Very well let's assume that these worlds exist for a moment, are they a threat?"

"No, the Roman world called David, 'Honoured Traveller' and had waited eighty years for him. They can't travel themselves. Danny's and Todd's world doesn't really know about it except for a few of our friends. The portal hides itself so it can't be found by accident."

"Very well." Sir Anthony said, "I'd like to visit these other worlds. His Majesty will also visit. Is there a problem?"

Sir Anthony had noticed a look of alarm cross Godfrey's face.

"His Majesty might find it difficult on Danny's world." Godfrey said, "They'd laugh at him if he tried to behave like a King."

"Surely they recognise nobility." Sir Anthony exclaimed.

"The Roman world would treat him with all due honours but if we visit again, they'll expect some sort of message. I don't know about Danny's world but they have a queen." Godfrey explained, "They'd laugh at us if we claimed to be from another world or else we'd have to tell them about the portal."

"Yes I see. As you say, it might prove undignified for His Majesty, however I should like to visit the world where you obtain all your information."

Godfrey excused himself to find David and Todd who were playing cards with Jethro, Isabella and David's mother.

"I'll have to come as far as the portal to confirm that he can make one trip." David said, "When do you intend going?"

"If you'd ask Mr. Barton whether he's got those medical books

I'd rather not go." Todd said, "I will though if Billy doesn't want to."

"I'll ask him." Godfrey replied, "What's wrong Todd?"

"Nothing except I phone my Dad and he asks me if I've got any money for a bottle of something. He never asks me how I am, he just asks whether I'm getting any money."

"You could ask Isabella." David suggested.

"I could but I don't think that she'll want to go." Godfrey replied, "She'd rather get on with her writing. Do we need three people?"

"I'd prefer it but it's up to you." David replied, "Can you handle Sir Anthony alone?"

"Grown ups think that they know everything then when they discover a new world, it shakes them up. I'll take Billy though, if he's allowed. Am I getting above myself?"

"Look, the portal is still going on about this big job I've got to do." David said, "It bothers me a bit and I don't want Lord Carlton's kind of servants. They'd stand watching me get into trouble because it's not their place to interfere. Sir Anthony has decided that you should take him, so organise it as you think fit."

Godfrey nodded, "I suppose the weekend's reminding me that you're a duke and I'm just a stable boy."

"No, you're Sir Godfrey, my champion. You're defending me from Lord Carlton by demonstrating that all's well here."

Godfrey nodded gratefully. It occurred to him that David was a duke more than just by inheritance. He might only be fourteen but he was a leader, who knew what he wanted and expected others to follow. Although one of David's closest friends, Godfrey still expected to work for his wages though it was considerably more interesting than farm work. He had been given a task that was way beyond anything that a mere farm hand could be expected to do yet he was expected to carry it out while others were expected to assist. Maybe Lord Carlton's servants understood their duties better but David expected far more of his servants, including being able to trust them. It was that trust that allowed him to read in the comfort of the library, Billy to run the offices under Wilson's tuition, and Tom to become Jethro's secretary.

Sir Anthony was an honoured guest of the Duke of Barabourne, so Godfrey was still nervous. Sir Anthony examined the portal carefully, satisfying himself that it was secure then relaxed as they rode to the Royal George.

It was mid-morning so the pub was shut, but Godfrey turned

their mounts into the field as they waited for a taxi. Sir Anthony watched Godfrey make the call to book it but all he saw was the boy talking into a flat case. Cars passed them which distracted Sir Anthony yet while they were waiting, he managed to speak pleasantly with the odd rambler who passed by.

Worldly-wise, Billy opened the taxi door with a flourish holding it politely as Sir Anthony got in before adjusting the seat belt for him. Godfrey got in beside Sir Anthony while Billy got in the front seat, asking for them to be taken to the library.

They did not talk much on the journey, content to leave Sir Anthony to take in the sights. Like Godfrey, he could see the part that electricity played on this world and understood why David was so keen to introduce it on theirs. He was an engineer and professional curiosity competed with a first-time traveller's usual fear. Sir Anthony was content with Billy's companionship so Godfrey headed off on various errands.

"Why hasn't he done anything about communications?" Sir Anthony asked on one occasion as they studied a television on display in a shop window.

"It's something we've learnt, sir." Billy replied, "When you go back, try explaining where you've been and everything you've seen. It's like when someone tells you that they've seen a ghost. It's difficult to believe because there's no way of proving it. David's idea is that his next crackpot scheme will be accepted once everyone starts saying how easy electric light is."

"Wise words from one so young." Sir Anthony smiled.

"Nah." Billy retorted, "Danny laughed at him for saying he's a duke. Now his family visits for holidays. Proof, see?"

"Yes, I do see and it's still wise words." Sir Anthony said, "Be honest, do his people slack off because he's so soft?"

"He's not soft." Billy retorted, "Some grumble because they can't slack off. Mr. Wilson and Godfrey sees that they don't. If Mr. Wilson thought that I was slacking off, I'd get a clip round my ear quick enough and David wouldn't stop him."

"I can see that this world is far more tolerant." Sir Anthony said, "Wouldn't you rather stay here?"

"I work for David." Billy said, "If I worked for Lord Carlton then I would, but if I worked for him I wouldn't dare say that you should be checking up on this world, and not questioning me about David."

"Fair point." Sir Anthony chuckled, "Since we're not choosing to remember our proper places, then I'll tell you this. His Majesty had to take Lord Carlton's petition very seriously. It specifically mentions Godfrey and you. I can see that the work you're all doing is producing results, the stable lighting for example is a serious application of your ideas. Incredible as it is for me, I now see what they're based on."

"His Grace's ideas." Billy interjected."

"No all of you." Sir Anthony corrected, "He couldn't do it all on his own. What I was going to say is that his social experiments seem to be working as well. You're a fine young man, and willing to accept David's position as your master. On the face of it, you're insolent and forget your position but in reality you speak openly and honestly which I can respect and it is what David wants from you."

Billy nodded thoughtfully as Sir Anthony concluded, "You're as much an experiment as electric lighting and you seem to be working."

Billy grinned, "That's good to know, sir. What I don't get, is why so many of his people are scared of him."

"We could spend a year discussing that subject." Sir Anthony replied, "I was lucky with my employers and now, I try to treat my people properly. He could have you whipped or worse, so you should fear him. He could dismiss you and ensure that you never found another job so you should just obey him. He knows what he's doing, responds to what you have to offer so you respect him. Most don't see beyond fear and obedience."

"Wise words from a toff." Billy exclaimed cheekily, glad to see Sir Anthony laugh cheerfully.

It was that evening when they had safely returned that Sir Anthony spoke with David.

"It's amazing." Sir Anthony said, "I have written to His Majesty and assured him that Lord Carlton's fears are completely unjustified. I have also informed him that your ideas on electricity, no matter how wild or improbable, are grounded in fact. I have suggested that the Admiralty would be wise to make resources available to you to develop communications."

He paused, "You know the fable of the goose that lays the golden eggs? I have further suggested we accept the golden eggs as they are laid and we should protect the goose from those who do not understand. I also explained that although I consider your other place to be safe, he may surrender too much of his dignity to visit."

David nodded as Sir Anthony concluded, "His Majesty may well surprise you. He is warmer and far more approachable than you might believe. He may expect you to fully understand court etiquette but he would not expect Billy because he was not brought up for it."

David nodded, "I understand. I'll be on my best behaviour."

"Ah!" Sir Anthony exclaimed, "That's not what I meant. I was trying to say that His Majesty may well prefer Billy to be his guide. He has a good understanding of the work that you're doing, and His Majesty could accept him being himself but you would have to be very much the courtier."

"Good for Billy." David laughed, "I'm surprised though."

"Because he's not like Lord Carlton?" Sir Anthony asked, "His father would have sided with him. He is genuinely worried that the empire is at risk. Can you imagine the problems if your projects were based on an illusion?"

David nodded and Sir Anthony concluded, "I've endorsed your methods even if Billy's the rudest servant that I've ever met but as I pointed out, he serves you with all his heart."

Relieved by Sir Anthony's remarks, they all felt happier about the impending visit. Sir Anthony was proved right when His Majesty insisted on Godfrey and Billy showing him around. The king watched indulgently as Godfrey demonstrated the new brake and explained how he made improvements to the light bulb. He was duly impressed when he saw the lighting in the stable, agreeing that with all the straw and other flammables, it was far better than oil or gas.

There were disturbances to the itinerary. Godfrey found himself apologising to David's mother that His Majesty's tour prevented him from lunching with her. Instead, David was summoned to allow His Majesty, Godfrey and Billy through the portal.

David, after a tense meal with his mother, spent his time in the staff-room, waiting nervously for their return while Wilson tried to fuss over him. For once even Wilson was caught out when they burst in unannounced. David, surprised and relieved to see them laughing cheerfully at some shared joke, tried standing for his monarch but was waved back down.

"You were right." King Charles said, "It was not a suitable place for me to visit but it was a lot of fun. It was also very strange being so completely anonymous. You were also right in that no-one seemed to be aware of your portal. I now understand, the importance that you attach to electricity. It dominates everything over there and the results are incredible."

The King paused, "I watched their traffic and I have never known so much outside of London but I was struck by the order. Nearly everyone obeyed the rules, the Highway Code is it called?

Anyway, it is of no matter. It was a different sort of order but it was order. Your relationship with these lads is also a different sort of order but I agree with Sir Anthony, it works."

"Thank you, Your Majesty." David replied, still uncomfortable at remaining seated while Billy and Godfrey just plonked down in the nearest chairs.

"A good few of our nobles would use your portal to replace me, Your uncle, Lord Carlton for one," the King said, " Is there any way in which he could get control?"

"No, Your Majesty." David replied, "He claims that I'm not being raised to suit my station but his efforts to become my guardian have failed so far."

"My father would have demanded the portal destroyed, rather than allow threats to *God's Proper Order* and his view was that any problem could be overcome provided we maintained it. You are slowly introducing changes based upon your experiences and I agree with you that we need to change."

"Yes sir." David replied.

"Sir Anthony mentioned that if you came up with too many incredible ideas then you would become a laughingstock. He may be right, but... what is it called, radio... needs to be looked at so I shall speak to Admiral Sir Rodney Greenway. If he sends you a couple of impoverished midshipmen who would benefit from your patronage, it would be enough to say it was a navy project. It would mean that you'd be entitled to funding and have access to navy resources. Understand, we would regard radio as the most important project that you have. The fastest overland communications we have is by vacuum tubes run by the railways. Once a ship is out of sight, communication with her becomes impossible. Can you do it?"

"Develop radio, you mean, sir." David said, "Todd could give us a better idea of what's involved."

"I see. He's from the other world, isn't he?"

"Yes sir."

"Where is he?"

"He thinks that he should make himself scarce." Billy interrupted, "So should we, now that we're back."

David looked nervously towards the king, appalled by his servant's breach of manners. The king caught his look.

"Billy, would you go and fetch him please?" He asked, "Wilson, would you ask Lord Westerham to join us and will you return? I think that we should clear the air. David, I believe you chair what you call a heads meeting. Perhaps we could have one now and no, I do not need to sit at the head of the table though I would like to speak."

There was considerable confusion as they gathered around the table. David expected them to sit, preparing whatever they needed for the meeting but no-one would sit before the king while he was content to watch the proceedings. It was Billy who spoke first.

"We do things arse-about-face here," he said, "It's the underling's who sit down first 'cos they're scared that they've forgotten something and want to check."

The king laughed, "There's a reason for all good etiquette. Gentlemen, please continue as you usually would."

Both Wilson and Jethro were decidedly uncomfortable as they took their places, while Godfrey and Todd were used to the bizarre. Finally, King Charles took a seat, pointedly choosing one near the bottom of the table and apparently content that Billy sat beside him.

"Sir, you wish to say something." David said.

"Thank you, David. Sir Anthony described the portal as the goose that lays the golden egg and that we should be content with the eggs and not claim the goose. I think that I agree. It should concern me if you were considering your own alliance with it against me but I find that difficult to believe. The very openness that your friends display would make a conspiracy difficult. I've mentioned research into radio and you will have more strangers wandering around. If everything is as it appears to be then you should have no problem but it would make a conspiracy harder to conceal. Do you accept that I need to keep an eye on you?"

"Yes sir." David replied, "Spies have to fit in with surroundings so I assume that they'll be able to contribute."

"Touché." The king laughed, "Now Lord Carlton and his brother. I'll ask again, are they likely to gain control here?"

"Uncle?" David said, indicating Jethro.

"If you're requesting new projects then our activities are going to seem even more tempting." Jethro replied, "I'm sure he'll want a piece of the action."

"A piece of the action?" King Charles repeated, "An interesting phrase but I understand and it can't be allowed. He'll seek support from the more traditional Lords and there might be more resistance to change. We have already drawn up contingency plans for the evacuation of London. We might have to implement them during the next smog. It's that serious and it's why electricity is so important.

You are not the first to suggest the potential of electricity but other projects have failed because it would be demeaning to be interested in a fairground toy. The commissioners still think that I'm just indulging you. They'd had their usual cosy chat and intended to dismiss you before lunch. That's before I decided to intervene. The senior members decide what should be done then inform the junior members. Juniors who do have something to contribute forget their place if they try."

David nodded as the king continued, "This is why I'm so interested in your friends. I don't believe that you could control so many projects without help and I don't see how the accepted way would work."

"I kinda thought that you wanted all the toffs in control." Billy said.

"I do," the king replied, "It's God's order, but it's too rigid. If you fail with your electricity, then Lord Carlton will condemn you as an irresponsible idiot with childish fantasies. If you succeed, then you'll vindicate your methods and then we can tackle other problems. That is why I'm spending so much time here."

"The portal also has tasks for me." David said, "What happens if you both want something at the same time."

"The same thing that happens when you go gallivanting off now. Your subordinates understand what to do, they'll not wait for you to return to make a decision which again, is the usual way."

"Now I intend to send a vacuum to summon Lord Carlton, while you summon your friends on the other world. You know, messages in tube sucked through pipes seemed like a marvellous invention until I saw what else is possible and we need it. I'm happy for you to demonstrate your working methods tomorrow so be yourselves; just make sure that your equipment works though apart from sabotage, I don't think anything will go wrong. If all goes well, then I'll be seen tolerating your breaches of manners while you're demonstrating what your methods can achieve. However, if it does all go wrong tomorrow then I'll find it very difficult to refuse Lord Carlton's petition."

"I'll round up as many hands as possible." Godfrey said, "We'll patrol the grounds tonight. Everything else is ready."

"When your king is staying, it's not necessary." King Charles smiled, "There's a ring of agents around the area. David could invite them in if you're worried."

"We'll do it." Godfrey exclaimed, "We can't afford to take any

137

risks. I know what you're thinking David, but I'll explain to the people that there's too many strangers around. They'll be okay."

"That's for me to decide." David snapped angrily, "I'm not turning my home into a prison complete with warders."

"With respect, Your Grace, *Sir* Godfrey is right." Wilson said, "If you do decide to go out at three o'clock tomorrow morning, will it really be imposition if you're asked to identify yourself and state your business?"

"I still won't do it." David pouted.

"That's not like you, David." Jethro said, "Now state your objections calmly and quietly."

"All right, I suppose it is sensible. Godfrey, pick some hands that can accompany these agents. If a stable-boy's just sneaking back after an evening with a village girl, I don't want him detained because no-one knows who he is."

"That's better." Jethro said.

"Very well." King Charles said, "If we could move on. I want some demonstration of radio within three months and you may consider it a test of your operating methods as much as anything."

The rest of the table just stared at him and it was Billy who spoke.

"You want to see if it all breaks down if we're pushed," he said, "That's your experiment, isn't it?"

"Well done, Billy," the king grinned, "Any thoughts."

"Yeah, kidnap someone from the other world," he laughed, "No, David wouldn't do that but we'll need help."

"Easy Billy." Godfrey said, "You're pushing it."

"Sorry." Billy muttered, "Everyone just seems more nervous than usual."

"That's understandable." King Charles said, "I wish some of my court shared your enthusiasm."

Chapter 12

Despite King Charles' efforts to put everyone at ease it was still difficult to relax and it was no better the following day as guests arrived. As Jethro and David feared, Billy, Todd, Darren and Danny clustered around the king while he strolled through the gathering guests receiving more conventional curtseys and bows. It quickly became obvious to the boys that the rest of the guests were expecting to see a failure. Lord Carlton looked angrily at the *urchins* pestering the king, smugly confident that the king would be furious when the whole project collapsed into farce. For now, he had to concede that his sovereign did seem knowledgeable even without the impudent promptings of the boys.

All in good time. He was ready to take control and rescue his king from a humiliating fiasco. It was just after four and nearly dark when Wilson sent footmen round the guests asking them to assemble at the front of the house.

The king mounted the steps to stand in front of a small dais.

"Are we ready, Your Grace?" He asked.

Nervous, David replied, "We are, Your Majesty."

The king was also nervous. He was placing a lot of trust in a fourteen year old boy and he took a deep breath as he pushed the switch.

Every window in the house lit up while street lights erected along the drive provided a ribbon of light disappearing into the distance. For a few moments the guests were entranced but just as suddenly everything was dark again. Lord Carlton almost yelled in triumph as he hurried forward to rescue the king from his embarrassing predicament but the lights came back on again.

Other lights came on, illuminating the lawns and Billy came running up to the king, not bowing but anxious to deliver his message.

"Your Grace." His Majesty called out, "The message is AOK. If I remember my briefing, I believe it means that the generators are now running as expected and the demonstration can continue after we have dined. If I understand this young man correctly, the load was increased too quickly and the breakers tripped. I believe that it was an oversight and the breakers prevented any harm but if it had been gas or steam power, we would be facing a serious leak or explosion. I would have preferred a demonstration of the safety features at some other time but it was useful, nonetheless."

David breathed a sigh of relief while Lord Carlton seethed in impotent anger. The king's remarks had turned a mistake, which Lord Carlton could have exploited, into a minor hiccup and another chance had slipped by.

It was cold with a touch of frost in the air yet guests chose to wander around admiring the view. Wilson led a team of footmen carrying braziers. Each one roasting chestnuts, potatoes and winter food. One of the engineers set up a table to run David's original demonstration while Wilson took small groups around the house to show off the interior lights.

A select few dined with David's mother. The guests included all of David's young friends, the King, Jethro, a few friends of David's mother and the most senior engineers. As always when David's mother was uncertain about the guests, she had arranged a buffet. Lord Carlton was also included but stood stiffly waiting for the king to catch his eye. Instead, His Majesty seemed to prefer to talk to Godfrey and Isabella. Youngsters including David, rudely interrupted them and even David's mother approached him uninvited. As always, Billy chose to show off though this time even Wilson was pleased with him.

Somehow, the adults found themselves with servants keeping their plates and glasses filled while at the same time they managed to feed themselves. The servants were the rest of David's friends all anxious to help make the day a success.

"Whose idea was this?" Jethro asked.

"We talked about it." Billy replied, "You can't have a king, a duke and a lord getting their own food, can you? Besides, I bet it's something David can't do. Carry plates and glasses without dropping any."

"Don't challenge him tonight." Jethro laughed.

It was when the house guests got into the steam broughams that Lord Carlton realised how much he had been sidelined. He was relegated to a brake, driven by Isabella while David had joined a whole gang of *urchins* who had run off in unseemly haste towards the village.

In fact, it was the first time that David had seen the village lit up and it was the culmination of all his efforts. Even his mother conceded that he had the right to be an excited fourteen year old.

The less privileged guests were just as excited and cheerfully strolled down the lane after the vehicles. Most of the village was standing around looking wonderingly at the street lighting, then watched bemused as the high and the mighty descended upon them.

Finally, cold and tired, the guests began to disperse while David and a whole gang of boys continued to play football on the green, their game illuminated by the newfangled lights.

Lord Carlton had been invited to stay the night but he left the next day, as soon as he could. The king walked beside David, now definitely the duke as they entered the church and relished the cheers and applause as they left. He chose to stay for lunch before leaving and David knew that he had his king's full support.

Something that David never discovered was the conversation between King Charles and his wife Queen Anne when they were alone together.

"I was wrong and Sir Anthony was right." He said, "You would have enjoyed yourself."

"And did everyone remember their place?"

"Oddly yes," King Charles replied, "I watched His Grace the Duke of Barabourne get himself thoroughly muddied playing with servants and commoners from the village. The following day, I watched the same rabble standing respectfully and knuckling their foreheads if he deigned to speak to them."

"Do you really approve of him mixing with commoners like that. His family must have been appalled."

"I think I agree with his guardian," Charles replied, "He doesn't need to be the duke all the time, any more than he needs to wear the robes but it's all there when the occasion demands. However, he has access to incredible knowledge and I'm insisting that he begins a new project. It's called radio and may prove to be the key to breaking the stalemate with the French. I can afford to be indulgent if he succeeds."

"And if he doesn't?"

"The project is to be able to send a message to India so that it arrives in less than a second or to a ship in the middle of the ocean. He and I have an advantage. We know it's possible but the trick is convincing others. Without his common touch I don't think that it would be possible."

"It's still very indulgent of you, my dear," Queen Anne said.

"Maybe but he's at the centre of mysterious events. If it was anyone else, I'd consider him a threat to the throne so maybe it's as well that he doesn't behave like my other peers," the king replied.

It was about a week later that a very nervous midshipman

found himself being greeted by Wilson. He was fifteen, having begun his training at twelve, relying on a scholarship. Officers tended to have separate incomes so scholarship entrants tended to be treated like poor relations. He was shown into the library where Jethro and Tom were sitting.

"Make yourself comfortable." Jethro said, "Did you have a good journey?"

"Yes, thank you, Your Grace." he replied.

"I'm Lord Westerham when I'm on duty but just Jethro when I'm not. It's one of David's bad habits that I've caught."

"Er, yes sir. I'm sorry," the midshipman replied.

"David, that's His Grace, is preparing for a journey so he's a little pre-occupied. The others will look after you though... and speak of the devil..."

He broke off as Billy arrived and looked the newcomer over.

"So you're the Navy guy?" He said, "Got any work clothes or are you too hoity-toity for that?"

The midshipmen glanced at Jethro.

"This is Billy," he said, "According to His Majesty, the rudest servant in the country but well worth listening to. What have you been told about us?"

"Not much, sir." Midshipman Clark replied, "I'm to report to His Grace on His Majesty's orders. No-one said anything but the impression I got was that someone has a hare-brained scheme for long distance communications and His Majesty is obliged to go through the motions of examining it."

Billy took out a mobile phone and rang David.

"I'm just demonstrating a hare-brained scheme in communications. Would you speak to the navy boy, please."

Billy listened for a few moments then handed the phone to Midshipman Clark with an instruction to say 'Hello'.

"I'm glad you've arrived." David said, "Change into civilian clothes and tell Billy to bring you down to the portal. We'll have a late lunch at the Royal George."

The midshipman duly relayed the instructions to Billy. Looking puzzled as he heard David's disembodied voice and looking even more puzzled as he tried to understand the message.

"I'll show you to your room then fetch a brake. It looks like David's going to explain everything."

David had spent the week, spending as much time as possible at the portal. In many ways it felt as if he had been wasting his time but at least he seemed to be communicating more easily. One thing that he had learnt was that the portal was reluctant to give too much information so that David formed his own opinions and ways of handling things.

The midshipman was a case in point. David asked whether he should be shown everything or just enough to do his own job.

The portal replied, *You must judge him for yourself. It's natural for him to want to improve himself but does he want to improve himself at the expense of everyone else?*

In answer to a question about the next world, the portal responded, *"You are now their god. Factions argue over how to serve you. Leaders will lose face if you say that they a*re wrong."

David decided to treat the midshipman in the same way as he had treated the others; show him everything and leave him to prove it to others which was why he had arranged to meet him at the portal.

There was a layer ice under the recent snow fall making conditions treacherous and Midshipman Clark struggled to keep his footing but stopped to stare at the brake. It had a boiler far larger than such a vehicle normally needed, it had the large lamps which he had never seen before and instead of smooth solid rubber narrow wheels, it had wide wheels with a deep tread.

"Godfrey's patenting the tyres." Billy said proudly, "He's going to have his own business and everything."

Midshipman Clark was duly impressed with the confident way in which Billy drove in conditions that were too hazardous for conventional vehicles and even horses could slip. They found David sitting in a garden chair, in his shirtsleeves in a patch of green grass leaving the newcomer to wonder how he was keeping warm. He stood and put on a coat as the others arrived.

"You must be Midshipman Clark." he said, "I'm David."

"And?" Midshipman Clark snapped, "His Grace is expecting us so stop loafing around and take us to him."

He paused, thinking and David was content to let him figure things out.

"Are you His Grace?" He asked eventually, "His Lordship referred to him as David but you look more like a farmhand even if you're not acting like one. His Grace doesn't seem very formal but I was warned not to forget that I'm just a scholarship boy so I'm worried about keeping him waiting."

"I am the Duke of Barabourne but don't worry. You'll find that here, winning a scholarship means more than having a title. You've met Billy, officially he's the boot-boy but he lazes around so much that we've had to take on another." David grinned as Billy stuck out his tongue, "If you need anything, want to find your way around or want to know about any of our projects, ask him."

David paused, "We haven't even shaken hands but you are welcome. I'm hungry, how about you?"

"Yes sir." Midshipman James Clark replied, "I've been travelling since six."

"We'll have to walk from here." David said, "OK, boot-boy, damp the fire and follow us. We'll let you eat with your betters today."

"Stuff you, David." Billy riposted, "We're going to another world so I'm going to be your food taster. You can't eat until I say you can."

David turned to the bemused looking midshipman, "Like I said, titles don't count for much round here."

"It's not what we were told at Dartmouth, sir." Midshipman Clark said then putting on a pompous sounding voice recited, "Upset His Grace and you may as well resign your commissions."

"A gentle hint that you're a scholarship boy." David laughed, "Call me David, not sir. What's your first name?"

"It's James but Jimmy will do, sir," he paused, "Sorry, I'll try but it takes some getting used to."

"You wait 'til you get to the Royal George." Billy piped up, "You'll get used to anyfin then."

Billy was right. Like every other visitor, the sight of petrol driven cars, electric light, jukeboxes and the rest left the midshipman flabbergasted. The regulars who knew David greeted him cordially and with an easy familiarity and like many others, his view on the world changed. When they returned, they were just a group of boys, talking animatedly between chasing each other with snowballs.

They were still cheerful as they gathered in the library that evening though the conversation drifted on to David's impending trip.

"This trip sounds dangerous." Midshipman Clark said, "I'll come along if I can help. I know how to shoot."

"Godfrey's my chief bodyguard." David said, "Talk to him but thank you, Jimmy."

"Father was against me applying for Dartmouth. He said it would be different if we were at war, but in peace time the officer's mess is just a gentlemen's club that doesn't like outsiders. I suppose I'm thinking that if I don't go along with everything then you won't want me."

"David's got an uncle who wants to take over." Godfrey said, "If he did, I'd be lucky to keep my job here, so would Billy. What I'm saying is, your dad would be right about him but do you think that he's right about David?"

"No, I suppose not. I thought he was just a farm boy when I first saw him and I was quite rude. He wouldn't speak like that to anyone so I'm sorry."

"You were quite right to snap." David said, "If a farm boy had been idling instead of bringing you to me he'd be hoping that Godfrey didn't find out."

"Fair enough but it's all so different. I'm sorry I must sound so stupid."

"No you don't." Billy retorted, "All us common folk feel it a bit but it's Mr. Wilson who really stands up to David because he never stops being the butler. I'll have a lemonade, please Wilson."

"Certainly Master Billy." Wilson replied, "May I remind you, sir that I'll be inspecting those cupboards again, first thing in the morning. I'll borrow Godfrey's belt if you've left them in your usual mess."

The rest chuckled at the exchange then Jimmy said, "I wish my Father could meet you all. He'd never believe it if I just write."

"You've been allocated an engineer's cottage I believe." Jethro said, "By all means invite your family, we can find them another cottage for their stay. Billy your brief seems to extend to the new village, will you see to it? If it was just a short visit, then they could stay in the house. You're only in a cottage because we need rooms for guests, especially over Christmas."

"Mr. Grant and Mr. Thompson run things." Billy explained, "I'll have a word."

"Could I suggest something?" Midshipman Clark asked, "The army could be interested in Morse code and the telegraph thing. Could you speak to someone about it."

"Good point." Jethro said, "Let's get it working and set up a demonstration. Get Billy to show you what we've got and we'll take it from there."

Leaving the midshipman to settle in and learn about their activities, David turned his attention to the stone circle world. The Winter Solstice was approaching and David was trying to learn more of what was expected of him.

"They are gathering," the portal typed, "There is considerable animosity. You cannot delay your work any longer."

"Show me who's gathering." David commanded.

A holographic image appeared and David gasped at the scene showing a stone circle about 10 metres in diameter bounded by fifteen evenly spaced stones. David had seen pictures of other circles and he noticed just how regular and even these stones were. Each one was about two and a half metres high, square with each face half a metre wide but it was not that that made him gasp.

The ring was surrounded by a wicker fence and beyond that the ground was covered with thick snow. Inside the fence there was none, though there were signs that it had been cleared. What jolted David the most, was that the men and women working inside the ring were all naked. Two more arrived, wrapped up against the winter weather, disappeared into a hut just outside the fence. They emerged as naked as the rest then hurried through a gate in the fence towards the centre of the ring.

David stared at the naked figures, his curiosity, emotions and need to observe conflicting with the embarrassment of finding many of them attractive. Suddenly, David's attention was drawn to a girl, possibly a year or so older than himself. She exuded sexuality and obviously affected any man who looked at her. David just stared, unable to move. Had he not been so smitten, he might have noticed the high proportion of people with red hair and fair freckled skin but he continued to stare until the girl looked in his direction and smiled.

David jumped back, startled then breathed a sigh of relief as a boy appeared in the hologram and walked towards her, blocking the view. He recovered his wits, and studied the hologram further. He could see the portal in the centre of the ring and above it, an ornately carved, wooden table. A hole was drilled into the centre and dozens of thin narrow grooves radiated out. What appeared to be cuffs were fixed by chains on the long ends of the table.

"Is that table an altar or something?" David asked.

More accurately a sacrificial table The blood of the messengers will drip onto my terminal.

"Messengers?" David asked.

They are being sent to ask why the gods have forsaken them.

"Oh!" David exclaimed then a thought occurred to him, "They're going to sacrifice a human."

Two humans. The girl who so stimulated your body and her husband.

"Husband?" David exclaimed, "I thought that sacrifice victims had to be virgins."

In this society, they would be difficult to find, however, their love for each other is considered pure and they'll travel together.

"We've got to stop it." David exclaimed.

Yes. Be sure. If you save them both, you won't have the girl.

"I know. Bring them across now."

Those who do not see it will believe that they have run away. Two more will be selected but there will be war.

"I know that I should make my own decisions but I can't without understanding what's going on. Explain it all to me."

That world believes in many gods. There are groups that argue which is the most important. The group that sees you as the most powerful god dominates.

"Sees me?" David exclaimed, "They don't know me."

They knew my creators and you are their successor. They see my terminal as the pathway to you.

"Which it is." David said.

Yes but not as they understand. Other factions have different ideas. One believes that my terminal is another god stabbing Mother Earth. Those that believe that I'm a pathway are strongest because many grandparents remember creator's last visit.

"Let me guess." David said, "If the messengers don't succeed then the pathway believers will be weakened and some other group will try to take over."

Or the families of the messengers will be blamed and murdered because their children were not pure enough. Their clans will seek vengeance and blame the pathway believers and civil war will break out.

"The two messengers are my age aren't they? How come that they're so ready to die?"

The stories of the creators appearing and disappearing are plentiful and believed. Study them more carefully.

"They won't like it if anyone tells them that they're wrong." David murmured thoughtfully.

No they would be killed for spreading a false message.

"This sacrifice is meant to occur at the Solstice. If they're tied to the table and then the whole thing disappears, would that do anything?"

It would create a vacuum for self-seekers to fill.

"If I went across?"

Then you would be in danger.

147

"I gathered that." David laughed, "Would it do any good though."

Only you can decide.

"Very well. I'll say that they make better messengers unharmed. I've been sent to find out why they saw fit to disturb the gods."

The messengers are telling them.

"No. I'll say that the priests or whatever gave them a message to pass on but the gods needed more. Would that work?"

Question vague. Extrapolation attempted. You are an observer for the gods sent in response to their message. It will encourage more sacrifices.

"Do you have a better plan." David asked irritably.

Yes.

"You mustn't tell me though. You can't influence me."

Correct.

"Then we're stuck with mine. I'll deal with sacrifices when I understand things better. I don't suppose that the creators got things wrong or couldn't plan for everything."

Why do you suppose that they are no more?

"So only you are perfect."

How do you suppose I learned not to interfere?

"Oh!" David exclaimed.

Later when his friends including Danny and Darren were gathered, he described events carefully playing down his fascination with the girl.

"How come the place was so warm?" Darren asked.

"I don't know. The portal can give out a fair amount of heat but not on that scale. It had been cleared because there were puddles and one or two still had touches of snow around them."

"So the ground must have been cold." Danny offered.

"Yes, there were mats or something laid down." David exclaimed, "I hadn't thought about it before."

"Air curtains." Todd said, "Like the ones at the mall only bigger."

"Maybe." Danny said, "Stopping these sacrifices is more important."

"Agreed. I've got to do it without making anyone feel bad. I'm stopping a civil war as well."

"So we go across so that you can talk to them." Godfrey said.

"No, I go across. I stay near the portal and you watch. We'll have an emergency word to bring me back if anything happens."

Godfrey frowned but Danny interjected, "It makes sense to me. You'll see more in the hologram and we can all watch and be ready to yell."

Godfrey was still obviously unhappy but nodded in agreement.

"What really worries me is whether I should be naked when I go over? I don't really want to strip off like that."

"I don't blame you with a body like that." Danny giggled.

David blushed as Billy snapped, "Can it. He ain't so bad. You're the weedy one compared to him."

"All of you can it." Godfrey commanded, "OK, we all go in for a bit of mickey taking when we're swimming but this is work. We support each other."

The others nodded.

"Sorry." Danny whispered.

"It's done." Godfrey said, "I reckon he should wear shorts and a vest or T-shirt, kind of like a badge of rank."

"Find out if he'd offend any other god." Todd said, "Is it like the Roman world where they waited for a traveller or is it a temple to all of them."

"He's a messenger not a god so he wants to appear ordinary. He should go naked, rather than challenge anyone." Darren said, "When in Rome, do as the Romans do."

"Shut up, Darren." Danny said, "You're too young to understand. David can't go around naked."

"Why not?" Darren asked, "You go skinny-dipping don't you, it won't be me who's the kid if you make him feel bad."

"I'll think about it." David said, "After the portal suggested it, I watched the couple who are going to be sacrificed and they're scared which is not surprising. I don't think that they're volunteers but they treat the adults with the utmost respect. I think that they're more scared of being disrespectful than of dying."

"I've got an idea." Billy said, "I go through and I'm naked and I order them all to prepare for David who arrives in shorts and vest."

"No." David exclaimed, "You'll be in too much danger."

"Then so will you." Billy exclaimed, "Besides, I'll have you telling the portal to pull me out, not someone it may argue with. It'll give you a chance to sus things out before you arrive."

"It makes sense." Godfrey said, "Thinking about it, we should have taken this world more seriously from the outset but it's too late now. We'll just have to go very carefully."

There was not much that they could do until the stone circle

149

filled in readiness for the solstice and David began to understand the mystical side of the circle. Crowds gathered just outside the wicker fence, wrapped up against the cold and the snow, staring in awe at the *holy ones* wandering around naked. At least David assumed that they were priests or something but he couldn't be sure. Whatever they were, they were demonstrating a mastery or a contempt of the elements.

The sacrificial couple now obviously frightened, held hands and looked at each other, offering quick reassuring smiles. It was as if they kissed each other goodbye when they were escorted to the table. David watched as they lay down and were cuffed to the table. Even before the chief priest could approach, David gave the signal and the table together with the couple disappeared. David's friends quickly threw blankets over the pair while Godfrey got busy with a pair of bolt-cutters.

David glanced at Billy, who stripped and nodded. Even before he had time to feel the cold, Billy was standing in the circle facing the priests who stared, frozen in stunned amazement.

"You can put that knife away for a start." Billy said sharply, "The Messenger isn't going to come through while you're planning murder."

The priest with the knife recovered first.

"Who are you?" The priest asked, "You're no god."

"No, I'm not." Billy replied, "Neither are you so why do you think that you have a right to kill people."

"The Divine Pathway needs life," the priest replied, "We must supply it."

"It certainly doesn't need blood." Billy retorted, "You've got the wrong idea about it."

"So you say but who are you to say what's needed?"

"How about, I'm someone who can travel along the pathway and my master is waiting to arrive."

"Your master," the priest sneered, "If he's so powerful, why is he scared of my blade?"

"Scared? I said that my master is a messenger. I didn't say that he was powerful. He's taken the two kids you wanted to murder, though. They're alive and well and he wants them to stay that way as well. Why are you so scared that you need a knife."

"To bring you here and I succeeded," the priest exclaimed.

"No, you failed because you only got me." Billy said.

"The boy is right, Cradawg." another said, "Obviously the

150

pathway does not need our blood so put away the knife. He may also be wrong for I suspect that he is more than he says he is. Can you help us, boy?"

"I don't know what you want." Billy replied, "Neither does my master."

"You say that you have our messengers alive and well," the priest said, "They will tell him."

"They will tell him what you think you want to know." Billy said, "He's coming to discover what you really want."

"You believe that we don't know?" Cradawg yelled angrily.

"We don't know if you know."

Cradawg was obviously getting more angry while the watchers giggled at the conversation. Rather than putting the knife away, he was now holding it threateningly.

"Easy my friend. He arrived along the pathway so he deserves some respect. We can't expect the same reverence that we expect from our own youth," the other priest said, resting a hand on Cradawg's shoulder before turning to Billy, "Do you have a name, boy?"

"It's Billy. What's yours?"

"You may call me Bran," the priest said, "You call the messenger, your master. Are you a slave?"

"No, I'm many things but not a slave."

David and the others were listening and watching via the portal.

"He's going to mess it up." Todd exclaimed, "He's being too cheeky."

"Maybe! They are angry at the way he's talking, but it is diverting them from religious ceremonies and reverent sacrifices." David said, "It could help."

As if echoing his thoughts, Bran continued, "Those who tread the Divine Pathway are not like us and their ways are different. Tell me, Billy, how does your master expect you to behave?"

"My master expects me to be honest." Billy replied, "I don't mean to be rude but your friend wants me and my master to be scared of him so that we don't disagree with him. I hope he sees that it's not going to happen."

"A good answer." Bran laughed, "Very well, what do you know of us?"

"Nothing." Billy replied, "We're here to learn. The first question is, my master wishes to arrive dressed but does not wish to offend you."

"Why don't you know?" Bran asked, "If you travel on the

divine path, surely you should know what the gods' demand."

"For a start, what you call gods, we call creators." Billy explained, "The creators expect you to make your own way, they won't command you so they won't come. Since we're not gods or creators we have to learn about you before we can tell you what's needed and then you can ignore us if you want."

Bran laughed again.

"High Priest Cradawg believes the opposite or rather that we do have a choice, obey the gods or be annihilated. What do you say to that."

"Sometimes there are two paths to the village." Billy replied, "Take a third one and you could fall over a cliff."

"I'm not sure if I understand." Bran said, "This is a temple dedicated to the elemental gods, Wind, Fire, Earth and Air. They keep us warm in the winter and we show our respect by not thinking that we need more than they offer. If he is not a god himself, then your master should show respect but he may be taking one of your different paths hoping that it's not leading to the cliff edge."

Billy grinned and looked pointedly at Cradawg.

"If Bran says he may come then so be it," he said, "I look forward to meeting this giant who the gods listen to."

Even Billy was startled as the ground shook and the air around the portal terminal shimmered until it became opaque. As the shaking eased and the air cleared, then figures became visible. They were unrecognisable at first then Billy could make out David, dressed in his shorts and vest, Godfrey and Danny who were naked, and finally the two sacrifices who were wrapped in blankets which they quickly dropped.

Once again Bran laughed, "I assume that the clothed one is the all-seeing and all-powerful giant. Welcome, I am Bran, Chief Priest of this temple and this is Cradawg, a friend and believer in the Truth of the Divine Path."

David bowed formally to Cradawg.

"You defend the Path against others who believe that it has no place here," he said.

"I do and now I am vindicated." Cradawg replied, "Offering our own messengers brought you here."

"True but only to stop you."

"No! Our message has been delivered."

"Billy's right. We'll not listen to a message drenched in blood. We're children so we'll learn from teachers not from killers."

"I say that you are imposters who have intruded onto the path." Cradawg exclaimed angrily.

"Enough." Bran snapped, "The gods' breath is already tiring so it's time to go. May I offer our visitors the hospitality of my home?"

"Thank you." David responded.

"You have other duties." Godfrey interrupted, "You need to return."

David turned, annoyed with Godfrey's interruption but catching his frown and quick shake of the head. Obviously Bran caught it too for he said, "Your friend is cautious, there's no sin in that. Sadly the gods appear to be moving away from here for their breath is becoming weaker. It may be gone completely before long and then we fear that the divine path will disappear for ever. It may be the last time that we meet here."

"And you wanted us to be trapped here?" David asked.

"No! Oh I see, I explained things badly. The breath will last awhile yet but not until the next great festival and I was offering you time to understand us."

"Your two messengers will confirm that the other end of the path has no protection but it still functions. I'll return on the night of the next full moon. That's about three weeks. We might be all dressed, just in case."

"If that is your way." Bran said gravely.

Once they were back on the other side of the portal, David looked questioningly at Godfrey.

"I didn't trust Bran," he said, "There was something about him. I'm not sure but he wanted the sacrifice to go ahead and when it failed, blame Cradawg."

"But he seemed so friendly with Cradawg." Todd exclaimed.

"He'd get others to start rumours, pretend to help Cradawg and they'd still be friends when he failed." Godfrey explained.

"How did you work that out?"

"I didn't." Godfrey replied, "It was a plot in one of Isabella's stories but I was watching Bran and it came to mind but I'm not sure why."

"Okay." David said, "I think that Todd's world calls it body language. I agree that he didn't behave like a priest who was having all his beliefs turned upside-down though I suppose that he could just have been shocked to see us arrive and tried to deal with it."

"An unbeliever," said Billy, and grinned. "He's just pretending, right?"

Godfrey smiled at Billy and nodded.

"Yeah, Cradawg was angry that we're just kids instead of all knowing gods. That bit where we were talking about what he wanted and what he knew got silly and that made him angrier because it was irreverent. Bran didn't care. I think that the difference is that he'll stab you in the chest and Bran would stab you in the back."

"Portal, why did Bran say that the god's breath is failing?"

Todd should be able to work it out.

"Air curtains?" Todd asked.

Yes.

"Just air curtains?"

No, but the force fields are fully functioning.

"Things like Hoovers have filters which get clogged. I suppose something like that is too simple for something like that."

You suppose wrong.

"Todd?" David asked.

"Air has to be drawn into a fan or something. There has to be a filter to stop debris damaging the blades. Over time stuff clogs it up."

"What was that about force fields." Danny said, "I bet you'd have to be a rocket scientist to clean them."

You lose bet.

"Right." David said, "The portal seems to think that we can repair the heating system so we should. Maybe though, we should do it at night when there's no-one else around. The trouble is, I don't want them to think that they'll gain by killing that couple."

The others nodded thoughtfully so David continued, "Assuming the portal tells us what to do, we'll go tonight."

As answer, a roll of papers appeared. When Danny and Todd looked at them, they proved to be schematics which they could study.

"It's even got an on/off switch in the stone nearest the gate." Danny exclaimed, "It's a real 21st century stone age ring."

"It can't be 21st century and stone age." Todd said, "It's a modern stone ring though, all digital."

Midshipmen James Clark was with them.

"Is this going to be some sort of landing party?" He asked.

David nodded, "No cutlasses though, we'll just take screwdrivers and spanners. I'll take Danny and Todd to do the work as well as Billy and Godfrey to act as lookouts. Would you like to be the third?"

While James grinned, Darren pouted looking sulky.

"Why can't I come?" Darren whined.

154

"Because I want someone monitoring the portal." David replied, "I know it's boring but someone's got to do it. I'll try to rotate trips but not today."

Darren nodded, only partly mollified. They waited until dark then opened the portal. The party hurried through only to stop and stare.

Chapter 13

The two messengers were there, tied with hands above their heads to a crossbar supported by two posts. They were facing each other, their feet were tied together and there were ropes holding them tightly together. As he recovered his senses, he looked again and was sure that they had been tied to make any movement sexually arousing and they were shivering.

"Danny, get this place warm. Jimmy, cut them down and free them." David commanded, "Godfrey, Billy, scout around. Todd, can you do anything while they're switched on?"

Todd nodded, hurried to a stone and placed his palm on a slight indented disc not far from the ground and counted to ten. David was sure that Todd only found it because he was looking for it, the indentation was so slight but Todd continued to press the disc on other stones in some peculiar order. Finally, they all watched amazed as hatches in the stones clicked open and rods slid out. Using the rods as a ladder, Todd climbed to the top of the first stone, opened a grill and reached inside and pulled up with both hands. Twigs, rotten leaves and other debris poured over the sides of the stone. He leant in again and this time pulled out a round mesh, using his fingers to brush it clean.

"OK David," he called out, "Do you want to start on another one. It's safe but don't go poking around below the filter position."

"OK! Is it really that easy?"

Todd shrugged, "Back home, someone would be telling me to leave it to the adults. They'd be worrying that we might fall off the ladder or get our hands chopped off in the fan blades but this part of it really is easy. I've done Dad's vacuum cleaner and it's the same principal only bigger."

David complied as Todd put everything back then clambered back down to the ground. As they worked, around the stones a slight background hum faded and the ring steadily warmed up.

The two messengers were still shivering but they refused any sort of covering. Finally, Danny called David over.

"They're trusting the gods to warm them," he said, "Actually they could be right. I seem to remember that they should warm up slowly and they were only brought here at sunset. I don't think that they got too cold."

"Fair enough." David replied, "Any idea what's going on. I thought Cradawg agreed not to sacrifice them."

"It's not Cradawg, it's Bran." Danny explained, "He wants everyone to think that they were taken by the Wind God and not by the Divine Path. He sneaked them up here so when they were found it would just seem as if the god's had taken them."

"Bran is the priest to the Wind God so he ends up looking good while Cradawg is left looking stupid." David said, "I think that Bran would claim that while kindly old Wind God needed to hear the message first hand, he was not punishing Cradawg for getting the wrong idea."

"Could be." Danny said, "What do we do now?"

"Work out how to look after those two." David replied, "Do they need some time or can I talk to them?"

"They're OK, but they're a bit scared of you." Danny replied, "You lead us and we insult the gods and defy the priests."

"Very well, you speak to them. Ask them whether I can find Cradawg and invite him here."

Danny returned to the couple then hurried back looking a little surprised.

"Iain said that he'd take me." Danny said.

"No, I'll go." David said.

"No way." Danny said firmly, "You're in charge and have to run things."

"I hate being in charge." David said, "You're right about me staying but I should ask Billy. He wants to be the servant and Cradawg will recognise him."

"There's a problem." Danny said, "Iain reckons that Bran took their clothes. It wouldn't seem so magical if it looks as if they walked here."

"Very well. Fetch Godfrey and Billy and will you and Todd report to Jimmy. He should know about placing lookouts."

"Sorry, Godfrey but I need you to donate your clothes to Iain. All the rest of ours would be too small. Billy, would you be willing to go with Iain, and find Cradawg? It could be risky if Bran catches you."

Billy's face split into a broad grin, "My own adventure. 'Course I'll do it."

"Travelling to other worlds isn't an adventure?" Danny asked.

"Yeah but this is like being a spy with just a guide. I won't be able to just yell to the portal for help, will I?"

"No, and it's not a game either." David said, "You be careful or I won't send you."

"I lived in a sewer for a while. That was before I got in the orphanage. I never got caught thievin'."

"I'm a Justice of the Peace so that's a bit too much information." David laughed, "I get the point. You know how to be careful. Danny, send a message through the portal. Ask Darren to fetch some more clothes for Godfrey. This'll please him; tell him to use the brake to save time."

Godfrey seemed unconcerned at stripping off, though Billy thought that he looked quite handsome, in boxer shorts and t-shirt. His outer clothing looked a little big on Iain who was more worried about dressing inside the circle.

"Don't worry." David said, "You fear the cold, that's respect enough."

Iain nodded but hovered near the edge of the circle anxious to leave. The first part of the journey was ordinary and it was only as they approached the village that they became cautious.

"Bran's men could be out." Iain whispered.

Billy nodded but he was also puzzled for the village was lit by electric light. They were lucky though. The few people who were about, hurried past ignoring them though Billy followed Iain's lead by stepping aside for any adult.

They headed for the centre of the village and arrived at a green. Where the other houses had been comfortable looking cottages, the ones surrounding the green were far grander. It seemed to Billy that they took the long way round to a house and when Billy queried it, Iain replied, "I didn't want to walk past Elder Bran's house."

Billy expected them to find the back or servants entrance but Iain confidently rang the bell on the front door. Again, it appeared to be electrical which seemed to conflict with naked folk, cavorting in a stone ring.

A servant opened the door, Iain announced themselves as Messenger Iain, and Divine Traveller Billy. They were immediately taken through to Cradawg. Billy quickly explained what was going on.

"Bran never learns." Cradawg chuckled, "He'll never understand that he can't fool the gods."

"He'd have finished you if we hadn't come to fix the air curtain." Billy retorted.

"If the gods wanted it, then yes. Instead, they sent engineers who stopped him and restored their breath."

"I don't get it. You know the gods don't keep the circle warm for you."

"Are we going to have another what we know, what we don't know argument? The gods do keep the circle warm for us. They persuaded those of the divine path to build it for us, and now they've sent you to repair it."

"I don't get it." Billy said.

"But that's not the purpose of the visit, is it?" Cradawg said, "You came to warn me, and to ask me protect our two young messengers."

Billy nodded.

"And I will. I believed that shedding their blood would be a strong message to the gods and I was right. They brought you here. I accept that we had to show that we were serious, but I cannot imagine you wanting children killed in your name. If we try again, we'll expect you to intervene and so we won't be sincere. Do you understand."

"I think so." Billy replied, "At least, I've got a rough idea. You still seemed keen to kill someone when we first arrived."

"It's been centuries since the last human sacrifice. In many ways, it seemed wrong to me, but the Council of Elders were becoming desperate. I was about to perform one of the most solemn of ceremonies when this cheeky imp or demon called Billy arrived. I agree that you were a messenger, but you could have come from hell to distract us."

Billy grinned, "And you don't like kids being cheeky, do you?"

"The solstice is for serious contemplation. Don't you have times like that?"

"We call them Sundays."

"Very well, you're human not a demon and you're not celebrating the day of the sun. Go back to the circle and wait for me. I'll gather up some men and come out at dawn. God's breath won't sustain us all until dawn."

"I think that we've repaired it. It was even warm at the edges when I left." Billy said.

"To have done it so quickly. Now that is magical. Very well. For once, obey an elder, and I'll gather up some men." He looked at Iain, "Maybe you and Megan should be known as elders. It seems that the gods look upon you very kindly."

Cradawg's attitude still confused Billy. He was reaching for a telephone as the boys left, yet reminded his helpers that the gods would give them all the warmth that they needed once they were back inside the circle.

"How come they don't expect the gods to provide food and water at the circle?" Billy asked as they walked along.

"They do." Iain replied.

Billy did not say anything else. This world was far more complex than anyone realised. He had instinctively liked Cradawg in spite of the knife and wanted to know more.

David was relieved to see them back but was a little worried when Billy asked to speak to him alone.

"This place is really weird." Billy said, "If Cradawg agrees can I stay with him, please? I'll sus the place and tell you all about it."

"You'll miss Christmas at Barabourne." David said, "I'd like you there."

"Nah." Billy exclaimed, "Your mum will be glad if there's one less of us. You'll be greeting all those bigwigs like you usually do, you'll be better off without me."

"Talk to Cradawg, and if he agrees, visit in the New Year. Ever since His Majesty accepted you, even Mother sees you as part of the household. Look! I said before, I will not be ashamed of you, and Christmas is when my household should be together. It is important."

Billy might have argued more but Cradawg and a small group of men arrived, glancing around, puzzled.

"Only the Elders should know how to seek the god's breath, it has its old strength back and it no longer wheezes." Cradawg looked at David and grinned, "That means the motors aren't running at full power just to maintain a reasonable temperature, doesn't it."

David nodded, a little surprised, as the newcomers hurried to the hut to strip off before returning.

"We do not understand how those air screens are produced but they're still a gift of the gods as are you," he said. He saw David frown so continued, "No, I don't mean that we should keep you. I mean your help is a gift."

"My friends are a little shy about stripping unless we're swimming but it's nice to get our winter gear off."

"So your gods are not all seeing."

"Yes, we only worship one God and he knows everything."

"Then it's pointless being shy, He probably knows what your body is going to do before you do."

"I suppose so."

Cradawg glanced at Godfrey who was still only in his

underwear, "He seems to have made a fair compromise. Modesty for your god and acceptance of the gifts from ours."

"Yeah, I think he'd be freezing anywhere else. We have to go home for a couple of weeks but Billy would like to come and stay with you then. He'd like to learn about your world."

"Let me speak to Iain and Megan." Cradawg asked and walked over to them. He returned a few moments later.

"They've come here to die twice now. It's not good for them but I've suggested that they live here, for a time. I'll tell Bran and the others that you favour them and that harming them would make you angry. You know how to repair the equipment which puts you in the god's favour and makes you powerful. Understand, our ways are different and they were not restrained. They were ready to die for us. Now you're contradicting what they were taught so they don't fully trust you. Don't expect too much from them"

David looked puzzled.

"Bran would have killed them and this time it would have been murder, but you arrived in time to save them again. If they stay near the divine path, then you'll keep an eye on them. What will happen when you lose patience with those who would harm them?"

"Is my protection enough?" David asked.

"Billy will always be welcome in my home." Cradawg replied, "If he could come and go as he pleases, then your protection would be more visible but he could also carry out his duties to you."

Billy grinned happily as they explained Cradawg's suggestion, then hurried off to tell the others.

"He's also blessed by the gods." Cradawg said, "They gave him to you and now he wants to prove himself worthy. I know, you say that Billy is his own man and you don't own him but look into his heart. You will see."

They were all tired and Cradawg promised to look after Iain and Megan so it was time to go home.

Chapter 14

Christmas was a busy time for Barabourne, though David was lucky in one respect, it was everyone else who was expected to visit and pay their respects to the duke rather than he make the visits.

He was not surprised when his mother said that she wished to see him but was surprised when he was told that he need not change.

"Isabella is to wed in the new year," the dowager duchess said once he was settled.

"I didn't know that she had met anyone. Who's the lucky boy?"

"Godfrey. Will you see to it that he proposes before Christmas, please?"

David would have said that, after the last year, nothing could surprise him but he just stared at his mother. "You want me to have him to propose to her. Has he not done so already?"

"He is a sweet boy and he does have prospects," his mother said, "Isabella's publisher expects her to publicise her new book far more than her first one which means her father will find out. He is quite likely to take her home and stop her career. Sybil is adamant that it won't happen. Isabella's living in your house, and you're the head of the family so if you give your consent he'll be the one defying you if he objects."

"It's these stupid laws where women are treated like property. Ownership of her passes from father to husband." David exclaimed.

"Exactly. I was lucky with my husband, Sybil was not and Godfrey has experienced the same strange influences that you have. He'll treat her as an equal and will encourage her."

"Look I sympathise with Isabella but I'm not going to force Godfrey."

"Of course you're not. Isabella says that he wishes that they could marry but believes that not even you would break the social barriers that much. Of course, when the barriers are down, and marriage becomes a real possibility then it may not seem so attractive."

"Very well, but there's something that I'd like to do first but I want Billy, Godfrey, Uncle Jethro and Wilson to be here."

It took a little while before they were all assembled and settled and David could begin.

"All the patents we've taken out are in the name of a company and all my friends are shareholders as is Barabourne itself. You all know that but I think that it's time that I let Billy and Godfrey go as direct employees. I think that they should come and go in this house as my guests and they can have an allowance offset against dividends from the company. It's borrowing against future income but I think that it's fairly safe."

David paused before turning to Billy, "You won't need my permission to visit Cradawg."

David turned to Wilson, "They'll need rooms appropriate to guests. Do you have any problems?"

"No, Your Grace." Wilson replied, "If anything clarifying their status will be easier for everyone. However, might I suggest that they be given a cottage in the new village. I'll arrange staff to look after them but rooms would be available for true guests and not residents."

David paused uncertainly, for once looking nervous, "I'd like a private word with Godfrey, please."

They went to the stables and mounted up. Instead of his usual canter, David chose a slow walk.

"This is going to sound so weird coming from someone my age but what are your intentions towards Isabella?"

"I understand, you have to warn me off." Godfrey responded, "I'm surprised that I've been allowed to see her for so long."

"Just answer my question." David said, "Please, I'm not sure how to handle this."

"Very well, I'd marry her if I could." Godfrey said, "I know her father would never allow it but I love her. What's this all about, she's not expecting, is she?"

David laughed, "In a way she is, but don't worry, there's no father but there'll be just as big a scandal when it's due."

David saw the look of horror on Godfrey's face, "Sorry, I'm teasing you. According to my mother, you're a sweet boy who will offer Isabella a very equal marriage. If I was to give my consent, then it would be on the understanding that you encouraged her writing."

"Can you give your consent?" Godfrey asked, "Would you?"

"Do you want me to?" David asked, "I can withhold it and everyone would understand. No-one else need know that you asked me to."

"I don't need a let out. It's what I want. May I go and find her?"

"Don't you need an engagement ring?" David asked. It was meant as a joke but Godfrey crumpled as if he was about to burst into tears.

"I can't even afford that for her," he sobbed, "How can I look after her?"

"So the marriage is going to be more equal than you expected. It seems to be the first problem that you're going to share. Don't worry, she's not going to let such a sweet boy go for that."

Godfrey's rude gesture in reply should have got him the sack but David just laughed as Godfrey galloped off. David returned home at a more sedate pace. It was later in the morning that his mother made her first visit to his offices, looking curiously about her.

"I've never seen a couple looking so happy," she said, "I'm so glad that you're allowing it."

"Her father isn't going to like it but I bet I have to deal with Lord Carlton. What happens next.?"

"I should like to offer my mother's engagement ring as an engagement present. It would have gone to your eldest sister but you never had one so do you object?"

"Just how much have you talked with them?" David asked, "You seem to know a lot about them."

"I would have liked a daughter, and I could only have hoped that she would have been like Isabella. Now what are we going to do about a dowry?"

"I don't know." David exclaimed helplessly, "What about a dowry? Wilson, you advise me on household affairs, what do you say?"

Wilson had followed David's mother into the offices in case they needed anything. The dowager duchess frowned angrily at a mere servant becoming involved, but kept quiet in case she had an ally.

"My experience of weddings is that you should close your mouth, open your wallet and be a good little duke by being seen and not heard."

"Really Wilson. That is no way to talk to your Master," the dowager duchess exclaimed as angrily as was ladylike, but then she relaxed as David laughed out loud. After all, she could not have asked for better advice.

"I think a house in the village would be acceptable, don't you?"

"As a dowry?" David asked, "Why?"

"The dowry should reflect the worth of the bride which, considering her status and her prospects as an authoress is substantial. Rather than Godfrey being humiliated as the poor relation receiving largess, it would be Isabella who would be insulted if we do not recognise her value."

"You make it sound like a cattle market." David pouted.

"Dowries are much less common nowadays but make no mistake. There are families across the country planning on how to make their daughters irresistible to you," his mother said, "Considering the bonds you form with your friends, I would be surprised if some were not grooming their sons as well."

"Mother." David exclaimed, "I don't do that sort of thing. They're just good friends."

"And loyal servants who do more than any servant can be expected to do," his mother added, "I do understand and I also understand that it may be different in the other places you visit. However, Godfrey and Isabella are here and we should use our ways to make them happy."

Later, Jethro spoke to him.

"You aren't going to allow this marriage, are you?" Jethro asked, "It'll split the family and I'm not sure that Isabella should be making decisions like this."

"Isabella has a good mind." David said, "Her judgement is just as good as ours. Are we going to make things that much worse between us and her father?"

"No, I suppose not." Jethro conceded, "It's just that allowing her to marry a stable boy will be seen as the worst of all insults."

"He is also a knight, charged with protecting me by His Majesty. What surprises me is that Mother approves."

"I don't doubt that she observed His Majesty very closely while he was here. If he approves of your activities, then she will. Understand, your mother is a very determined woman who wants you to succeed. Social order preserves stability and stability makes your position more secure. She can also see that your activities, rather than unsettling things, will make Barabourne even more secure. Add to that the romanticism of helping star-crossed lovers, Isabella's mother's wish for her to be happy, and I suspect that England would fall before we could stop her."

"And as Wilson suggested, I should close my mouth, open my wallet and be seen but not heard."

"Did Wilson dare say that in front of her?" Jethro asked, "I've given you the problems as I see them, I agree with your answers so the decision is yours. You are very much the duke, far more than even your father would have been at your age. What are your plans now?"

"To do what my mother tells me." David grinned, "Godfrey

wants to spend time with Isabella, Billy wants to spend his time with Cradawg while my three other-world chums can't tear themselves away from the brakes. I'd rather have one of their cars to play with."

"And Todd is also busy in... what does he call it, R & D... ah, yes, research and development. Is there no mischief that you can get up to?"

"I'd like to go to Cradawg's world as well but Billy wants to show us what he can do. He says he's preparing a report which he'll give me after Christmas."

"Aren't there any other village boys, you could play with?"

"No. I'm all right." David said, "I want to be quiet and not have anything to sort out. I might take Jasper out later. I wonder if Jimmy Clark can ride."

"Are you sure that you're all right?" Jethro asked, "It's been quite a year for you. You're not suffering some sort of reaction, are you?"

"Probably." David said, "I sometimes feel as if it's all happened to someone else and I feel a bit tired but I shouldn't complain, should I? I'm not penniless, struggling to survive, am I? I think that I'll lay down for a bit and I'll be all right."

Jethro was concerned though so he strolled round to the stables where he found a massive snowball fight in progress. David's friends were part of it and it seemed as if they had involved the younger stable hands.

Zack the stable foreman hurried over.

"I'm sorry about this, My Lord," he said, "I should have stopped it."

Jethro might have said something but Danny, Darren and Todd hurried over.

"Is David OK?" Danny asked, "He's not getting fed up with us, is he. We could go if he liked."

"No. He's just a bit down at the moment. I not sure how I'd have coped with everything he's been through." Jethro replied.

Danny nodded, "Sorry about the snowball fight. I know we shouldn't disturb the staff."

"Yes, I should be annoyed with you but I've got an idea. Move your games nearer the house somewhere near his bedroom window. Find those braziers we used before and cook yourself some food. Let's see if some harmless fun will cheer him up. Midshipman Clark, use your officer skills to arrange it. Danny, would you come with me please? Better still, would you run on ahead and find Wilson?"

Soon after, they were all settled in the dowager duchess's drawing room.

"Wilson, who do you consult about the Christmas ball?"

"Why, His Grace and Her Grace, My Lord."

"Celia, who did you consult about Isabella's marriage?"

"David, of course."

"And I consult him about managing our businesses while His Majesty and the portal set him tasks and it is all quite proper because he is the duke. Last year you consulted me as guardian and trips to other worlds was the stuff of fantasies. David would have been away at school where his only worry would have been avoiding the teacher's cane."

The others nodded, waiting as Jethro continued, "We were unhappy at the way he mixed with the estate boys during the summer but he chose his closest confidantes well and he could play as boys need to. As winter has set in so he's been confined to the house more and with less contact everyone seems to settling back in the old ways."

Jethro paused, making sure that he still had everyone's attention, "Now I should be delighted that things are returning to the proper order but I'm concerned that David is losing the release valve that he needs."

"You are quite right," the dowager duchess said, to Jethro's surprise, "I hadn't realised just how many responsibilities he has assumed until you just mentioned them but he's coping, isn't he?"

"Yes but they may be tiring him."

"I think that I may be ahead of you." David's mother said, "I've invited friends for a Christmas Eve soiree and suggested that David would enjoy the company of people his age."

"So they stand around in their best clothes listening to adults discussing the state of the world." Danny retorted.

"Yes, I see. It's not helpful, is it?"

"If I may suggest, Your Grace." Wilson began, then as the dowager duchess nodded, continued, "The young visitors may wish to appear suave and adult, especially if there are members of the opposite sex present. However, they're as fascinated by the latest mechanical devices as any commoner. Maybe David, could be persuaded to show them around."

"And if the estate hands happened to arrange their own party out by the stables." Danny added, "Dad's collecting me that afternoon, I wonder if he could fetch some fireworks."

"And some of those disposable coveralls." Wilson said, "The young visitors may wish to protect their best clothes and they will cover everyone's status."

"See to it that an adult takes charge of the fireworks." David's mother said, "I don't want excited youngsters blowing themselves up. And see to it that there's plenty of cider. I also suggest that the older staff forget the usual warnings about them being on their best behaviour. You seem surprised, Jethro."

"I am. Danny, you won't be here but will you help?"

"When are you going to tell David?"

"I think, when the preparations are well under way and all he has to worry about is his part in the evening. The Christmas Ball will be an ordeal for him but that is his duty though I think that we might consider ways of brightening the Servants Ball on New Years Eve."

"I really am surprised." Jethro exclaimed, "It just does not sound like you."

"My son may be making himself ill through overwork. I understand how important it all is so we've got to keep him well. Unfortunately I can see no other way of giving him the respite that he needs."

"You're scary." Danny exclaimed then blushed, "Sorry."

"I shall take it as a compliment. When it comes to my son's welfare, then I hope that I am, as you say, scary."

The meeting broke up and Danny hurried round to where the noise was, to find an impromptu football-match in full swing with David in the thick of it. During a break, David strolled over to him.

"Planning something with my mother and uncle are we?"

"Not really." Danny replied.

"Tell me and don't tell me that it's a secret." David snapped irritably.

"Your mother wants to organise the sort of do that we put on for the king." Danny replied, "We were thinking of a bonfire and fireworks in one of the fields and all the guests our age being taken there on a wagon all lit up with electric light."

"Very well but it's going to be too cold to be out there too long." David said.

"You wouldn't approve of the estate boys having their own party in the stable, would you? What would happen if you and your friends stumbled in on it?"

"I can't see Mother approving of that but it might be fun. Let's see what we can do."

David hurried back to the football while Danny sought out Jethro to tell him what was said.

"All I could think was, don't let him think that we're ganging up on him." Danny concluded.

"Good for you. The servants can set up the field. You deal with the stable."

Barabourne was at the centre of travel to alternate worlds. It was also beginning a revolution that would change their own world but both projects were too big. Giving David a good Christmas was something everyone could understand.

A few moaned of course, but they were ignored. Most saw that the brighter boys on the estate could study with David and had better prospects. Again through the youngsters, older folk could approach the *big house* with their problems. Much of the estate consisted of farms which were rented out. Two tenant farmers were gone. They claimed for a bad harvest while even a town boy like Danny could see how badly the farms had been neglected. Another tenant had lost everything in a fire. David led in helping them to rebuild from the ruins and the family was about to enjoy their own good Christmas.

Normal country life had continued, the estate was flourishing and for most it was more than a job, it was where they lived, and their social lives centred around their neighbours. Although very much a feudal lord, David was popular and most liked the idea that they could do something for him.

David had been depressed and at first, the noise below his window had irritated him. Seeing the potatoes being cooked, chestnuts being roasted he suddenly felt hungry. He might have sent for something from the kitchen but the boys' excitement was infectious so he wandered down, *but only to grab some food,* he told himself. The ball headed in his direction and it seemed only natural to kick it. Suddenly he was in the middle of the game, taking in lungfuls of fresh air and burning off youthful energy. Even his mother saw a difference in him that night.

"I should have found those medical committees that I mentioned. It would save me sitting here being told how wild David is becoming. He isn't though, is he?" She asked Jethro when they were alone.

"He should be away at school, growing up with his peers." Jethro replied, "At least that's still my first instinct but it's not practicable considering everything that's going on. Again, considering what's happened to him, he's relaxed rather than wild."

David's mother nodded, "Those boys do seem to help him. I thought that Christmas Eve would let him find more suitable friends but I fear that instead, it's going to scandalise the county set."

"His friends are against fox-hunting and he agrees with them more but although he's not riding on Boxing Day, he's willing to greet the hunt."

"His friends from the other world." David's mother exclaimed, "They have such strange ideas. And you don't need to remind me; I know that David will do his duty. He'd be the perfect host on Christmas Eve if I insisted but it won't do him any good. You think that I'm too rigid as well, don't you."

"David himself says that he needs you and Wilson to maintain the status quo. I might sneak away for some cider and roast chestnuts in the stable, but I'll put a damper on things if I stay too long."

"Then we won't stay too long." David's mother said, leaving Jethro to stare, puzzled but all he was aware of was David's mother having a long conversation with Godfrey, the next day.

The plans were not quite as Danny had expected for he had forgotten the problems with travelling on that world. He had also forgotten that David would be expected to attend the midnight mass at church. Some guests would have been travelling for a couple of hours in a horse drawn coach. Horses were considered safer, more sure footed on an icy road, more likely to find their way home at night. The soiree was planned for the early evening so that they could at least arrive in daylight.

They were also lucky that the weather had turned milder so briefly the guests assembled in the drawing room and everything was as it should be except for a strange device on a table beside the window. As it got dark so it started clicking and Todd wrote down a message while everyone watched.

"It's a message from the field, Your Grace. They're ready but wish to know how many to cater for."

"Very well." David replied, "We've arranged a few fireworks in lower field. If any of the younger guests would care to join me, then they'd be welcome. I'm afraid transport is a little basic so perhaps older guests would care to watch from the balcony. It's quite muddy after the snow so we'll supply a coverall to protect your clothes."

Guests could hardly refuse to allow their off-spring to accept an invitation by His Grace and were all intrigued by the telegraph, marvelling as messages clicked to and fro.

The youngsters donned the disposable coveralls, puzzling over the material, then stared at the brake which was hauling the wagon. It was one of Godfrey's designs, larger than most brakes with wide wheels, and headlamps. It had a third, adjustable lamp that the driver switched on to show the steps onto the wagon. Landowners among the dowager duchess' guests could see the sense in lighter more manoeuvrable tractors and began asking Jethro about them.

"Potholes are a problem but the lanes on the estate are fairly well maintained." Jethro explained to a curious guest, "Their real strength is on soft ground. They can go where horses would struggle to pull a cart. Of course, on a good road they can outrun a horse, especially at night."

"They're the work of the stable's charge hand." David's mother interrupted, "He continued after receiving his knighthood, but now that he's becoming a member of the family... Oh dear. Please excuse me, I shouldn't have said anything. I think it's the cold, shall we go back inside."

Jethro laughed to himself, David's mother would never have made such a mistake. He was sure that it had been quite deliberate but she had got everyone's attention.

"Barabourne's not been the same since David's disappearance. He had the strangest of experiences, I really can't describe them, they're so strange but he has all these wonderful ideas about electricity. Then His Majesty became interested so David needed to find help and he sought out the brighter boys on the estate but dear me. You can't imagine what it's been like with so many forgetting their place."

Jethro was impressed. It was not how he remembered events but still he listened as she continued.

"What with stable lads being knighted and allowed to do whatever they like, I expected Barabourne to descend into chaos. It hasn't though, but Jethro and I have an impossible task bringing up David to remember his station. He really does seem to care more about brains than about position so would you believe it, we have a boot boy who can advise the king. It was going too far to give him shares in all those companies, though.

Jethro wanted to applaud, especially as guests appeared to be checking the servants, looking for a boot boy who might be standing in as a waiter.

"Yes my dear." One of the guests exclaimed, "What about the stable boy joining the family. Has there been an unfortunate incident?"

"Oh dear." David's mother sighed, "I think that we should

reveal at least part of the scandal. Isabella, is also falling into bad ways by becoming an authoress, may I present her as John Sanders author of *A Lady Is Curious*. She has written another book and will be expected to take part in all that ghastly publicity when it's released. I'm wondering whether a polite little gathering here might show those dreadful publicity people how it should be done.

Jethro was still admiring the dowager duchess's performance. He had long suspected that she was far more worldly wise than she let on and her speech had proved it.

While pretending to be shocked and bemused by everything, she had hinted that anyone involved with David could become rich. Further she had offered her friends a very discreet, genteel book signing and still left a hint of romance and scandal to come. In a world without television, cinema or radio, authors were celebrities and being a select guest at the launch of a new book would be an honour. As he thought about it, Jethro realised what else she had done. If they wanted their own electric light, then David's servants and low class friends would be worth talking to. In turn, they would have to turn a blind eye to the very behaviour that David's mother had been complaining about.

The flash and bang of a rocket distracted everyone and again the adult guests hurried to the balcony to watch. Jethro could see the glow of the bonfire and watched as more rockets were launched. One thing that he had to concede, fireworks on the other world were of much higher quality.

David was enjoying himself; he was part of an excited group who were enjoying a novel event. The disposable coveralls had done their job and David's guests did not realise that they were mingling with mere estate boys, at least until they returned to the stables.

One thing that Barabourne now had in excess was hot water, the consequence of so much steam driven machinery so guests were greeted by a pleasantly warm space, the smell of cooking food and the sound of music.

"It's the stable boys' project." David replied in answer to a query, "They always complain about the loft being cold and now the stables are warmer than parts of the house. Todd's the expert but a couple of the lads are learning fast. Do you know what the hardest part was?"

There was an expectant silence and a few shakes of the head.

"Convincing them that they wouldn't get into trouble for experimenting. I'm glad they got over it because they're going to modernise the house."

Some of the lads were playing fiddles, drums and flutes while others were singing. As everyone began removing their outdoor clothes, it became clear that there had been a breakdown in the social order. The guests turned to look at David who was unconcernedly chatting to a farm boy. The circumstances were novel enough for the female guests to find the estate boys attractive while the male guests were fascinated by the electrical gadgets that had been put on display. Some just glowed and crackled, though there was also the telegraph used for training to try as well as the original demonstration of electric light. Since the stable lads had the most 'hands on' experience, they spoke knowledgeably, impressing everyone.

When Billy arrived, and approached David, his first words were, "Pinching cider again? Don't let cook catch you."

To David's surprise, Iain and Megan were with him.

"I'll explain when it's quiet." Billy said quietly, "Don't worry, they know that they've got to keep their wedding tackle hidden."

Other male guests were following David's lead in taking off dinner jackets and ties while the girls dresses seemed a little looser and the noise was getting louder. The party was going well when the adult guests arrived.

Chapter 15

The music faltered but David's mother spotted an adult hand who had been tapping his foot to the music and headed for him.

"If I have to wait for someone to ask me to dance then I'll wait all evening. Shall we?"

David watched in amazement as his mother asked for a lively jig and almost pulled the hand away from the wall. Jethro stood next to David.

"Now that's something I never expected to see," he remarked.

"Me neither." David replied, "She's good though. How come?"

"We want you to rest this Christmas. Her guests will have to leave soon and you'll have to prepare for the Midnight Mass. For now, relax and have fun."

"I'm not a child and I don't need fussing over." David snapped irritably.

"I'm your guardian and I am concerned that you're doing too much." Jethro replied, "That concern has resulted in your mother accepting that you need your estate friends. I suggest a little diplomatic tiredness and fussing might be useful. Are you really upset that your mother's way of fussing is to dance with Richard?"

"OK, you're right and I have felt a bit down" David said more calmly, "She is enjoying herself, isn't she? Let's do the same."

Adult guests looked on aghast at the chaos, at least on the surface. Underneath, they saw the folk who His Majesty listened to and who were the driving force for the new industries that David was creating. One guest broke ranks to stroll over to the telegraph display. His face broke into a delighted grin as he found himself talking to Midshipman Clark, relieved that it was not a stable boy, he began an animated conversation. The rest surrendered to the situation, though with varying degrees of nervousness, and cautiously mingled.

Only Jethro knew just how carefully David's mother had planned things. Using the genteel surroundings of the soiree she had carefully piqued the guests interest. Wilson had been instructed to make the punch a little stronger than usual, and they had left the comfort of the saloon only when everyone was off guard.

Godfrey had organised events in the stable but had remained in the background. After the last of the guests had gone, David's mother sought him out and they spoke quietly until David was called over.

"Godfrey will send you back to the house in time to tidy yourself for church," she said, "Tomorrow you'll be working, but on Boxing Day, apart from greeting the hunt you should rest."

"Mother…" David exclaimed exasperated but his mother interrupted.

"You are fourteen years old and I am very proud that you are so grown up. However, sometimes even grown ups don't know when they're overdoing it. Accept that it is something that you must learn, and in the meantime be guided. Of course, if you are adult enough to cope with everything, then you should act like the duke more."

David grinned, "You're wrong you know. Lord Carlton will still be here so I won't be able to rest."

"Ever since His Majesty visited, your position has been assured. Godfrey and I will deal with Lord Carlton's brother."

Jethro could not resist interjecting as he turned to Godfrey who was standing nearby, "Your future father-in-law. You realise what that makes Lord Carlton, don't you?"

Godfrey grimaced as David laughed.

"You and Godfrey will deal with him, Mother?" David queried as he considered the conversation.

"Godfrey will discuss his stocks and shares. I'll discuss how he obviously has the king's favour."

In later years, David would say that dealing with relatives was the same as dealing with other worlds. Isabella's parents, uncle and brother arrived while the family was at church. The staff was ready and used the time to take them to their rooms. Always seeking to dominate, Lord Carlton chose to greet the family at the main entrance.

David was sharing a brougham with his friends.

"It seems we're the guests and he's the host." David muttered, "Let's go with it. Me first, then Mother and Uncle Jethro. Godfrey next then as an officer, Jimmy. Let's have Megan and Iain next followed by Todd and Billy. Let battle commence."

David and Lord Carlton approached each other with the same wariness that two dogs circle each other ready for a fight. However, Lord Carlton had no choice but to accept David's proffered hand and greet him. As duke, David stood beside him acknowledging the other arrivals. David could almost feel Lord Carlton's increasing anger as he was expected to greet David's friends as guests.

Lord Carlton watched as his brother and sister-in-law were whisked away, wondering at what gossip that he was being excluded from. David's friends gathered round him and Jethro leaving Lord

Carlton and his nephew, Jeremy, isolated. As cheeky as ever, it was Billy who tried to include them but only managed to elicit a few grunts.

They remained surly during Christmas Dinner and retired as soon as possible to get ready for the ball. That evening, David could be nothing but the Duke of Barabourne and not even Wilson could fault him. He greeted the high and mighty of the county with all the confidence and maturity that a duke should show. For Billy, Todd and Midshipman Clark it was a surreal experience as they circulated, speaking to magistrates, Lord Lieutenants and sheriffs. As Billy remarked, "I bet they don't they don't know that I've been stood in front of their mates."

"Where're Iain and Megan?" Todd asked.

"Shagging in their room." Billy replied.

"Oh!" Todd gasped, "How come they came across?"

"Bran's getting desperate and nasty." Billy replied, "They're still innocent and pure despite being married. It's that they only do it with each other that makes them special. It still makes them good sacrifices."

He paused as the others nodded before continuing, "Cradawg got his head in the clouds, you know, he really is all priestly. It made sense to him that the Divine Path needed some sort of fuel and blood from living people made sense. Anyway, he got himself all worked up into believing it then, when we turned up, he had to stop believing it again. Now Bran's getting all worked up that we're gone for another lifetime and he's blaming Iain and Megan saying they must have slept around."

"Yes but wasn't he the one that didn't believe in it." Todd asked.

"Cradawg reckons that Bran believes in whatever makes him popular. He started saying that they were prisoners in the circle until their deceit could be exposed."

"What about you?" Jimmy Clark asked, "How does he explain you coming and going as you like?"

"I don't know." Billy replied, "He's muttered something about me being too wild to travel on the divine path. I am a problem and he wants to do something but he doesn't know what."

"So you phoned me and Godfrey for permission to bring them through." Todd said, "I reckon I know about computers and cell phones but it's weird how the portal makes it all work."

"You might know about computers, but I don't." Jimmy exclaimed.

"You will." Todd laughed, "How about giving David a break?"

"Nope!" Billy exclaimed, "He's working and we're the ones just swanning around. We mustn't disturb him. He'll come over when he's ready. Why are you still standing here Jimmy-boy. That girl keeps looking at you. The least you can do is to offer to dance. What about you Todd? No-one you fancy?"

Todd shrugged, "David and Jimmy know this sort of stuff. I'd just make a fool of myself. What about you?"

"Blokes don't dance with blokes." Billy replied, "At least, not here. I'm all right."

Todd stared, briefly shocked then smiled. A thought occurred to him.

"Is that why you like visiting Cradawg?" he asked.

Billy smiled, "We don't dance but what we do is normal over there."

"Oh!" Todd said, "Go for it. You're not thinking of staying there are you?"

"Nah! Cradawg says I'm bound to David." Billy caught Todd's look, "Don't look like that, not that way, it's not serving him but being there for him. I think I get it."

Servants circulated with a message for the guests to gather in the main hall. David called for attention.

"My uncle Richard has an announcement," he said before turning to Isabella's father.

"Hmm, yes, hmm, very well, Isabella, Godfrey, come here please," he began, "I am delighted to announce the marriage of my daughter Isabella and Sir Godfrey Lowe. Would you raise your glasses and drink to their long life and happiness."

"Long life and happiness," rang around the room together with cheers and applause. As the applause died down, Richard spoke again, "Hmm, I don't see why you shouldn't kiss your fiancée."

Neither David nor Jethro knew what David's mother, his wife and daughter had said to Richard but they were amazed when he concluded, "It seems that I have another reason to be proud of her. Apparently she is an accomplished authoress. I don't read much myself but I understand that her stories are very well received. I'm not sure that my ideal choices for a husband would have allowed such activities so I'm particularly pleased that she's found a suitor who will encourage her."

As he finished he offered his hand to Godfrey and they shook, Godfrey grinning happily. Jethro considered Richard to be a weak man and a bully. He'd beat an employee who couldn't fight back and his wife was terrified of his rages. Jethro guessed that he saw advantages in forming closer ties with the dukedom, possible links with the royal palace and opportunities for his family to become very rich. Richard was also content with his own little world, resisting any change unless it made him more comfortable and the new alliance would make it easier to get electric light.

Once married off, Jethro thought, he would forget Isabella as a problem solved, and if any of his cronies commented on her behaviour simply reply, 'I agree. I wish her husband would show some authority'.

Jeremy was surprised at the announcement but he was drunk as usual and just looked for the nearest tray of drinks.

It was Lord Carlton who took the news badly. He was convinced that he could run the dukedom, then the kingdom, then the world better than anyone else. All he could see at that moment, was that David had taken control of part of his empire, Richard. Lord Carlton understood other things like treachery, blackmail, and corruption; while hunger for power cut across his innate snobbery. Taking a deep breath, and controlling the sick feeling that he was about to do something disgusting, he strolled across to Billy and Todd.

"No young fillies that take your fancy?" He asked, "I could make some introductions if you liked."

"Thanks but we've both got two left feet and the sense of rhythm of a tomato." Todd replied.

"Tomato?" For once Lord Carlton was genuinely amused, "Flat and squashy, and definitely no bounce."

"I don't know why I said that but you've made it make sense."

"Happy to oblige." Lord Carlton replied. He nearly added that he could introduce some girls that danced like that but just in time he checked himself from making derogatory remarks about his class. It would have been a great chance to put the two boys at ease but it slipped away as he said, "You must do very nicely out of your friendship with His Grace. Maybe we could also do some business."

"David's Uncle Jethro deals with the business side." Billy said, "You should talk to him."

"I'm thinking of more private business, on the side, that His Grace shouldn't know about. It could be very lucrative for you."

"Now I get it." Billy said, "We can't discuss it here. Maybe somewhere later."

"A good idea." Lord Carlton replied confidentially, "I think that we understand each other."

He strolled away to find more suitable company leaving Todd and Billy alone again. Todd looked at Billy quizzically.

"He wants us to spy on David, pinch plans or something. He thinks that I'm interested so he won't go after anyone else."

"I wondered why you agreed. It was a bit obvious wasn't it?"

"That's Carlton for you." Billy saw Jethro glancing at them and discreetly crooked his finger to beckon him over.

"Lord Carlton?" Jethro asked, "I saw him talking to you."

"Sorry about the summons, I reckoned you could be curious but we couldn't go rushing over to you." Billy began before repeating the conversation then adding, "I reckon he thinks we're gonna be his spies."

"Well done, Billy." Jethro said, "You can be very proud of yourself. Now we don't want to bother David, I'll tell him once we've come up with a plan. Why don't you take him for lunch at the Royal George? Get him confused and see what he lets slip."

Billy grinned, "You sure. You want one of us rough commoners tricking your hoity-toity noble cousin."

"In his case yes. Just look out for David. Carlton's looking this way so I'll move on."

"Anything that I should know about?" Lord Carlton asked as he strolled back to them.

"Nah! Just telling him about Todd's squashed tomato dancers."

"Very well." Lord Carlton said, "We should talk more."

"You've got some messages to vacuum." Billy said, "Tell me to get steam up on a brake to take you to the station. Make it the day after tomorrow and say you'll miss lunch because you want to wait for the replies. I know somewhere where we can talk in private. Now scarper or everyone will wonder why you're so pally with us."

Briefly Lord Carlton looked furious at being spoken to so rudely but then he smiled, a broad, genuine smile that lit his face.

"For once, I'm not dealing with an idiot. Good thinking."

"He'll never cope with the Royal George." Todd said after Lord Carlton strolled off.

"Yeah, I know." Billy said, "Jethro wants us to deal with it and not bother David. I've got a better idea. These phone things record don't they? We'll go to Chasebourne village."

"Just be careful." Todd grinned, as Jimmy Clark rejoined them, "How come you didn't go home for Christmas?"

"Dad's a priest. If someone's in trouble then he'll do anything

179

to help but in return he expects obedience to the church, obedience to the law and in my case obedience to navy discipline. He'd have forty fits if I didn't refer to David as His Grace all the time and Billy should be calling me, sir. I want us to stay on speaking terms but, I wrote and said that I had duties here, which I do, and he wrote back telling me that it's a cross I was strong enough to bear."

"You don't want to invite your family then." Billy chuckled.

"I'd invite my mother and sister." Jimmy replied, "If David sent a formal invitation then Dad would say that it was their duty to come but I don't think that he'd cope."

"Leave it a bit, then ask David." Billy said, "Don't give him a new problem until after Christmas."

To his surprise, David was enjoying himself. It was the first major event where neither Jethro nor his mother were by his side and he circulated as the duke and very much his own person. He enjoyed the attention he received as one of England's most eligible bachelors and managed to speak to the girls that he found attractive. He also agreed with his mother. A few of the boys were trying to catch his eye as well. To his disappointment, providing he kept to small talk about the weather, the King's health or other trivia everyone was happy. However, the eyes of all his suitors seemed to glaze and the conversation lapsed when he mentioned his interest in science or politics. The exception was one of the plainest girls in the room who replied, "Yes, your ideas on alternating current are revolutionary."

Her mother tried to intervene but was unsure how to interrupt without appearing rude. David guessed that she was preparing some well-chosen rebukes when mother and daughter were alone again.

"It is difficult to have a sensible conversation here. Perhaps you'd care to come for tea. Jodhpurs would be suitable if you wished to be shown around," David replied.

David had to admit that the smile transformed her face while he enjoyed watching the mother's confusion. Her daughter's crass, unladylike conversation had got her the most coveted invitation in the room. He beckoned Wilson over and told him of the invitation.

"I'd like an afternoon when I'm unlikely to be disturbed, Wilson," he said before turning back to the girl, "It's rude of me but I do have little time to myself. That's why I'd like Wilson to arrange it through my mother."

He paused, uncertain what to say but had caught the girl's sense of fun so he continued, "Forgive me but it's Olivia isn't it. I know, I should know the names of all my guests so please excuse

180

more bad manners."

Olivia laughed happily, "I believe yours is David isn't it?"

David laughed with her, suddenly aware of her bosom heaving with the laughter.

He blushed, suddenly all his confidence gone as he tried to lift his eyes to her face. He could see her amusement at his struggle and he blushed even more.

"Could we take a stroll on the balcony." Olivia asked, "It's becoming very stuffy in here. I'm sure I'll faint unless I get some fresh air."

"Yes of course."

"I'm not very ladylike you know." Olivia said when they were alone, "I'm flattered that you find my breasts so interesting. If Mother noticed, then she'll insist that my gowns are cut even lower."

"Oh!" Suddenly David felt deflated, "I'm sorry."

"Don't be. I'd like more than your eyes sizing them up but let's keep it between ourselves."

David just had to bend forward to kiss Olivia but his nerve failed him.

"Shall we dance?" he asked instead. Suddenly the dance floor seemed to be safer territory.

"No." Olivia replied, "Let's not be too interested in each other. At least in not in public and cause all the silly gossip. I'm looking forward to our afternoon together though."

David smiled and this time, overcame his fear as he kissed on the cheek.

David remained the perfect host though Olivia's mother noticed with considerable satisfaction, David's constant glances towards Olivia. David enjoyed the ball more than he could have believed possible.

The following day, Billy told Jethro of his plans who said, "It's a little underhand."

"We can destroy the file thingy so no-one ever hears it but if he starts getting underhand then I'll be underhandier."

"What a delightful word." Jethro laughed, "I agree, so what can I do?"

"Nuffing." Billy replied, "Jimmy Clark and I will deal with it. I shouldn't have told you nuffing but we're not letting David down and someone had to know, in case we stuff it up."

"I understand." Jethro replied, "Please be careful"

The plans changed slightly. Billy delayed the meeting and took

Jimmy to see Darren, feeling like a seasoned traveller as he took Jimmy through the portal then phoned for a taxi. Like all first time travellers Jimmy sat quietly taking in the sights but they returned knowing a little about networks, streaming and routers.

The following day no-one questioned Jimmy taking a brake to set up some sort of telegraph experiment while a little later, Billy picked up Lord Carlton from the main entrance. When they arrived at the pub in Chasebourne, Billy said, "Let's get comfy and you can tell me what you want."

Lord Carlton glared at him, "I shall get comfortable, you will stand for your betters and you will address me as 'My Lord'."

Billy looked startled.

"Make no mistake." Lord Carlton continued, "You're my servant now and you will behave accordingly."

"Stuff that..." Billy began but was startled by a slap to his head.

"If word of this meeting gets back to His Grace then you will be in deep trouble." Lord Carlton said, "Stop drawing attention to us and behave."

Although Billy was relieved that his plan was working, at that moment, it all seemed a bit too real as he meekly followed Lord Carlton into the pub and stood beside his chair.

Once Lord Carlton was settled with a mulled wine beside the fire he looked up at Billy and said, "I hear a lot about patents. I want details of any about to be released."

"There's not many at the moment..." Billy began but Lord Carlton interrupted, "I'm not interested in the ramblings of a street urchin, I want the papers. Next, you will find ways of damaging those machines. I want people to believe that they are unreliable, dangerous even. Now, good servants are rewarded and you will be paid but for now I want proof that you're worth bothering about before I go home. I dare say that you understand the alternative."

"I don't have much choice, do I?" Billy muttered.

"No, you don't." Lord Carlton smugly replied. The conversation effectively finished at that point and Lord Carlton felt extremely pleased with himself until Jethro asked to see him in the library. Puzzled that the midshipman was present he sat down beside the fire facing Jethro.

"I still find an open fire cosy, don't you?" Jethro said, "I believe that you're interested in the patents that we have in the pipeline. Here's one that may interest you, though it'll be many years before we're ready to patent it. Jimmy, your demonstration please."

It was impossible to describe Lord Carlton's shock as his recent conversation with Billy echoed around the room.

"Apart from you and Billy, only two people have heard your conversation so far. That's me and young Jimmy there." Jethro said, "We'll keep it that way if you leave now. A brake's waiting to take you to the station and if you hurry, you'll catch the last train."

"What about my servant? He'll need time to pack." Lord Carlton exclaimed.

"I have no argument with him. He can stay tonight and follow with your luggage."

Typically, Lord Carlton should have blustered but he was still shocked by hearing his own words coming out of nowhere to condemn him. He stood up and left the room. Not long after, they heard the brake chuffing away as Billy hurried in.

"Well done, you two!" Jethro exclaimed, "Just out of curiosity, were you tempted, Billy?"

Billy was serious for a moment.

"Everything here is about thinking things through," he said carefully, "I considered it but it never seemed like a good idea."

Jethro nodded, "I understand. In fact, it was a good answer. Thank you."

"If we started being polite, we'd still be thanking each other for stuff, next Christmas." Billy said, "More importantly, you find a reason to invite Jimmy's mother and sister but not his father."

Jimmy glared angrily at Billy but listened as Billy explained

"It might be tactful to invite them all." Jethro said, "I'll have a word with him and warn him that the natural order has been adapted to cope with all of His Majesty's demands. Perhaps not that but something like it. Now Billy, is there anything that you want?"

"Yeah but it's too big."

"Try me." Jethro persisted.

"I slept on the streets and I had some good mates. We'd look after each other," he paused, tears in his eyes, "I bet some are dead and others bin hanged."

He was sobbing freely now, just staring into the distance.

"I hear my fellow peers saying that down-and-outs would rather be on the streets instead of being clean and fed so why waste money on the system." Jethro said quietly, "I also hear pretty shameful stories about how almshouses are run. You want to do something about it and find your friends."

Billy nodded, "I told you that it's too much."

"It's a project that David would approve of." Jethro said, "If we went up to London, could you find one of your old friends?"

Billy nodded cautiously.

"You have no idea just how rich David's projects are going to make us, you included." Jethro said, "You could back your own projects to help people."

"But that's later. Could I try to find Jamie, now?"

"Who's Jamie, a friend?"

"No, my brother." Billy replied, "I know I can't do anything until that other world is settled but could we do something then, please?"

"You should have said before, Billy." Jethro exclaimed, "Give me all his details, everything that you can think of. I'll instruct our London agent and he can make enquiries."

Billy rushed across the room to hug Jethro who was even more startled when Billy just settled into his lap, arms around his neck. For a time Billy just sat sobbing quietly.

"Why didn't you ask before?" Jethro asked.

"I was a boot boy, I'd have got the sack." Billy replied, "I was saving what I could and I was going to run away. Then I got involved with David and we've been kinda busy but I've been thinking about him a lot over Christmas."

"Very well." Jethro said, "Let me see what I can do. Do you think a £500 reward would help?"

"No way." Billy exclaimed, "You'd have every kid in London lining up to claim. Use it to buy information in small doses, like the police do with informers."

"You realise that you might not like what we find."

"I know. He could be doing life, or be dead or crippled in a fight. He might have emigrated. He's my brother and I want to know."

Before Jethro could respond, David entered. He looked at them before settling in a chair opposite Jethro and Billy.

"What's going on?" David asked, "If I accept that you want me to rest, will you at least keep me informed. What have you been up to?"

"Lord Carlton tried to bribe Billy." Jethro replied, "Billy and Jimmy succeeded in turning the tables so Lord Carlton left rather than be humiliated. Billy wants to find his brother."

"Tell me about the bribe." David said.

"No. It's not a matter of keeping unpleasantness from you but a matter of honouring our side of the bargain."

"Fair enough. I'll give Billy some cider. When he's drunk, I'll tickle the information out of him." David paused, "Billy's brother? I didn't know that he had one so I guess that needs some explanation. Billy doesn't seem able at the moment, so will you explain, please Uncle."

"Billy has a brother. They were separated when they were waifs on the streets and I've promised to find out where he is."

"I know he can't come here." Billy said, "He was rough before, he might be worse now."

"Yes, he can come here." David said, "We might have to lock him in a shed at night to stop him stealing the silver but my foster mother on the other world knows about this stuff. Let's find him first."

Billy nodded contentedly not worrying that he was still sitting on Jethro's lap hugging him. David left them, content to read quietly in his own room. Although important to Billy, Jamie was a distraction that David did not want. What occurred to him as he sat, quietly reading, was that he was not needed for every problem and that his friends and family could act decisively on their own. He thought back to Godfrey designing the brake. It was all down to do with them using their initiative which was what he wanted. He realised that he had been slowly forgetting it, and that his enforced rest was indeed helping. He also realised that it might be fun, adopting a little ducal aloofness, and watching events.

In fact, it took less than a day to find Jamie. Although Jethro was impressed by the efficiency of the agent, Mr. MacArthur, the agent himself had to admit that it was luck. Finding a street urchin was completely new territory for Mr. MacArthur and he had no idea how to go about it until he remembered an incident on Christmas Eve as he was leaving his office. The police arrived in force and bundled anyone who looked destitute into wagons before moving on.

"Don't you worry about them, sir." a police sergeant said, "They'll have good food and a warm bed for Christmas while respectable citizens like yourself won't be pestered by them begging."

As a result, Mr. MacArthur knew of a large group of candidates in one place, together with a role of their names so he started at the prison where they were held. Confidentiality was less of an issue on David's world, Mr. MacArthur was obviously a gentleman so he was allowed access to the prisoners records. Allowing for a little sloppiness in the records, at first, there were two likely candidates. He rejected the first without any problem. J. Whitely turned out to be John Whitely and was thirty-five years old. The second was a James Whiley, the right age and he even had a brother of the right age. However, the brother was named Timothy and was in jail for attacking an old lady while trying to steal her purse. Mr. MacArthur might have given up but he spotted another file, badly stained but with a barely readable name. Jamie Wallis.

"Sorry about that, sir. Someone spilt tea over it then rewrote the name," the jailer said as he opened the file. "And he got the name wrong. It is Whitley you're looking for, isn't it?"

"No, it's Whitely but it's close. May I see?"

Mr. MacArthur knew a little from an account that Billy had sent him. Although Mr. MacArthur knew that justice could be rough on the poor, the police tended to investigate thoroughly though those investigations could be *adapted* if required. However, he was able piece together Jamie's story who currently faced five years hard labour.

When Billy was eleven and Jamie, thirteen, they had both been caught in another general clampdown on the homeless. The two brothers had been separated and sent to different orphanages. Billy had been lucky, placed in an orphanage run by good people before being sent to Barabourne. Jamie was less fortunate. As quickly as possible he was sent to a cobbler to learn a trade not caring that the cobbler was a drunk and a bully.

Jamie had only been with him for two nights when the cobbler realised that his wife was hiding at her sister's, he could not afford a prostitute so he turned his attentions to Jamie. They were in the kitchen, Jamie panicked, hit him with a saucepan and fled. He was confused, upset, not on his guard and was arrested soon after. Accused of assaulting his kindly master while trying to rob him, he was sentenced to a year in reform school.

His life there consisted of physical education, bible studies and work to get him used to *earning his keep*. It consisted of three hours in the morning, three hours in the afternoon and three hours in the evening screwing one piece of metal into another piece, 360 units per shift. When he asked what they were for, he was caned for being argumentative. He was released by being pushed out of the door which was slammed behind him.

He survived by begging, stealing when he had to, and finding warm corners to sleep in. He was arrested again and sentenced to a month's hard labour.

When Mr. MacArthur found him, he had just turned sixteen and already had two convictions. All they could charge him with was vagrancy but he faced hard labour, this time as an adult, at Dartmoor.

He was lucky in that court officials wanted a Christmas break so he was being held until the New Year. It was not that he was being sent for that puzzled him, it was the cautious tone in the gaolers' voices. He was taken to another room where he found a tall distinguished gentleman waiting for him. Jamie did not recognise Mr. MacArthur and struggled to think when the man asked, "Does London Bridge mean anything to you?"

It took time but something stirred in his memory. He thought of the code that he and Billy used to be sure that messages really did come from each other.

"Billy, sir?" he whispered, scarcely believing it possible

"I'm Mr. MacArthur, the Duke of Barabourne's London agent," he said, "I'm to give you a message from Billy. It's 'London Bridge. You'll be all right. Trust us!'. Do you understand it?"

As Jamie cautiously nodded, Mr. MacArthur turned to the warden and bobbed his own head.

"You are being bailed and remanded into the custody of the Duke of Barabourne." the warden said, again sounding cautious as well as surprised, "It must be some mistake. I can't think why His Grace would be interested in the likes of you so you'll be back here soon enough but make the most of it."

Jamie stood not moving as he tried to take everything in finally just nodding again.

"Do you trust me?" Mr. MacArthur asked.

Jamie hesitated but nodded still not confident enough to speak.

"Please be sure." Mr. MacArthur said, "If need be, you can be held here until Billy can come. We'll be removing those chains and if you run once we're outside then I'm afraid that neither His Grace nor Billy will be able to help you."

Again it took time for it to sink in but then Jamie whispered, "I won't run."

Mr. MacArthur smiled, "I've met Billy once or twice. He's a remarkable young man."

Once again, Jamie needed time to formulate his thoughts.

"Billy works for this Duke. He's got a good life. I'll fuck it up."

"Billy is His Grace's friend. He acts as servant when needed but he has his own mind and he can speak it, sometimes quite bluntly."

For the first time, Jamie reacted and smiled, "That sounds like Billy. He's got a good life. I'll fuck it up. I always do. That duke bloke won't want the likes of me around."

"I don't know. You do have one thing in common with His Grace, you know."

Despite himself, Jamie responded, "Yeah! What?"

"You like to hit perverts over the head."

Jamie stared, his shoulders heaved as if he was sobbing before whispering, "No-one believed me. I'm still a fuck-up though."

"One step at a time." Mr. MacArthur said, "Let's get you out of here and to His Grace's town house. You'll feel better for a bath, clean clothes and a decent meal. Ah! I saw that look. All the doors have locks on the inside."

Jamie smiled again but this time, Mr. MacArthur saw something of Billy's innate cheerfulness.

"What's this duke like." Jamie asked, "What did you mean by Billy being his friend? A nob like that wouldn't even look at him."

"I find Barabourne a strange place." Mr. MacArthur said, "His Grace is genuine and is exactly as he seems. He's not expecting you to be an angel so be yourself and you'll be all right. Shall we go?"

From then until getting off the train on his way to Barabourne, Jamie's day was a blur of comfortable even sensuous sensations. There was the warmth and soft seats of the steam-carriage, the carpets in the big house he was taken to. He was nervous of the bath, expecting it to be icy cold but it was at just the right temperature. No-one cared that he emptied and refilled it twice as the water became cleaner and cleaner. He was sure that he dozed but as he relaxed so his stomach rumbled.

Unsure about clothes, he wrapped towels around himself and padded barefoot looking for Mr. MacArthur vaguely embarrassed when a maid found him and led the way.

"Ah, good." Mr. MacArthur said, "This is Mr. Reynolds, a tailor. I know your fears but would you allow him to take your measurements?"

Jamie now felt safe with Mr. MacArthur and nodded. Finally, Jamie was allowed to sit at the table to be served the largest meal that he had ever had. He dressed in the off-the-peg clothes that Mr. Reynolds sent round and felt like a different person as he followed Mr. MacArthur out of the house for the drive to the station. He was aware that they were travelling first class but everything was still so unreal.

It all had to be a dream and he was going to wake up back in the cell.

Mr. MacArthur might have found him morose and moody but had been warned. Because he was watching sympathetically, Mr. MacArthur saw how Jamie slowly became more interested in the changing scenery. It was that which convinced Jamie that it was not a dream. He had never travelled by train before and had never been outside London so it would have been impossible to imagine.

Once off the train and on the platform, he was still warm in his new clothes and still happy to go with Mr. MacArthur as they left the station. Waiting outside was a steam-brake with a boy a couple of years younger, waiting beside it who hurried over to greet them.

"Hello David." Mr. MacArthur said, "Is everyone else busy then."

"Billy wasn't sure what time you'd be arriving and he had an urgent errand he needed to run. Godfrey's been press-ganged into helping with the wedding arrangements. The rest are preparing to demonstrate the telegraph to His Majesty. I was glad for something to do."

"Right. If you sign this, then legally Jamie will be in your charge." Mr. MacArthur said, "Don't worry, Jamie. That's just complying with the terms of the bail. Technically, you're a prisoner until His Grace signs the final papers."

"Oh! I haven't felt like a prisoner. Thanks for everything, Sir."

"You're in David's hands now, I'm going to see about a return train."

They all shook hands and Mr. MacArthur hurried back into the station.

"I'm going to leg it." Jamie announced, "Will you get into trouble if I do?"

"You'll only end up in prison again." David said, "Why run?"

"Because I don't want to stuff it up for Billy. I'll do something stupid, end up in gaol anyway and Billy will be in trouble too. I don't know what Billy said, but I'm just a worthless shit and when that duke bloke finds out, Billy will be sacked as well."

"There's something I want to tell you, but not here. How about we get a cider in the pub while I tell you and then you decide whether to run."

Jamie nodded. In truth, he wanted to stay and enjoy more of the friendliness he had experienced. It was as they entered the pub that Jamie tensed for the whole place fell silent. He sighed, waiting for the disaster.

189

"I wish you wouldn't all do that." David laughed, "You're terrifying my friend."

Jamie was surprised at chuckles spreading around the pub as the conversations picked up again but watched as a youth sidled up.

"I'm not really skiving, Your Grace," he said, "My hands were so cold, I couldn't feel anything and I was cutting myself more and more."

"For the record will you show me?" David asked.

The youth held out his hands.

"I'd say that you should have finished sooner. Go and see Dr. Hastings then tell the estate office that you're to have light duties, somewhere warm for a few days."

He turned to Jamie, "He's been chopping up dead wood for firewood. It can get bloody cold in the woods especially when the wind's blowing."

Jamie nodded uncertainly as they headed for the bar.

"Good evening, Your Grace," the landlord said, "You know that I shouldn't serve you, don't you."

"I only want a cider each and it's important enough to pull rank. Besides, that's the constable over there and I thought he was on duty until nine."

"That's right I am, Your Grace," the constable said, "I'm doing my rounds and needed a warm up as well. Just one cider is it?"

"Yes. This is Billy's brother and Billy will kill me if I don't get him home soon."

"You've got him then," the constable exclaimed, "That was quick. I'd only vacuumed my own search requests this morning. Why don't you come and sit with me."

Jamie really was terrified now but did not know where to run to. Besides, it was still all so friendly.

"You don't have to be scared of me. I used to work in the city and I couldn't take it any more. My superiors could either accept my resignation or find me somewhere out of it all so here I am. You're bailed to His Grace, and we all like our David and we don't like anyone who hurts him." The constable held out his hand, "Remember that and we'll all be friends. How about we seal it on another cider?"

Jamie looked at the constable, relaxed and nodded before turning to David.

"Why is everyone calling you Your Grace. Why was that guy so worried about not being at work."

"I'm the duke bloke that you're so worried about." David

replied, "I already know all about you and it's all right. Billy is my friend and I want to help him. You'll have to go back to London to attend court but my solicitor will represent you. He won't be used to vagrancy laws so you may have to help him but he'll confirm that your address is Barabourne. Do you still want to run."

Jamie burst into tears, shaking his head and it was the constable who pulled him into a hug.

"I'm going to stuff up and spoil it for everyone." Jamie sobbed.

"Do it by accident and everyone will help you," the constable said, "Do it deliberately and I reckon that I'll be arresting Billie for your murder. You'll be all right."

David had expected all sorts of problems but not that the life had been crushed out of Jamie so completely. David looked around and saw that everyone was pretending to mind their own business but the little drama was too much to resist. Jack the landlord was hovering nearby.

"How do you like being the first pub with electric light?" David asked.

"Well enough, Your Grace." Jack answered, "As you can see, we turn them off in here except the ones behind the bar but people come from miles to see the ones outside. Even the king came in to inspect them. I never thought that I have the honour of serving him. I heard that Billy had told him that it was expected. I can believe it of the young scamp."

"It's when him and Todd get together." David chuckled, "I can't tell you much but there is a reason for allowing it."

"That's to do with your strange journeys and none of our business but we all understand. Before, young Silas would have carried on working until his hands were torn to shreds and you were right kind to him just then."

Soon it was time for them to leave and now that Jamie was calm again he was able to walk to the brake. They travelled to the house in silence and Jamie followed David into the main hall.

Chapter 16

At sixteen Jamie, should be street-wise and feel as if he could deal with anything but his day had been a mixture of hope and fear. He saw Wilson hurrying towards them and only saw trouble. It was easiest to assume that Wilson was David's father arriving to turn him out. The cider also proved to be a mistake for this time, he was sick, emptying his stomach over the floor. Seeing what he had done, he collapsed to the floor losing control of his bladder in his fear.

"I never expected to have that sort of effect on a guest, Your Grace." Wilson said as he beckoned a footman, "A chair for the young gentleman and towels for him to cover himself. David; kitchen, find someone to clean the floor but come straight back. Your guest needs a familiar face. When he's regained his strength, take him to his room and help him into bed."

When David returned, Jamie looked deathly white but he smiled briefly when he saw David.

"I told you that I'd stuff up. Do you want me to go now?" He asked.

"Only to bed." David replied, "I don't know how long Billy will be but he'll want to see you so let's get you ready."

Jamie nodded and allowed himself to be led to a bedroom. Wilson nodded to the small bag that Jamie had been carrying and David dutifully picked it up.

"OK, into the bathroom and have a good soak." David said, "There's a dressing gown and towels. I'll unpack your bag."

David's valet would have been impressed with the way that he put away the few possessions that Jamie had. He took a pair of pyjamas and tapped on the bathroom door.

"May I bring in your pyjamas so that you can put them on in there."

"Will you leave them outside the door, please?" Jamie replied, "Can you leave me for a bit, please? I'll be all right."

There's a bell-pull beside the bed. Ring when you're in bed and I'll come and see whether you want something."

David sought out Wilson.

"Does he need a doctor?" He asked.

"Possibly but let's see how he is in the morning." Wilson replied, "He is ill but some illnesses just need rest and good food.

Billy tends to stay late when he visits Cradawg. When he does return, I'll inform him of his brother's arrival but if he's asleep then he shouldn't be disturbed. Now how about you? You don't need this extra problem."

"You know Wilson, I think I do." David said, "I'm getting involved in this political row between Bran and Cradawg. We're doing something for the crown and the government by installing electricity but am I doing anything for people? Will they benefit? I feel as if I'm doing more good with Jamie than all the rest put together."

"I think that I understand, Your Grace." Wilson said, "You're giving the rich new toys but you want to give the poor and the destitute new chances."

"This is my world, and I'm learning more of its problems. Trips to other worlds will always be exciting but those visits are making it clearer what needs to be done here and that's where my true duty lies."

"There's many who would not see beyond the smell of disinfectant in the main hall and I see a footman going up the stairs. I don't think the young man needs another stranger at the moment."

When David reached the room, Jamie was fast asleep. David gathered up the wet towels and the rest of the laundry and quietly left. He suddenly realised that he had never noticed what happened to it when it was taken away. He hurried back to Wilson who was obviously amused.

"Learning something about running the house, are we?" He asked.

"Silly isn't it?" David replied, "I should know how to deal with some dirty laundry. Jamie's asleep so I left him to it."

David's last task was to intercept Billy when he arrived.

"He's in a bad way." David said, "Physically, he's very thin and he's a nervous wreck. I'll show you to his room but if he's asleep, just sit with him."

Billy nodded and hugged David then stepped back, looking worried, "Supposing he don't recognise me?"

"Play it by ear and go carefully." David replied and Billy seemed happier. He need not have worried. Jamie must have woken up because, as he closed the bedroom door David heard yells of delight as they saw each other.

Billy and Todd looked after Jamie while Billy continued visiting Cradawg. Megan and Iain spent their days greeting visitors to the stone circles and nights cuddled up in their room. In theory, only

Christmas day was a holiday. In practice, those that could afford it saw it as a holiday with their families so little was happening in David's projects.

The New Years' ball, also known as the servants ball proved to be fun. Normally everybody desperately warned youngsters to be on their best behaviour and everyone stood around trying to behave. This year the village and estate boys clustered around David. Older staff were more reticent but spoke more freely with David's mother and Jethro.

The evening began well with Jimmy's look of shocked surprise when he arrived to see his father standing with Jethro while his mother and sister were happily chatting with Godfrey, Isabella and his own mother.

"Billy arranged it." Jethro explained, "Or rather, he persuaded me to collude with a bishop to arrange the Reverend Clark's visit."

"A formidable young man." the Reverend Clark said, "He's made it clear that we're to get know each other."

"That sounds like Billy. He never does anything by halves."

"Neither do you." the Reverend Clark said, "It's why I was always proud of you but I was worried that it would get you into trouble. I glad that you've found like-minded individuals."

"I thought you believed in maintaining order and keeping everything in its place."

"It's safer." the Reverend Clark replied, "How much did you struggle with prejudice at Dartmouth?"

Jimmy nodded, "I'm happy here. Have you met David yet?"

"Not as formally as I'd like but it seems that you have a lot in common. Your mother and sister seem to be more interested in the forthcoming wedding so I shall watch and learn from a detached distance. I'm here for a fortnight so we have plenty of time to talk."

"Come over and meet them all." Jimmy paused, "You know that I do believe in God don't you? I tried to do things your way but there was always so much to explore and now there's even more."

"We haven't long arrived and I'm still tired from the journey so for once, it's me who doesn't want a long philosophical debate."

Without thinking, Jimmy stepped forwards and hugged his father. On Todd's world it would have seemed natural but here, people were more restrained and the Reverend Clark was unused to such a display of affection. He glanced at Jethro who smiled and so he hesitantly returned the hug.

Jimmy looked up and smiled. He stepped back and said before

bowing his head, "It's a new beginning would you bless it?"

Once again, the Reverend Clark was surprised. Where it had been assumed that the parson's son would become an altar boy and generally take part in the church, Jimmy had always been reluctant, partly because whenever he was in trouble someone was bound to say, 'And you, the parson's son'. However, it was obviously important to Jimmy so he made the sign of the cross and said, "Lord, bless our search for understanding."

Jimmy looked up and smiled again, there was nothing more to be said for the moment so he headed for his friends.

"I'm glad that you got on so well." Jethro said.

"Billy was right." the Reverend Clark said, "The servant's ball is a good time to relax."

"That's the scary thing about Barabourne. The boot boy is usually right." Jethro chuckled.

Silas, who was known as the shyest boy anyone had ever met, proudly showed his bandaged hands but nervously said, "I can't work until I'm better. I'm sorry, Your Grace."

"There may be something you can do." David said.

"Oh yes! Anything Your Grace. Tell me what to do."

"Amos Stevens is getting on a bit and won't be able to manage Coldharbour Farm for much longer but he's too proud to admit it. He's got no children so when it happens he's got no-one to look after him or his wife. Maybe we can convince him that I want you to have the chance to take over the tenancy providing you agree to look after him when he gets too old. In the meantime it'll still be his farm and his part would be to teach you."

It was a lot for Silas to take in, he grinned, "I get on with him but you wouldn't really give me a tenancy, would you, Your Grace?"

"Why not? I want to convince Amos that it's the natural process. You know, the land passing on to the next generation."

"Oh thank you, Your Grace." Silas gushed.

Others had overheard the conversation and were impressed. Some land owners would have just thrown Amos and his wife out so it was important to understand what their own old age would be.

Everyone went to bed cheerfully ready to face the new year.

Jamie's case was up on the first Monday of the New Year. The family solicitor, Sir Douglas Mayhew agreed to represent Jamie though as he said, he was more used to patent law and conveyancing, agreeing that Jamie probably knew more about vagrancy law though as it turned out, it did not matter. Sir Douglas greeted them at the court.

"The magistrate is Sir Cloudsley Pomfret-Smythe. A pompous name for a self-righteous, self-important prig. I've never appeared before him in court before, but we both belong to the Athenaeum Club so I know something about him. Be warned, he does not waste time on, and I quote, 'Scum who should be never allowed near respectable folk'. He regards the court as his personal domain and he uses it for his crusade to cleanse the city streets. He'll take it as a personal insult that I'm speaking for Jamie and the fact that we're entering a not guilty plea will add fuel to the fire."

He turned to Jamie, "I do not regard you as scum and you have my full support but you must understand what we're dealing with."

"Now I have spoken with the police solicitor, a Mr. Johnson, and he's a good man. In fact, he's glad that for once, prison and hard labour isn't the inevitable outcome. However, despite that, don't expect a shining example of English justice in action. If it was, he would merely stand and say that he'll offer no evidence. Sir Cloudsley will not be pleased and will not let it pass."

Sir Douglas paused again, "There's one more thing that will upset Sir Cloudsley. I informed the clerk of the court as soon as I was instructed so our case is being heard before the other wretches and their fate would seem to be in our hands. It's not only Jamie who will be cocking a snook at Sir Cloudsley.

Incidently, I've also received instructions from your agent. The purchase of those warehouses will proceed as quickly as possible."

He looked across to the clerk of the court.

"Good, it seems that we're ready."

They all trooped into the court and stood for the magistrate. Barely had they sat down when Sir Cloudsley exclaimed, "Why on Earth is a man of your position wasting time on this rubbish? The boy's a useless loafer and the sooner I have him at Dartmoor the better."

Sir Douglas stood up.

"For the benefit of the court, I am Sir Douglas Mayhew and I am representing James Whitely in this matter. I was instructed to examine the case by His Grace the Duke of Barabourne and on doing so, I saw the merit in accepting further instructions from Mr. Whitely. I will not argue whether the young man is a useless loafer since it is not a punishable offence. As to your eagerness to send him to Dartmoor regardless of guilt or innocence, I may consider it a matter to send to the Lord Chancellor's office. "

Sir Cloudsley glared angrily at Sir Douglas before turning to the other solicitor.

"Very well, let's go through the motions. Mr. Johnson, will you present your case, please?"

In his turn, Mr. Johnson stood up, "Has the defendant entered a plea? It doesn't matter though because we have no evidence to offer."

"What is this? Collusion? Explain yourself, sir."

"Mr. Whitely was arrested along with some three hundred others under the vagrancy act. The police took their names and fingerprints and remanded them to Pentonville. It was only at Pentonville that they were asked about addresses and next-of-kin and Mr. Whitely named his brother William.

"We have no statement that Mr. Whitely was begging, neither can I submit an inability by Mr. Whitely to offer an address because he wasn't asked. In short there is no formal evidence to prove that Mr. Whitely was a vagrant. The third point that Sir Douglas made in his bundle was that Mr. Whitely can now produce one of the most respectable addresses in the country. I would also point out, that in your eagerness to send Mr. Whitely to Dartmoor, you omitted to have the charges read out and have Mr. Whitely enter a plea. I assume that Sir Douglas would appeal on that alone."

"So you want me to let this scum free again. Why? Are you going to share out the best of the girls for your harems?"

Both David and Sir Douglas leapt to their feet but Mr. Johnson was already standing.

"That is outrageous, even for you. I withdraw from this case and I shall also send a complaint to the Lord Chancellor's office."

He gathered up his papers and left the court.

"I shall also be registering a further complaint, and one on behalf of the duke." Sir Douglas said.

Sir Cloudsley jumped to his feet and stormed through to his chambers. The clerk of the court looked at Sir Douglas and Mr. Johnson.

"Strictly speaking there should be a new hearing. However, Mr. Whitely, you are accused of vagrancy. Sir Douglas, how does your client plead?"

"Not guilty."

"Very well. It's recorded that the prosecution offered no evidence." he said, "It would seem from his remarks that Sir Cloudsley accepted it. That makes *not guilty* the only possible result and the case is closed despite the irregular procedure. In the circumstances, I shall also have to forward a report expressing concerns about his behaviour but I'll point out that the interested parties agree that justice has been done."

Once outside the court, David looked at Jamie who was trembling.

"It's all right, Jamie." David said, "It's not you who's in trouble now. Remember what the doctor said, you're suffering from complete nervous and mental exhaustion. Let Todd and Billy take you home so you can rest. Sir Douglas and I are going to rescue the rest of the round-up."

"I've heard you talking. You're going to put them in warehouses." Jamie said, "They won't like that. They're cold and draughty."

"Yes I know." David said, "We know that some won't be able to work but we're hoping that some will be able to start making them habitable and we'll supply the tools and materials. At least they'll be fed."

Jamie nodded and looked towards Billy who said, "Come on. I'm getting hungry and Mrs Fuller keeps saying that you need building up. We'll stuff our faces while David works then go to the station together."

"Interesting friends, you have." Sir Douglas said, "Billy's definitely a rough diamond."

"I'm more interested in that hearing. Are all the courts like that?"

"Sir Cloudsley is in a league of his own, I must say that hearing was nothing like anything that I've experienced before." Sir Douglas replied, "However, Mr. Johnson and I agree on the outcome and if we raised too much of a fuss, young Jamie would face another hearing. Magistrates have considerable autonomy and it's a basic principle that all judges are independent and neutral. To interfere with them, loses that independence. Professionally I have to agree with that position. Privately, I believe the system to be corrupt. Have you heard the saying about power tending to corrupt?"

David nodded.

"I was friends with your father for many years. We shared our concerns about the squalor and poverty that blights our cities. You remind me of him in so many ways but there's more to you. You have a confidence that things could improve but the people you're helping are used to our sort doing enough to ease their consciences then losing interest. If it's in your mind to tackle the corruption, then plenty would support you. However, you'd also add to the opposition that's already forming against you and you must think in terms of changes taking years."

Sir Douglas paused again as he changed the subject, "What I'm really concerned about is that you're over-stretching yourself financially. You're investing massive amounts in this electrical business and although the early results look good, you are gambling everything on unproven science. What happens if electricity delivers less than you expect? We can't discuss it here in the street but if you'd care to come back to my office then we could prepare a more cautious approach."

By answer, David took out his phone, found the camera function and scanned the street before showing the resulting video to an astonished Sir Douglas.

"This thing is primarily a communication's device but that part only works at Barabourne so far. We're only scratching the surface as to what electricity can do and there're years of research and patents ahead of us."

"I see. I've heard electric light described as a passing fad but it's not, in your opinion."

"You know that we're already generating an income from licences and franchises. Come down to Barabourne sometime and I'll show you around."

"Thank you. I will. You should rejoin your friends." He saw the frown appear on David's face. "You'll not be welcome at the warehouses and I will make enquiries to establish the support for reform. You can't do anything except offer your patronage."

"Fair enough." David said, "I've got enough to do so we'll return to Barabourne."

Back at Barabourne with Jamie being cared for and Billy spending time with his brother in between visits to Cradwag David turned to his own needs. He wanted to visit the Stone Circle World but he also wanted to see Olivia again.

Billy still visited Cradwag and it was nearly two weeks before his own visit to that world was due. He would invite Olivia again. Her first visit had been far nicer than David had expected and he was becoming attracted to a girl whose immediate ambition was to learn to drive.

"My mother wants to marry me off." She had said on her first visit when they had gone for a walk alone, "I'm fifteen and ready to breed. At least that's how my parents seem to think but I'm not ready.

Even if I was, I'm supposed to make myself alluring enough to attract a man, and then resist his efforts when I've succeeded. I don't see the point of that."

David was slightly shocked, but liked her plain speaking and nodded in agreement as she concluded, "That's all my mother has ever told me about courtship. How about you?"

"I'm not sure what I'm supposed to do." David admitted, "A part of me wants to carry you off to my bedroom, so you've certainly been alluring enough."

Olivia smiled happily, "Ah, the rest of you is a gentleman so I won't have to resist you and a part of me thinks that it's a shame."

David grinned in his turn, "You're so easy to talk to."

"No I'm not, otherwise you'd have mentioned the wild passionate sex that we'd have in your bedroom."

David might have blushed but he had seen too much of Iain and Megan's world and instead he laughed.

"One of my duties is to produce the twentieth duke." he said, "I don't mind, but I've got relatives who also see a wife as a mare for breeding. They also expect the maids and female staff to be eager to please them. I don't think that I want to be like that. You made wild passionate sex sound like fun and I could enjoy it with you but..."

He trailed off uncertain what was bothering him.

"But you don't want the baggage of being a father yet, so sex is a bit scary." Olivia finished for him.

David nodded, "Silly isn't it."

"You are going to carry me off to your bedroom but not today." Olivia said, "Let's leave it as something to look forwards to when we're ready."

David stopped to kiss her on the cheek but Olivia grabbed him and their lips met. She let go.

"Anything we do will be passionate but it'll be what we both want." Olivia said.

That had been last week, and now he anticipated another meeting with excited nervousness and as usual, it was Wilson who summed up their budding relationship.

"She seems well able to support His Grace in his ventures," he said, "At least I'd be left to run the house in peace if they wed."

In any other establishment Wilson would be sacked for his comments but they were the only public concession he made to the new relaxed attitudes. Jethro's opinion that David's mother was far more worldly-wise than she ever let on was enhanced as she watched the odd incident where Wilson reproved David, but she made sure that Wilson did not see her. She should have been shocked but Jethro thought he had caught a slight nod of approval though Jethro still had his own concerns.

"Is this still part of what the portal expects you to do? You're not going off on your own tangents, are you?" Jethro asked when they were alone.

"No, I don't think I am." David replied firmly, "I don't fully understand but it's OK for cultures to be cautious about new ideas but our world rejects them out of hand. Did you know how bad the courts are? You've mentioned homelessness but have you seen how bad it is? I wouldn't have done if the portal hadn't got me to know Billy and the others."

"Very well. As long as you are clear in what you are doing, I have to agree. You were lucky in finding your friends though."

"I'm beginning to wonder if it is luck." David said, "I'm wondering what the portal is really capable of."

"Go on."

"Remember that the portal said that a crisis was due back in the Autumn then, when it discovered that I was busy, the crisis was delayed. Godfrey suddenly knew the Highway Code on the other world and could drive over there. Even His Majesty seemed more relaxed than I expected. There's other stuff."

Jethro nodded, "I've got the idea. What do you think?"

"I don't know." David replied, "Did Billy really relax enough to finally talk about his brother?"

"Very well. Let's remember that you're a fourteen year old boy and you've admitted yourself that you can't cope with everything. Neither can you go charging around, sword in hand, smiting your enemies."

David grinned as Jethro continued, "Despite your age, you are one of our country's leaders and you're certainly leading. You probably don't know this but Godfrey had been in trouble with the constable for fighting. Now he puts his energy into designing road vehicles. Once he's married, he'll settle down and you'll need a new champion. I can't answer all your concerns but my point is that you affect the way people behave as well. There's plenty that don't respond but you bring out the best in those that do."

"So is the portal just bringing out the best in me?" David asked, "Or is this all my imagination?"

"Ask it whether it planned on getting you lost on another

world." Jethro replied, "I would say that it was there that the changes in you began and I have to admit that now I'm more used to them, I prefer them to the old ways. I assume that you wouldn't object if I asked Craddock in here for a game of chess, would you?"

"What, the under-footman? No, of course not but isn't it a bit odd? You would never have even known that he played chess before."

"Before I was about to lose my leg, do you mean?" Jethro asked, "You return after being lost for weeks with all sorts of magical gifts including medicine to save my leg. Then you ferreted out Allen and dealt with it. Everything, including your new attitudes to staff seem to work. You were changed by your experiences and I was influenced to accept them because you saved my leg. I'd say the word may be influence rather than control. Do you want to resist any of the influences shaping your life?"

"No, I suppose not."

"Be careful, look out for anything that really does seem as if you're being pushed but beyond that, go with the flow as Todd would say."

"Thanks Uncle."

Although he visited the stone circle on the promised date, it was an anti-climax. Bran contented himself with sending a junior priest while Cradawg was there. According to Billy, the next significant event would be the spring equinox.

"Very convenient." David said when the portal confirmed Billy's findings.

"You are concerned. Explain." The portal typed.

"Things seem too simple as if they're planned and people are being manipulated."

"They are." The portal replied, "Explanation. You are being trained. Have you heard, 'Power tends to corrupt. Absolute power tends to corrupt absolutely'?"

David nodded, "Sir Douglas used it to describe the courts. I don't want to be like that."

"On your own world, portal would give you absolute power. You are not helping stone-circle world, Billy is. You are not needed. Go and play with your Navy friends."

"Oh!" David gasped.

"Physical reactions indicate jealousy, anger and embarrassment. Do you wish to sulk or understand?"

"Explain." David responded sulkily.

"Good. Ego attacked but you are trying to cope. You chose

Billy, portal did not. He is a good choice. Now he saves world while you cannot. You help midshipman. He will change attitudes, you will not but you give him the chance. Others will receive credit. You will not but it's you who your friends respect."

"So I should stay in the background and not get involved." David asked.

"Training needed; when to be in background; when not."

"But today's lesson is that I know I can't do it all but sometimes I get big-headed and think that I can or that I have absolute power."

"You understand. You have the right character but so did others. You have the right support but others did not."

"So Midshipman Clark will demonstrate the telegraph and stuff while I stay at Barabourne and do nothing because my part's done."

"You still need rest, waiting at Barabourne stressful. Go incognito, as servant."

David nodded thoughtfully.

"Idea stimulates you. Task important but you will be playing. Do you understand?"

"Oh! I see what you meant earlier." David laughed, "It could be fun."

Chapter 17

It took some time before David pieced together all the events at Dartmouth. Initially the midshipman returned alone to report back. As expected, he found himself standing in Captain Povey's office in front of his desk.

"I was informed that you would be away for at least six months." Captain Povey said sternly, "Since you're back early, I assume that you ignored my warning and displeased His Grace. I warned you that I would be unable to save you so what do you have to say for yourself?"

"Only that I'm to give you this, sir." Midshipman Jimmy Clark replied.

Captain Povey was fully expecting a list of wrongdoings and a complaint for foisting a scholarship boy onto the duke. He stared puzzled at the royal seal on the letter before opening it. Puzzlement turned into bewilderment when he read it.

"Is this a hoax?" He roared, "Tell me now before you get into real trouble."

"I understand that a confirmation is on its way, sir." Midshipman Clark replied, "But Admiral Sir Rodney Greenway's office is seeking its own confirmation. However, His Majesty is anxious to see the next demonstration."

"Next demonstration?" Captain Povey asked uncertainly.

"Yes sir. The first was little more than a demonstration across a field near Windsor. That's why we're going to try a field exercise."

"Explain this exercise."

"Enemy marines are to sail along the Dart to capture the college, sir. We'll have a big enough force to defend it but not if it has to be split up river and down. It'll be a night exercise so the semaphore and flags will be impracticable and normally we'd have to rely on lights. However, we plan to coordinate our defences with considerably more precision."

"By we, you mean His Grace."

"No sir. His Grace will not be present. I will command the defending forces."

"Preposterous." Captain Povey snapped. He might have said more but a seaman arrived carrying a signal. Captain Povey read it with increasing amazement before turning back to the midshipmen.

"It seems that I am to give you every support." He said more calmly, "You appear to be moving in very distinguished circles. Remember, if it all fails, you will be the scapegoat."

"Neither His Grace nor His Majesty are like that, sir but I'll do my best."

"Very well! What do you require?"

"I've been trained to use the equipment, but estate boys from Barabourne have also been trained. We'd like them to stay while we set up and demonstrate its operation. Once they arrive, then we'd like to install radios in two of the pinnaces. I'd also like a room for a command centre. We could use an empty cellar."

"Surely you need the top floor or even the roof to watch for your signals." Captain Povey said.

"It would be nice, sir but eventually we'll be able to signal ships thousands of miles away or in thick fog. A cellar should show that we don't need visual contact."

"Very well. Your task is to control the defending forces as a demonstration of this new equipment."

"Yes sir. The telegraph is tried and tested. The radios should work as expected but we've only got a week to iron out the bugs."

"Iron out the bugs?" Captain Povey queried.

"Someone was developing other equipment when it stopped working. Apparently insects had been attracted by the heat it was giving off and shorted it out."

"And if I ask what *shorted it out means* then you'll reply with something equally incomprehensible."

"I'm sorry sir. I'll set up a demonstration as soon possible and then I can explain properly."

After the midshipman had left, Captain Povey looked at the two messages again. It was all very odd but orders are orders and he would comply.

Midshipman Clark began work, pleasantly surprised at the cooperation that he received. Where Todd and Danny's world had taken a hundred years, Barabourne had taken less than a year to produce radio equipment. It did not matter, that on Todd and Danny's world, it would seem old-fashioned, roughly equivalent to 1920 amateur equipment, it was still a major advance on David's world.

Captain Povey was invited to the first tests of radio on a boat. To him, he was seeing a modern scientific marvel. He stood watching a steam pinnace sail up stream until it disappeared round a bend then jumped as the receiver clicked into life.

"They're ready and awaiting the firing sequence." Midshipman Clark announced. "Captain Povey, sir. The pinnace has six each red and green flares. Would you write down a sequence for them to be fired."

The captain complied and waited as Midshipmen transmitted the message then watched, increasingly impressed as the flares rose in the correct order.

"Not as much ironing as you expected, Mr Clark?" He said, "Congratulations. My office. Twenty minutes."

When Jimmy Clark was standing in front of his desk, Captain Povey said, "You intend fighting a naval battle by moving blocks of wood over a chalk drawn map on a cellar floor."

"Yes sir." Midshipman Clark replied, "The blocks will represent the different forces involved and will show where my lookouts are deployed."

"Yes, I know that." Captain Povey snapped, "While I agree that radio has considerable potential, smothering your uniform in chalk while grubbing about on the floor is hardly likely to impress their lordships. Allow me to help you prepare your command centre."

"Yes sir. Thank you sir,"

"Now why haven't you requested a ground force?"

"Sir? We're just supposed to intercept the boats carrying the marines."

Both Major Morris and I have received orders that the terms you set are too vague. The objective for the marines is to capture the parade ground. You've heard nothing I take it."

"No sir."

"Very well. Major Morris accepted that you wanted to demonstrate an accurate night signalling system and that the aim was to locate the landing party and then confront it with a powerful opposing force before it could land. His orders now are to take the terms to their limits and even exceed them. Now his new orders may well have come from the palace but you should have received your own signals. Both flotillas could be feints and while your command was reduced to chaos, the marines would just march in. Now I know how these things work so is there anyone who would have blocked your message or wanted it blocked."

"Lord Carlton. David's, I mean the duke's uncle. He probably hates me and he wants control of Barabourne."

"That would explain interference at the Admiralty, he could well have friends there."

"I should tell David. He's here but just as one of the village boys. He wanted to be on hand but he also wanted me to run the demonstration. He understands all the projects he's started but I've focussed on telegraphy and radio so I have a better understanding."

"You mean that His Grace is here but incognito." Captain Povey exclaimed, "He shouldn't be snooping around like that."

"He's not snooping, sir." Midshipman Clark retorted, "You know how important this is. He couldn't just sit at home but he won't interfere. Besides, if people do want us to fail, he may prove useful."

"Your career depends on this young man." Captain Povey said, "Because you don't have the right clothes for every function, you, like all scholarship boys, are seen as unsociable, dour and not part of the team. It doesn't matter that you're an excellent seaman and have my highest recommendations, you won't be noticed. For once, I can see that a scholarship boy gets the advancement that he deserves so I'll ask again, are you willing to place your career in the hands of this young duke?"

"Yes sir. I am." Midshipman Clark replied.

"The honour of this college, the duke's prestige and your future rests on this exercise. Are you willing to continue?"

"Yes sir, I am." Midshipman Clark replied again.

"Is there anything you need?"

Midshipman Clark hesitated as he considered the question then replied, "I need to bring more equipment from Barabourne and an introduction to a few of the right people locally. Poachers would be best but local farm boys would do."

Captain Povey grinned, "Shore patrols with local knowledge? That makes sense. Vacuum for what you need."

It was a hectic few days. Captain Povey kept his word and Midshipman Jimmy Clark could feel the anger against him as his fellow cadets were assigned to mere farm hands or laboured to create a command centre to Captain Povey's standards. Only Midshipman Clark was exempted rehearsals and parades in preparation for the royal visit but gradually as the training came together so the entire college realised that it was doing something special.

On one occasion Captain Povey told Midshipman Clark to send his assistant to his office with some papers. The assistant happened to be David.

"I'm impressed." Captain Povey said, "You're not like the self-important fops that we often get here as cadets. You really can do what needs to be done."

207

He paused, "If I said that Mr. Clark was thrown in at the deep end planning this exercise but now that he has the help of our instructors, he's excelling, would you agree?"

"Yes sir." David replied, "He really does understand electrical signalling."

"I'm not comfortable with you calling me sir." Captain Povey said, "I should be calling you, Your Grace."

"If you did, Jimmy would lose all authority. Once it's over then I'd like to attend a function where I can be properly dressed, but only because I'm a little tired of the invitations and put downs."

Captain Povey nodded, "Let me guess, 'come to dinner with us. I'm sorry I forgot, you can't dress properly'. If I say anything, then it's a bit of teasing and naval officers should be able to deal with far worse."

"That's right." David agreed, "I suppose I went in for something like it when I was at school but I understand now."

"If all goes well, we'll not be dependent on the railway's vacuum tubes for much longer. For that reason alone, the Navy would be indebted to you and I'll see to it that you have your gathering."

However, events conspired to handle the problem differently. As dignitaries arrived to observe the exercise, so the college marched on the parade ground, making salutes and standing to attention as guards of honour were duly inspected. Finally, Captain Povey ushered the king, lords of the Admiralty and Generals from the War Office into Jimmy's command centre where he was giving the equipment a final check.

He glanced up, saw the king, hurried round to bob his head and offer his hand as he said, "Hello sir. It's good to see you again."

Jimmy caught the sudden tension and shocked looks, and tried to withdraw his hand but the king grabbed it and they shook.

"At last. Someone who heard my request that I be just an observer." the king observed calmly, "I'm sorry that we changed your original exercise."

"I should have seen it, sir." Midshipman Clark replied, "My original plan only needed two signals. It was hardly a demonstration."

"Explain the situation, please."

"Yes sir. We're expecting two enemy forces, one sailing up stream from the sea and the second sailing downstream from Dittisham. Time is the key. The force from the sea could be here within five minutes of being spotted. We've got twenty minutes with the Dittisham force."

The king nodded as Jimmy continued, "Either force could land the marines. The only concessions that the exercise gives us is that the marines cannot deploy before it begins and we must be able to see whether they are on board. However, if there are no marines on board then we must expect a land attack and either way we must expect all sorts of diversions."

Jimmy paused, marshalling his thoughts, "We have to keep our land forces close by but we need to know which is the main attack before we commit."

"How do you propose to do that?"

"We've established observation posts along the river. The further ones are using radio and the nearer ones, the telegraph. We're using local boys who know the land to guide those light tractors that Godfrey's building to patrol to the South and have an arc of posts from the end of Old Mill Creek to Dartmouth Town."

"Very well. Your aim is to send a force to meet them before they get too close to their goal."

"Yes sir."

"This table with the map painted on it, is what you call the plot, and I'm supposed to sit in regal splendour on that raised dais. I think that as an observer, I should like to wander around. Would that be a problem?"

There should have been only one possible answer.

"Of course not, sir except if it gets a bit busy, er..."

"Then as Billy would say, you won't have time to flaff about and curtsey. I understand."

Again shocked gasps echoed around the room.

"Right." Jimmy snapped, "It's nearly eight o'clock. Roll call."

Todd tapped out a message to the radio while a Midshipman, the Honourable Andrew Worthington assisted by Danny sent out a similar one over the telegraph. The dots and dashes were incomprehensible to the rest of the observers but the king had also been learning and understood that the posts were reporting in.

David was still content to act as Jimmy's servant. He was surprised the king had not acknowledged him but it was nice, not to be the one in charge for once. He was also aware how much he had built up Jimmy's confidence so he was also watching a success story. However, it did not prevent the tension mounting as nothing happened except for the observation posts routinely calling in. It proved too much for one admiral.

"They must be nearly on top of us by now, boy. Do something

or I shall." he snapped.

Jimmy turned towards the king who asked, "Is there anything that you can do?"

"No sir." Jimmy replied, "We're getting regular checks, so we can't even say that the lookouts are asleep."

King Charles laughed cheerfully but said nothing.

Suddenly the radio receiver clicked into life.

"Enemy in sight. Marines on board." The call sign was from the post closest to the sea. It was followed by a second signal that their own pinnaces were sailing to intercept.

"Tell them to hold position." Jimmy snapped, "It's not going to be over with one signal, is it, sir?"

Before anyone could reply, the lookout post signalled again, "They're dummies. Being thrown overboard."

"Well done." the king said, "What now?"

The radio receiver clicked again, this time from up stream, "Enemy in sight. No troops."

Jimmy felt everyone in the room watching him.

"Tell our pinnaces to move position to the mouth of Old Mill Creek." he said uncertainly, "We can't do much until we find the troops."

Jimmy was worried now. He was sure that he was missing something and everyone was still waiting for him. Suddenly the radio receiver clicked into life. The boats from Dittisham were ferrying troops across the river.

"Signal the tractors. Make all speed to Old Mill Lane and patrol to the north of the Creek. Tell them to give their position regularly."

"That's a mile or more along narrow lanes at night." King Charles murmured then smiled, "Yes of course, Godfrey's contraptions."

"That's right." Jimmy grinned, "David, keep the plot up-to-date."

The king watched quizzically as David responded with a smart 'aye, aye sir'.

"He's on loan from Barabourne." Jimmy said.

"I have heard the reasoning and I can accept it. Explain your orders."

"They tried confusing us. They wanted us chasing up and down the river after one red herring then another. They didn't bargain on how much information we can transmit so we weren't fooled. We know where the enemy is but I still want to be cautious in case they try for another ruse. Those light tractors can travel at nearly thirty miles an hour, even at night, so they can intercept the ground troops. They've either got to go round Old Mill Creek or embark again on whichever flotilla we didn't intercept so that they can cross it."

"So Admiral Rogers. Do still think that radio is an interesting toy?"

"No Your Majesty, I regret though that the exercise was not run by a more suitable cadet."

"Is there a cadet more experienced in this field?"

"It doesn't seem that difficult. A gentleman would have coped and without embarrassing you."

"I'm not embarrassed. Now would anyone like to comment on the demonstration we're receiving?"

"Yes, Your Majesty. How soon can my fleet be equipped?" Rear Admiral Smythe asked, "I'll take young Clark as an acting lieutenant to organise it."

For the first time in a while, the telegraph began to click, so King Charles replied, "We'll discuss it later. If my Morse code is up to scratch, then we have a sighting. Jimmy?"

"Yes sir. They're cutting across the fields to the creek. All the shore posts were told to have a spotter looking inland."

"There's a line of trees on the bank there." King Charles said thoughtfully, "It'll be easy for them to hide, if they're awaiting transport."

A message clicked through, "Enemy in sight. Am in pursuit."

"Shit." Jimmy yelled, "That's what they want him to do. Tell the fucking idiot to get back on station. Wait for the transports."

Jimmy suddenly froze and looked at the king who raised his hand.

"A busy moment? I understand. Carry on!"

"Yes sir but I am sorry." Jimmy said, "Telegraph, tell the ground troops to expect troops coming from Old Mill Creek. Radio, contact the tractors. Give them the troop's position and tell them to cause chaos and confusion."

"There's no reply from our pinnaces, sir." Todd said, "Hang on. A call sign but nothing else."

"Which means?" Charles VII asked.

"The radio's working but there's no message."

"Message from Obs. 2." Todd yelled, "Enemy pinnaces entering creek. We've been spotted. Last message."

Another message arrived from the spotter boat on the river arrived. "Enemy force retiring to Dittisham. Friendly force in pursuit."

"We won't be able to deploy our ground forces in time." Jimmy said despondently, "We'll be meeting them on the parade ground."

"As I said earlier, radio is interesting but it seems to break down when needed most." Admiral Rogers said, "It might be worth waiting while they train more and this time, a full cadet should be in charge, not a scholarship boy."

Jimmy was close to tears, no longer able to contain his emotions as his plans collapsed but before anyone could react to Admiral Rogers both the telegraph and the radio clicked into life. Both messages said the same thing, "Enemy troops surrendered to tractors."

"How?" Jimmy gasped, "There's only a crew of six between them."

They were all left wondering until Major Morris, commander of the opposing force arrived.

"The object was to out-manoeuvre each other, not engage in actual battle. Our aim was to confuse the enemy while their aim was to block us. Somehow you were able to coordinate forces spread over several square miles. Our plan was to draw you away from the creek and one or other of our flotillas would ferry the troops across. We only partially succeeded but we were not expecting your mobile land forces. We spotted some of your troops dug in along the bank and then more arrived by those tractors. We've never seen anything like that before and assumed that we'd been blocked, according to the exercise rules. What we didn't know was that they were just a few observers. Neither did we have contact with our own river forces, and assumed that the creek would be blocked."

"I see." Midshipman Clark said, "You didn't know that one of your feints had worked and drawn our flotilla off."

"No, but it didn't matter." Major Morris replied, "You knew where we were. We weren't going to surprise you so your forces would always be ready for us. Congratulations. With your new signalling system, you knew where we were and very effectively deployed your own forces."

At that moment Midshipman, the Honourable William Gregson arrived. He ignored everyone standing at the table to march over and salute, Admiral Rogers.

"Despite failing to receive the correct orders, I chased the enemy up river and forced them to return to Dittisham, sir."

"Surely, you should report to Midshipman Clark until you're released from the exercise." King Charles said quietly, "You defied orders and left your station. I should like to know why."

"Who are you to question..." As he spoke, Midshipman Gregson had swung round, faltering as he finally recognised the man that he had swept past, "I beg your pardon, Your Majesty."

"Very well. We'll put it down to another of Jimmy's busy moments." Charles VII said, "Now why did you defy orders?"

"We were supposed to drive their boats off, not sit on our backsides. Midshipman Clark didn't know how to act decisively."

"Excuse me, Your Majesty." Rear Admiral Smythe, called out, "I was very impressed with Midshipman Clark's skill and determination, My flag lieutenant wants to move on to higher things in the admiralty so I have a vacancy if the Midshipman is interested. I'd prefer it if this new Midshipman was assigned elsewhere, far from me."

"So Midshipman Clark, it seems that you have three job opportunities. You're going to have to decide carefully."

"Three sir?" Midshipman Clark queried.

"Continue with His Grace, accept a flag lieutenant's position or become the first Telegrapher Royal."

"Wow!" Jimmy exclaimed, "Thank you, sir. If he'll still have me, I'd like to stay with David. This is just the start of radio and I'd like to be involved with it. I can still help Admiral Smythe to install it on his ships and airships, at least I assume that His Grace would let me."

David nodded, smiling.

"I understand." King Charles said, "And my offer to come to court? I'll only make it once."

"Thank you sir, I'll help you set up a station but I'd rather be at Barabourne."

"Can you tell me why?"

"Yes sir. I'm not the parson's son if I do something wrong and I'm not the poor scholarship boy. I'm just part of the team and I like it. I really feel as if I can contribute something there."

"You should be prepared to serve wherever your sovereign directs." Admiral Rogers snapped, "A gentleman would understand that."

"We hope that a gentleman would also consider how best to serve his sovereign." King Charles said, "We approve of Midshipman

Clark's decision. He shall still be known as Telegrapher Royal. However, a lesser rank of Telegrapher for the King will also be created. The first task of the Telegrapher Royal will be to recommend him."

"Sir, thank you but may I still refuse? None of it would be happening without His Grace. I'd feel as if I was accepting titles on his work."

"No! We are fully aware of His Grace's contribution." King Charles said, "You are the one who stood here and demonstrated its capabilities. We are not offering a reward for services rendered, but are giving you the task of making electrical communications acceptable."

"I'm sorry, Your Majesty. I didn't understand. Maybe I shouldn't be at Dartmouth, after all."

"No, you shouldn't. As a lieutenant, you cannot attend any longer. Admiral Smythe, allowing field promotions in exceptional circumstances does happen and I would consider revolutionising the navy's communications exceptional. Would you deal with the legal niceties please?"

"My pleasure, Your Majesty." Admiral Smythe replied, "You'll have my full cooperation."

"David, a word in private please." the King said and once they were outside continued, "He should not have refused my offer twice. This egalitarianism is going too far."

"Sir, you had given him permission to act in your best interests. He was in the middle of an exercise where he had to think quickly so do you really think that he could have calmed down quickly enough to answer you properly?"

"I accept that. Very well. The court will not accept someone who thinks so little of etiquette so help him find a suitable telegrapher for me. Treat it as a practical problem. I don't want a boy who is so eager to deliver a message that he pushes the Prussian ambassador out of the way."

"Yes sir. Thank you. I'll see that everyone behaves better."

"You and your friends have a refreshing passion for everything you do. Neither was it they who broke discipline in the exercise. I remember your reasons for not mentioning radio. Let people get used to one idea then move on to the next. Try to follow the same principle with egalitarianism while I try to convince my court that I prefer honest answers to deferential ones."

David grinned as he bowed his head.

Chapter 18

The *Battle of the River Dart* was a turning point.

One beneficiary was Midshipman, the Honourable Andrew Worthington. Although from a wealthy family he also suffered bullying mainly because of his stutter when nervous and because he was so poor at sport. However, he was intelligent and showed a keen interest in telegraphy. He suddenly found himself at Windsor Castle, closely involved with his sovereign who was eager to promote the new industries.

Electric light might be flickering into life across London, but it was an enormous project, too big for David or even Barabourne to handle. A committee was appointed which made the decisions. It was also a long term project and it would be years before it was complete, or the benefits could be measured.

On the other hand, the benefits of radio were already obvious. The army and the navy were desperate to get equipment and even the railways saw its potential for replacing vacuum tubes. On Todd's world, the Scouts, cadet forces and others had taught children Morse code so it was something that David's friends could learn and pass on. Amateur radio was relatively cheap and so it was something else that they could become involved with. It seemed likely that Barabourne would skip thermionic valve technology and would shortly start producing its own transistors.

The problems on the stone circle world rumbled on without reaching a conclusion. It was frustrating but Billy simply said, "If they didn't have a real problem to argue over, they'd invent one."

David did not have a better idea so he left it to Billy. He had experienced the most incredible year of his life, full of adventure and discovery but it was fading into the routine with nothing happening until Todd's father suffered a massive heart attack.

The hospital authorities found a photograph of Todd with a phone number written on the back but there were no other traceable next-of-kin, so they contacted him and naturally, Todd hurried to the hospital.

So far, it was all routine until the staff took in Todd's age, called social services to be on the safe side and John Hemmings arrived just after David and Danny. David watched him warily but Mr. Hemmings smiled and took him to one side.

"You worry that you are being manipulated," he said. "Before you ask any questions, they will be vague and I will have to attempt extrapolation. Is that sufficient to establish my identity?"

Although shocked, David nodded.

"We need to talk but there's too many people around. Will you tell your friends that we need to go to John's office so that you sign some papers? Make it clear that we will be gone for some time but you'll be back."

Not long after, they were in John Hemmings' car.

"We're heading for the portal, aren't we?"

"Yes but please, no conversation. It's not easy driving through this body."

They drove along the lane and as they reached the gate, there was the shimmer before they parked in a forest glade, in the middle of which, a fire was ready to be lit.

"Humans never evolved on this world. Animals have a natural fear of fire so we won't be disturbed."

Once they were settled, Mr. Hemmings said, "This man is weak and makes himself weaker because he does nothing to strengthen or stimulate his mind. He's happily asleep and unaware. He'll know that his work has been done for him but he's escaped the effort and that's enough."

David nodded, waiting.

"Todd's father's heart attack was foreseen. He will die in a day or so." As David started to speak so the man continued, "He knows what he has become and hates himself for it. If we intervene he may live longer, but he won't give up the drink and he will die after a year of self loathing. Todd will feel duty bound to look after him and give up his chances with you. When his father dies, he will have nothing on his original world and he will be a stranger in your home. If things take their natural course then look after him through his grieving and he will have a future with you."

David nodded again.

"It is good that you're not arguing. You understand and you must not tell Todd. Dealing with death is not easy and this is another lesson. We did not cause the heart attack but we are using it to train you."

"Who are you?" David asked.

"What's left of the creators and we need your help. Will you give it?"

David nodded though this time, far less certainly.

"Don't worry, everything is going well. You have created a secure base at Barabourne and have friends who will defend it because their lives are there. You must find other friends for your quest; people who need to prove themselves. You can search for them while you prepare yourself. You have a question."

"I thought that the creators had been destroyed and what quest?"

"Our civilisation has been destroyed and is gone for ever. We're the survivors and must build a new one."

"And then you'll take over the portal again?"

"No. We use it but on a different level to you."

"I don't understand."

"Has the portal ever mentioned mental control?"

David nodded.

"On our Earth, we have become scavengers trying to preserve what's left but we're slipping backwards and our planet is being destroyed. You cannot stop us from slipping back but you can save our planet."

"I can?" David gasped.

"You can but you'll need help. We consider Craig Williams to be a strong candidate. He is intelligent, interested in science and is anxious to prove himself.

"Our poets would say that your quest is to find a sun that has been buried and release it. Our scientists say that you need to find a nuclear device, launch it and detonate it so that it punches a hole in the force field that has been wrapped around our planet. It's easy, you just have to ask Roman World or Stone Circle world for one, don't you?"

David nodded again, though far less certainly.

"You are the oracle, the guide, the messenger of the gods. Why does someone so powerful need such a device? You're going to have to steal one."

"This is crazy." David snapped, "It's impossible."

"Think of the poetic description. A quest should be daunting and it needs a hero who can overcome all odds. Wouldn't you like to be part of such a tale?"

"I suppose so but it's not like that in real life, is it?"

"You mean real life is all work and no fun."

"No, but…" David trailed off uncertain what he did mean.

"I chose this place because no human has ever been here before. We could have made do with the cafeteria in the hospital. I suppose it's more secure here but don't you think it's also more fun?"

David grinned, "I bet a spy would love a hideaway this secret."

"If we had not interfered, you would have grown up to accept your privileged position as normal and would have fitted in with those you have come to dislike. We gave you a choice and you chose to see the world differently. We guided you to Danny and Todd, and you saw them as they really are. Billy was your choice, and if you like, our mistake because we did not see his potential. Whatever happens the decisions are yours and eventually you will move beyond what we can teach. "

"You're telling me that I still have free will."

"If I haven't told you more than that then this conversation has been wasted."

David grinned.

"Our training does not revolve around discipline and conformity. It revolves around you becoming a well-rounded individual. That is why play is so important and why I enjoyed the pun in the previous sentence."

David frowned, puzzled then laughed, "I get it. Revolving to make me well-rounded."

"Dealing with Todd will not be play. It will take all your skill and all your energy. Afterwards, give yourself time to absorb the experience you have endured."

"Uncle Jethro was worried that I was overdoing it and wanted me to rest. Is that what you're saying?"

"With Todd you will have to overdo it. Afterwards, restore the balance."

"Revolve and become well-rounded again."

"Nicely put."

"Thank you. Now about stealing this bomb?"

"That project is bigger than bringing electric light to London. Our plans take time and we'd like Todd to be part of them. He is your next mission should you choose to accept it.

"I'll be back, should I choose to accept it; they're from TV aren't they?"

"I'm saving John Hemmings liver; he gets the oblivion he craves but without the alcohol. That and trying to restore his faith in life is payment for use of his body. I find my myself watching a fair amount of television and can relax with the more amusing nonsense. Your friends will become worried about you. We should return."

When they arrived back at the hospital, John Hemmings took

his leave. Todd hurried over to him

"Trouble?" he asked.

David shrugged, uncertain how to answer sensibly.

"Can we get help from the Roman world or from Stone Circle one? They know a lot about medicine." Todd asked, "I know, it's asking a lot but he's my dad and I've got to ask."

Todd was close to tears and trembling, looking desperately at David who did not know what to say.

"We'll try." David said, "I've been thinking about it but it's not going to be easy. You see, the other worlds tend to think that we're all powerful so what will happen when we need help like that? We present ourselves as observers for more powerful ones so why don't we turn to them. The other thing is, he's going to have to come to Barabourne. We'll find him a place in the village and a housekeeper. I promise, I'll do what I can, OK?"

Todd nodded and unable to keep his emotions in check any longer, burst into tears, grabbing David and sobbing into his shoulder. David's own mind was also in turmoil as he grappled with his conversation with John Hemmings or whoever it was. He was guiltily aware that he was misleading Todd, giving him false hope but did not know what to say.

"I know." Todd replied, "I wonder if Billy could help, you know, talk to Cradawg."

"I'll find out." David said, "You've got to look after yourself. Where are you staying?"

"Here of course."

"Your dad's going to be ill for some time. How are you going to cope?"

"I'll manage. I'm not leaving here until I can see him. I'm grabbing a drink and going back."

They headed back to the ITU and David sat next to Danny as Todd sought out a nurse. Of all his friends, David got on with Danny the most. The Barabourne boys still thought of him as their lord and master and were a little wary of him. It was well buried but it could surface if David ever felt irritable or annoyed. Todd felt as if he finally belonged somewhere and felt obliged to help. Danny just saw the fun and adventure in travelling and had liked David while they had been foster brothers. On his own world Danny was friends with Craig Williams, the boy who had laughed at David in class. It was an unlikely friendship but Danny could see through the bull and bluster to the boy, vaguely ashamed of his father's weakness, and wanting to assert himself.

As Todd sat resolutely by the ITU door and Darren sat beside him, David guided Danny outside.

"I can't explain but something to do with the portal was handling Hemmings. It seems that I could save Todd's father for a time, but the longer he lives, the more he'll drag Todd down."

Danny briefly looked surprised but asked, "You do worry that the portal can manipulate us, don't you? Is that the proof you wanted?"

"Possibly. I've said that I'll find a housekeeper and a cottage for his dad but that means his dad cooperating. Todd will try to control his drinking and his father will demand to go home. I can see it all logically but that makes it seem like a maths exercise and it feels wrong."

Danny sat quietly, not knowing what to say but stood up to briefly speak to Todd who nodded.

"I've said that we'll try to get help." he said when he returned, "I also said that doctors don't like interfering with each other's treatments so it'll be difficult."

"That'll help. Thanks." David said, "Remember when we were talking about pesky brothers hanging around? I bet that you weren't thinking of this."

"It's different. I reckon that we should find Billy and see if we can have a word with Cradawg. Let's see if we can do anything."

They found Billy back at Barabourne and told him the news.

"Cradawg won't help. He's a healer on their world but he would also look at everyone's spiritual well-being and you reckon that it would hurt Todd and his father spiritually. What are you doing, making yourself feel better or Todd?"

David glared angrily at Billy but relaxed, "I think that I'm trying to help Todd, er, I'm not sure but it's making him feel as if we're doing something, er, you know, supporting him."

"But it's phoney." Billy said, "That creator guy said that you had to deal with it but you're passing the buck. I don't blame you though, I'd do the same."

"Sometimes I wish that you were just a boot boy." David said irritably but then relaxed, "OK, I didn't want to hear that but you're right and I don't know what to do."

"I'll speak to Cradawg. Us messengers don't have parents and we need a human to talk to so I'll see if he can talk to Todd."

David nodded, "That makes sense. See what you can do,

please."

"What about you?" Billy asked, "You gettin' tired again? Or should I stick to being a boot boy and not worry about you?"

"I'm all right." David replied, "Let's see what Cradawg has to say. Let's go back to Chasebourne, Danny."

Mr. Barton, at the library was still pleased to see David, mainly for the historical information that he brought, though he preferred to ignore discussion of the portal. David and Danny visited him to tell him about Todd and it was as they left the library that they encountered Craig Williams who glared at David.

"What? Have they let you out of the funny farm then?" he sneered.

"Can it, Craig." Danny snapped back, "Todd's dad is dying. We don't need your crap."

"I heard. Why worry? It'll be one less loser. Why do you hang out with them, they're all losers. Does this nutter still think that he's a duke?"

"Why don't you ask me?" David said.

"OK, are you a duke?" Craig asked.

"No, not here." David replied, "Danny understands what I mean, so does Todd, but you wouldn't want to."

Craig stepped forward to stand almost nose to nose with David. Danny stood, uncertain how to ease the situation, aware that Craig was no match for David He was also aware that although normally calm and friendly, David needed a physical outlet to the pressure he was under. The tension increased until Danny's phone rang. It was Darren to say that Todd's father had suffered another heart attack.

"I could see the machines through the door." Darren sobbed, "Even I could see that his heart had stopped."

"Craig, fuck off." Danny snapped as he hung up, "You want to be my friend then don't make it all worse for us. We've got to get to the hospital, now. We'll hang out later."

Craig was startled by the passion in Danny's voice, so he nodded and walked off without another word. When they arrived Todd hugged David again, unashamedly crying in front of Darren and Danny.

"They're trying," he sobbed, "but they're saying that all that drinking damaged his liver and it's failing. The smoking has damaged his lungs and it's all putting extra pressure on his heart. When are you bringing someone to save him?"

"Billy's gone to get Cradawg." David said, "Be honest, can

anyone help him?"

"We've got to try. Can't you see that? He's my dad."

"I know, but he may be too weak unless they've got a pill that will fix his heart."

"I know, but we've got to try. When will Cradawg's doctor get here?"

"The portal will send him your dad's file. We'll take it from there. Let's see if he can do anything first."

David was uncomfortably aware that he was still giving Todd false hope but Todd was too emotional to understand though he managed to nod.

"Back home it feels as if we can do anything but we can't, can we." he whispered, "He's my dad, though."

"I know. I felt so helpless when my father died." David said, "They might have given him longer here but too much of his lungs were gone. He would still have been dying but at the time, I wouldn't have cared, I just didn't want to let go."

Todd looked at him, "You know something, don't you. Tell me."

"OK! I have spoken to someone and they won't help. They don't believe that he'll give up the booze so they'll just prolong the misery and the pain."

"So you have tried. I knew you would. Can't the portal make him give it up?"

Suddenly David understood problems that had been niggling him.

"It can tell him just how bad alcohol can be, like it taught Godfrey the Highway Code. It can create situations like when it brought me here but it can't make decisions. How Godfrey used the knowledge he got or how I reacted to being on a different world was up to us. How would your Dad react?"

"I understand but I don't like it." Todd sobbed, close to tears again.

A nurse approached them and asked, "Is there an adult that we can speak to?"

"No." Todd replied, "It's just us. I'm OK if my friends can stay."

"Of course they can." the nurse replied, "We're doing everything we can but he is very ill. His blood sats are so low that we're becoming worried that he may be suffering brain damage. We have to ask, if he has another seizure should we revive him?"

Todd stared, trying to absorb the information then finally

whispered, "What do you think, David? Danny?"

"I'm thinking about my father." David said quietly, "There came a point when I wished that it was all over and at the same time, didn't want him to die. It took a long time to stop feeling confused and I've felt guilty about it ever since. That probably doesn't help but you've got to do what's best for your dad, not you."

Todd nodded and gripped David's hand, "How bad is the brain damage?"

"We can't tell until we can do tests." the nurse explained, "There are no certainties but I'd prepare for the worst."

Todd nodded again, "I'm sorry, I can't say it. Do what's best though."

"I understand and I'll speak with the sister. Since there are no adult relatives I'm sure that she'll allow you and your friend to sit with him." she paused, "You need a break first. Get something to eat and have a shower or something. I would say, get some sleep but that's not going to happen, is it?"

Todd managed a weak smile as he shook his head.

"Come on Todd." Danny said, "We'll go to my place. Mum will feed you and you can borrow some of my stuff. David can go home and come back tomorrow while I'm at school. Maybe he can sneak back before Mr. Rogers sends you assignments."

The nurse was puzzled by Danny's comments but she got the gist of them. All three boys seemed to be extremely sensible and were well-behaved, otherwise they would not be allowed into ITU. Mary, Danny and Darren's mother insisted her children get some sleep and go to school as usual. She accepted that Danny was too closely involved, and phoned the school to inform them of events. The day shift in ITU had been briefed and accepted the rotation of Todd's friends as they sat by the bed.

They were sent to the cafeteria while a doctor examined Todd's father and waited to speak to Todd who hurried back as soon as he could.

"We're doing everything we can but the prognosis is not good." the doctor said, "At best, he's going to need a lot of care for a very long time. Are you sure that there's no adult relative that you can contact?"

Todd shook his head, "I've got friends like Mr. Barton at the library but they are friends, not relatives or anything."

"You have a social worker, I believe." the doctor said, "Maybe you should contact him. The nurse will give you a list of what your father needs and someone needs to fetch it."

"I can do it…" Todd began but was interrupted as a nurse called the doctor. Todd tried to follow but the nurse stopped him and guided him to the visitors room. A little later the doctor arrived.

"I'm sorry Todd, his heart was just too weak." he said, "It just gave out. He didn't regain consciousness and just slipped away."

"He's dead." Todd whispered.

"Yes." the doctor said.

"It was a myocardial infarction," Todd said, "According to the monitor, his heartbeat became more irregular and he showed more signs of hypoxia. Ischemia isn't it?"

"That's very good." the doctor said, "Do you want to be a doctor but more importantly is there anything you need?"

"I knew how ill he was but I wanted to be wrong. I pretended that I didn't really know what I was seeing. This is important, how bad was his heart to start with?"

"I can't tell without the postmortem, but I'd expect to find advanced ASVD. Sorry, do you know what that is?"

Todd nodded.

"Loosely, it's blocked arteries. Doctor, I know of a place that has drugs that would clear his arteries and rebuild heart muscles." As David started, Todd waved him back with his hand, "But both treatments would have put a demand for oxygen and nutrients that the other could not deliver. He was too ill for even that, I understand."

"I've never heard of such treatments," the doctor said, "I'd agree with your assessment if they existed, though."

"I'd be furious with someone who could have fetched those medicines but didn't, even if I understand why they wouldn't have worked. Just go away David. I don't want you around."

David was shocked but silently left the room and waited outside. A little later the doctor joined him, looking puzzled.

"Just why is Todd so angry with you?" he asked, "What gives him the idea that those drugs exist?"

"I can't say." David replied.

"I can't say? Most people would say 'I don't know' and he does seem knowledgeable about his father's condition. What am I missing here?"

"Nothing that would help." David replied.

"Very well. The nurse is calling his social worker but he needs friends and you don't qualify for the moment but if it's any comfort, I think that he'll get over it. I'm sorry, I must go. Speak to a nurse if you need anything."

David waited quietly until Todd came out.

"Tell me honestly. Did you let him die?" Todd asked.

"I don't think so." David replied, "Billy is talking to Cradawg, the creators said straight out that they wouldn't help. I could have spoken to Marcus on the Roman world but I offended the Emperor by telling him what I thought of gladiatorial games."

Todd nodded, "I'm sorry for what I said. It's just that I want it to be someone's else's fault and not Dad's."

"That's OK. I think it's a rule. When you lose someone like this, you're not allowed to think straight."

Todd managed a weak smile then shuddered, fighting back tears as a nurse approached.

"We've removed the tubes and everything. Would you like to see him."

"No. It's not Dad any more. I'm thinking of Christmas, a couple of years ago. He promised to stay off the booze until we had dinner and it was fun that morning. It was the last time he kept that promise for anything."

"Then you should leave. I'll contact your social worker and he can arrange the undertakers."

"No. I'll do it." Todd said firmly, "I've got er, trust funds and I can borrow against them. That's right, isn't it, David."

"Yes of course. Anything you need." David turned to the nurse, "We've both got substantial allowances and we do save for something special. We can deal with it."

Todd smiled and gripped David's hand. He was still conflicted; feeling guilty that he had not done more to help his father, he felt bad that they had not spent more time together and sometimes his guilt caused him to blame his friends for not getting help. At the same time, he understood that it was the drink that came between them and had killed his father.

Dealing with death is not easy, even for an adult and although Todd dealt with the funeral arrangements, John Hemmings proved unusually helpful, and David was not aware of any outside influence. He barred Todd from visiting his father's flat and was even interested enough to speak to David.

"He didn't always make it to the toilet so his flat stinks and it's a tip. The landlord will need a professional cleaning service before he even thinks of redecorating. There might be small things like photographs but I doubt if he's left anything to pass on to Todd. I had

225

an aunt and no-one knew how much of a hoarder she was. Todd doesn't need to feel how we did when we found how she lived."

David nodded, waiting for Mr. Hemmings to continue.

"My records show that Todd lives at a place called Barabourne. It's all properly documented but we both know it doesn't exist. Frankly, I've got more important things to do than to follow up on a couple of kids that seem so well. Don't make me come after you."

David smiled to himself. It seemed that the creator's therapy was working though there was a long way to go. Todd remained angry with David and needed him at the same time as they arranged the funeral. It caused a rift but David knew that he had to be patient. Adults were reluctant to deal with young teenagers at first but David could speak confidently, they could phone Danny's mother and Mr. Barton for support so Todd could feel that he was looking after his father.

Todd woke up the day after the funeral feeling lost, no-one expected him to do anything and his father's affairs were settled. They were as simple as the funeral. Danny and Todd tended to call Jethro, *uncle* so he had attended. Mr. Barton was there as were Danny's parents but there no other adults. The rest of the mourners were Todd's friends. Apart from their flowers, there was just a minimal bunch from the office where his father cleaned. The landlady of the Royal George showed more concern as she reserved an alcove in the bar for them, and supplied an alcohol free punch for the youngsters. Even the food ordered was supplied in generous quantities.

Todd could appreciate how many people were there for him, and it was something of a shock to realise that no-one had attended for his father. It could have made him angry, bitter or even more guilty that he had not spent more time with his father but deep down he realised that his father's drinking had isolated him from the friends that he once had.

However, he had a life more interesting than he could have believed possible a year ago and the medical team were becoming excited over a new strain of mould. It did not sound exciting but it could be the culmination of a project that he had initiated and that was very exciting.

For a long time, he felt flashes of anger whenever he saw David or Billy, blaming them for not helping his father but over time they faded. The cider that the youngsters drank so much of contained alcohol but just enough to act as a preservative and for the rest of his life, Todd never drank anything stronger. Whatever negative feelings

Todd felt, he loved David as a brother and that love dominated as he settled into his new life.

If David saw Todd's grief as a problem being solved, and other problems rumbled on in the background he was more concerned with the tasks that the Creators had for him. The first was bizarre; stealing a rocket tipped with nuclear weapons. The second appeared impossible; getting to know Craig Williams. The third was far more pleasant. He was expected to *round out again* and that meant play.

Peter Apps

Peter Apps lives in England, and The Long Way Round was his first novel to be followed by Time Askew and Deja Vu To The Nth.

He was born in 1948 and has lived in Sheerness, Kent for most of his life. The Isle of Sheppey where Sheerness is situated has a long, rich history has always fascinated Peter. History might seem a far cry from Science Fiction but imagining life in a Roman settlement is imagining a world just as alien as a distant planet.

Although he worked in a series of routine jobs, he likes to do his own thing when he can. For example, all his computers are Microsoft free zones and prefers to use Linux. He has always had an interest in science, especially Astronomy. Now that planets have been discovered around other suns, he feels that the time is coming when we could discover intelligent life out there.

Other interests include classical music and jazz. He also likes to settle down in the evening watching a good film and enjoying a nice glass of bitter or occasionally visit his local for a chat over a friendly drink.

The author is just a click away by email, peter@sjtales.uk.

Science Fiction
By
Peter Apps

The Stuart Johnson Chronicles

The Long Way Round
Time Askew
Deja Vu To The Nth
Earth Against Earth
Across The Continuum Sea (2017)

Worlds Beyond

The Growing Universe

Other Science Fiction

Disastrous Science (Short Stories)
Meanwhile In Time (Novel, late 2017

~~~

Non Science Fiction

Contributions to
Quirky Humans And Others
(An anthology by the
Sheppey Writers Group)

www.ingramcontent.com/pod-product-compliance
Lightning Source LLC
Chambersburg PA
CBHW070447260626
47161CB00004B/1226